Penguin Books
The Animal Game

Frank Tuohy was born in 1925 and educated at
Stowe and King's College, Cambridge, where he
took a first in English Literature and Moral
Sciences. He spent a year lecturing in Finland
and was then appointed, exceptionally young, to
the Chair of English Literature at Sao Paulo,
Brazil. Six years in Brazil supplied him with the
background for his first novel, *The Animal
Game* (1957) and for *The Warm Nights of
January* which followed in 1960. A volume of
short stories, *The Admiral and the Nuns*,
appeared in 1962 and the title story subsequently
won the Katherine Mansfield Menton Short
Story Prize. The setting of his third novel, *The
Ice Saints* (Penguin) is modern Poland, a country
he came to know well while lecturing at Cracow
University. With this novel the author achieved
a remarkable double by winning both the James
Tait Black Memorial Prize and the Geoffrey Faber
Memorial Prize.

Frank Tuohy now lives in Japan, where he
holds a lectureship at Waseda University, and is
working on another novel.

Frank Tuohy

The Animal Game

Penguin Books

Penguin Books Ltd, Harmondsworth,
Middlesex, England
Penguin Books Australia Ltd, Ringwood,
Victoria, Australia

First published by Macmillan 1957
Published in Penguin Books 1970
Copyright © Frank Tuohy, 1957

Made and printed in Great Britain by
C. Nicholls & Company Ltd
Set in Linotype Juliana

To Deborah and James Farmer

Contents

Book One

I

Far away, on the precarious underside of the world, a young woman was driving along the broad federal highway that approached a city. Already around her the hill was carved into squares with the red earth of roads that spread like a net over the low surrounding hills. Occasionally one of the squares was occupied by a eucalyptus wood, a rubbish dump or a clay-pit. Then suddenly, miles away, the fertile point was struck; the squares pushed up into concrete blocks, proliferated, gone wild with their competition for the light, into towers. For no obvious reason, in the middle of the plain appeared the giant bone-white construction of the city.

As the highway curved to give her a full view, the young woman's heart seemed to pause a little. She had lived here most of her life, but the highway was new; the city was new – a little newer every day. Today it lay with its skyscrapers dustily sparkling under a sky white with heat. But she had often seen storms which seemed to collect over the city in preference to the barren exhausted plain; melodramatically, willingly, it seemed to attract the fire from heaven.

The Packard throbbed smoothly over a bridge. She glanced at the tawny surface of the water. Clumps of water-hyacinth were drifting past. Some young men in shorts were playing football, skying the ball with their bare feet and heading it towards one another : they were workers from the railway.

The car now entered railway country, that neutral territory near all great cities where weeds and cinders alternate with gardens and rubbish dumps, and where the flora and fauna are as individual as by the seaside. The woman slowed down as lines and lines of goods trucks appeared ahead of her. No wheels turned, no rail clanged; the sky was empty of smoke and steam. A railway strike had been in progress for five days.

Because of it, she had made the seven-hour journey by road. In any case she had felt it better to bring back the car, which was her own. But it was the first time she had driven alone along the federal highway, and she was tired. On the journey to the capital she herself had not been driving. 'He won't drive it any more,' she thought, and she felt a hurting pleasure that the Packard was entirely hers again. She had closed the windows against dust, and the car was full of her own perfume and the smell of leather upholstery. Her compact had spilt powder on to the shelf under the dashboard; each stub in the ashtray bore the crimson tint of her mouth.

She drove slowly between the long lines of goods wagons. She had grown tired of her own mind during the journey. Her memories of the man had stimulated her to anger, so that at times she had driven carelessly, often dangerously, or had stopped full of apathy and boredom to rest in the shade of trees. Now, for the first time that day, her curiosity was aroused by something outside her. She glanced at the few workmen she passed, and wondered if there might be trouble. 'I'm no bourgeois,' she thought, 'they'll let me through' – and indeed many of the country's Communists were as rich as her father. The strikers were hungry; she could admit it clearly and firmly. All the more clearly, perhaps, because the sensation was completely beyond her own experience – she imagined it as something like when, after riding on the *fazenda*, you wanted your breakfast badly.

She thought of those things only because, subconsciously, she was still carrying on an argument with someone she loved; like all Englishmen of his generation, he mocked at political action.

Now, almost a mile ahead, something was happening. The road was straight and she could make out a cluster of people, and above them a slow whirlwind of circling vultures, an inverted cone of darkness with its apex on the railway line.

Then the noise came to her. It was a sound of agony, the noise of pain in abstraction, without cause, as though the air were screaming. A noise no one could hear without running – either towards it to help, or away in fear and terror. The young woman drove on towards it.

The stillness of the people at the roadside perplexed her. How could they let it continue? Coming nearer, she realized why. It was the screaming of animals.

Vultures dived down and settled in a seething cluster on the curved roof of the truck. Their leathery necks peered over the ventilators, then, scrabbling with their claws, they lost balance and flopped down on to the ground. Squawking with frustration they took off again and joined the flock circling above.

She opened the window of the car to see more clearly. The smell hit her. It was like a physical blow, affecting even the eyes and the throat. The screaming was louder than ever and she had to drive through it. She accelerated and the small crowd scattered.

A few yards beyond the truck, she stopped the car. A man jeered, hooting. She didn't mind – it was nothing to do with the strike or the screaming, but was caused by the sight of a woman driving a car.

She put her head out of the window. 'Young man,' she called, after the manner of the country, to an old man standing near. Her voice was loud but friendly; by nature she was one of those who speak to the poor as if they are slightly deaf.

The old man approached, his flat bare feet scuffling like flippers in the dust. He held a frayed straw hat in front of him. He smiled shyly.

'Please tell me what is happening.'

'They're shut in.'

'What are shut in?'

'Pigs, lady.' He grinned, a round of gums with one lone fang.

'Yes, yes. But why?'

'The strike. Everyone has gone away.' The staring crowd behind agreed with him. The faces towards her had a wide innocent look: they were the faces of the poor who still cannot help respecting and admiring the rich.

'It's two days they've been here now. At first they were squealing and squealing. I live over there –' Between the lines of wagons the old man pointed to a mud-hut on the railway embankment – 'My woman didn't like it. But then they got quiet.'

She nodded quickly, encouraging him to go on.

'Then they got noisy again. Blood came out. You see they've started eating each other. Pigs eat anything, but if they eat other pigs they die. They will die, these ones.'

Of course she did not believe him. This man was a peasant, and the peasants in her country, dumped there from Africa and the Iberian peninsula, had none of the semi-instinctive knowledge of European country people: the huge empty territory still bored them after four centuries. She knew that the pigs would die, but it would take a long time, and she heard in her mind the screaming continue for ever.

'Why can't you let them out – one at a time, I mean?'

The old man roared with laughter. She caught the blunt stink of cane-spirit. 'If we let them out, they eat us too. Besides, the foreman has the key.'

What would he have done? she thought, remembering her lover. He had cultivated indifference to politics, to money making, to everything. But this experience would have affected him, wouldn't it?

'Where is the foreman?' the young woman asked.

'He disappeared two days ago.'

The young woman suddenly felt sick. She thanked the old man. In her hurry to be away, she let in the clutch too quickly. There was another jeering sound from the back of the crowd, but the old man bowed courteously. Half a mile down the road she stopped again and got out of the car. She took off her sunglasses and was neatly sick into the gutter. Sweating and shivering she returned to the car and sat for some minutes with her eyes shut.

For fifteen minutes now she had not remembered her stay in the capital, and now it was as if the thoughts returning to her mind found it different, and their presence there less significant.

A man-servant in a white coat came out of the house.

'My God in heaven, Paulo, I've had such a time.'

It had taken her an hour to get through the centre of the city, driving tired and tense among the crowds of office workers whose return home was delayed by the strike. During that time the evening had changed to night. When she entered the drive of her father's house, the headlamps threw huge dragging shadows of tropical plants on to the walls. She switched off the engine and leant her forehead on the warm steering wheel.

The servant accepted the greeting calmly. For him, the young woman was the best of the family; he was glad to see her back again, and his flat Indian face glowed a little as it inclined towards her. The woman who stood behind him, however, knew just enough of the language to grasp the meaning of the words and to misinterpret them.

Though it was quite dark, this woman was wearing tinted spectacles. Her hair, drawn back tightly in a knotted bun, made her face with its wrinkled hidden eyes look raw and ill. Sliding and stumbling down the steps on thick raffia sandals, she caught the other's arm and embraced her.

'Celina, honey.'

'Betty.'

But after the embrace, the grip on Celina's arm did not relax. She took the new weight to add to her exhaustion as she entered the house.

'We've just ben worrying and worrying, honey.'

Breaking free, Celina watched her stepmother totter back to the half-full glass that stood on a table. Clutching the glass seemed to steady her. She turned and said: 'Worrying and worrying.'

Celina did not answer. She was looking for signs of her father or brother in the room. Besides, there were too many things that her stepmother might think it her duty to worry about; in any case, the North American concept of tact remained an uncertain element between them.

'I would like a drink, too. As a matter of fact, I've just been sick.'

At once she wished she had not said it. She could feel the other's mind rocking with speculation. Betty flinched, hung her head down towards the rim of her glass, gulped some whisky and muttered: 'No, darling, no, don't tell me it's that.' Then she got up and slid to the bell.

'Paulo,' she said in English. 'More drinks.'

When Celina came back into the room a few minutes later, the servant was pushing in a trolley on which glasses and ice tinkled gently together. Celina poured herself a strong whisky with water. Then she sat down. The two women looked at one another warily.

'This strike, it's really terrible. Your father's friends say there may be a revolution.'

'Who says it?' Though she knew that her stepmother was only making conversation, she was suddenly interested.

'Senhor Eduardo. I forget his other name. You know I can't remember their names here, darling.'

'Unfortunately all they've murdered so far is some pigs.'

'Pigs, honey?'

Celina laughed. 'It's our imitation of Belsen. In a few years' time we may get as far as humans. Now it's only pigs. This is not an advanced country, Betty, compared with yours. Still only a colonial civilization.'

'Pigs – I don't see ...' Helplessly the older woman sipped at her glass. Perhaps she ought to laugh, for the girl might be joking about something. 'Your father says ... there, but he'll tell you.'

Celina drank deeply and felt more good-natured. There was a long silence, while Betty made signs of distress on the sofa. At last she found an acceptable formula.

'How was the journey, honey?'

'It was very good. There was some traffic on the road, of course, because of the strike. I stopped once for coffee and once to cool the engine.'

'You must be famished. How's the car going?'

'It is fine. Everything was fine until those pigs. It was them that made me sick, and I cannot stop thinking about them.'

'You're tired too.' It *must* be a joke about those pigs. Celina was such a clever girl; such a brilliant family.

'No, Betty, I want to tell you about this. Please listen.'

But Betty, though she heard the other speaking, went on with her own thoughts: 'Poor kid, it's that man has got her into this state.'

Celina felt the warm spirals of whisky in her brain. ' ... And I go on thinking of them there. Eating each other, each biting another and being bitten. Or is it only the weaker ones? What will happen? I expect the last ones will die of thirst. Does blood quench a pig's thirst?' The desperation was growing, her nails digging into her palms.

Like a praying mantis, the blank face with the sun-glasses turned to her. Betty's head was not quite still, but shaking a little. 'Look, darling, why don't you get some rest? I forgot to tell you, there's company to dinner. But if you're too tired, I'll send you up a tray. They'll understand.'

'No. I will come down.' Celina stood up. 'Who are they?'

'Some British couple. The Newtons. Your father met him at the Law Faculty.'

'I'll rest for a little and come down.'

Celina went to her stepmother and patted her on the shoulder. In this family, embracing and touching one another were frequent, the actions creating a warmth which, in its turn, produced emotion. Betty put up her long thin hand, on which the rings were like shackles, to cover Celina's, and squeezed it.

When Celina turned to go, her father was standing in front of her. He was smiling, his arms open.

'Papai!'

Moving from Betty's caress to another, far stronger warmth, she kissed him eagerly. The familiar smell of the old man, like an aromatic wood, made her nostrils dilate. Taller than he was, she squinted tenderly into his fine hair.

Because they were excited and moved, the father and daughter began speaking in their own language. In a few moments, however, they had both remembered her – the other woman whom they had always to be consciously remembering, since a fundamental misadaptation caused them to forget her. They separated unwillingly, to include Betty in the conversation.

'Our daughter is looking beautiful, but I think tired,' the old man said. 'Do you not agree, my darling?'

Celina's eyes burned at him, as if she wanted to say, 'It's you that are the beautiful one.' He had already dressed for dinner in a crimson silk smoking-jacket, and everything about him seemed to her like silk, the silver hair, the black chenille eyebrows, the tissue-smooth skin of the face and hands. His shoes were as perfect as a waxwork's.

Soothed by his presence, the two women each took hold

of one of his arms and paced him up and down the room.

'We are going to entertain some English people, Celina. You see we have whisky for them.' He picked up the half-empty bottle, frowned at it, and placed it among the others on the trolley. Betty's face took on a look of despair.

'I know,' Celina said quickly. 'I've already had some. I was exhausted after the journey.'

'My dear, we would have sent the chauffeur. But with this strike there were no trains. We could not get him there.'

He patted her hand and then his tone hardened again: 'I shall make a cocktail as well, of course. Perhaps the other lady will prefer something less strong.'

'Father, I am going upstairs to rest.'

'Our guests are invited for nine o'clock. They will show English punctuality, I think.'

'I'll come up with you, darling. Oswaldo, I'm going to dress.' Betty quickly exchanged her husband's arm for Celina's.

'Father's looking grand, isn't he?' she said, half way up the broad staircase. Then quieter, and squeezing again: 'Honey, it's just the biggest thrill to have you back among us.'

A soft layer of indifference fell and settled on the top of Celina's mind. She broke free from her stepmother at the top of the stairs. In her own bedroom she found that one of the maids had already unpacked for her.

Celina went over to the window and leant against the cool glass. She was home, and now she felt the full sense of disappointment and let-down. Nothing had been changed. She knew now that the man in the capital had only to ask, and she would return to him.

The house was built on the edge of a slope overlooking the city. In front the skyscrapers stood against the sky, with their bases illuminated by the lights of cinemas and bars, so that each seemed to rise out of a smouldering fire. From far off the sounds of the city penetrated her consciousness, and beyond them, half-caught half-lost, it seemed that she could hear the noise of animals, the echo of screaming and pain.

Perhaps she would not even wait for the man to ask.

2

A young Englishman came out of the principal hotel and stood indecisively on the pavement. He was short, with a boy's nose and hair that had been blond when he was a child: it was one of those faces that people find difficult to take seriously. The slight air of absurdity was increased by his English suit of dark flannel, his old Somewhere tie and his suède shoes. In the whole city you could not have found anyone quite like him, and this made him instantly attractive to those who made it their business to come into contact with foreigners.

Because of this, he had learned to be cautious about looking at things and people too closely. He seemed only half aware of the creeping man who offered him a smuggled watch, and he ignored the bootboys along the wall of the hotel, who called and beat out rhythms on their soap-boxes to attract his attention. A scraping on the pavement beside him caught him more securely. It was the legless torso of a Negro, pulling itself along on a little trolley. The free hand held up a sheaf of lottery tickets.

'The cow, the cow for tomorrow.'

Another seller, a hunchback, came from the opposite side. 'The pig. The last of the pig.'

At first this had been one of the small mysteries of the place. Wherever you went, at every street corner or open space, the destitute and crippled turned towards you and shouted the names of animals.

'Look at the butterfly!' they called – 'Here is the cat!' –

until you began to feel yourself the only human character in a living bestiary.

The explanation of all this was complicated. The animals' names stood for the last numbers on the lottery tickets: number five was the dog, the deer was number twenty-four, and so on. The shouters were selling tickets for the official state lottery. The names of animals, however, originated in the enormous, illegal and far more profitable 'numbers racket'. This, the Animal Game, had a lively underground existence, and a code and mythology of its own.

The effect of all explanations – especially from embarrassed natives who unwittingly heightened the impression that something rather disreputable was involved – was for the animals' names to remain mysterious and startling. By buying a lottery ticket, you would enter an animal world, where the possession of a human will would have no value.

'The cow for tomorrow?'

The young Englishman shook his head.

'The pig. The last of the pig.'

He walked across the road and took the first taxi on the rank opposite the hotel. He climbed into the front seat beside the driver and gave the address of the Fonsecas' house, in the suburb known as Jardim Florida.

The radio was howling a report of the day's football. The Englishman had had a couple of gins in the bar already. He looked forward to the evening ahead with some apprehension. He was not above preparing, in fantasy, the conversation that he hoped he would have during the evening. But the two drinks had confused him. 'I exist,' he imagined himself saying to the distinguished people he would meet. 'You have to accept me. I exist.' He leant back in the seat and closed his eyes. His head throbbed. He knew that the driver might take him a longer route but he felt it did not matter.

Suddenly the radio snapped off. The taxi-driver was a white man with thin hands and an Italian-looking face. He would talk, the other knew – the fact that he had chosen the front seat was in itself an invitation to this – and he braced himself for the effort of understanding. He had been in the country for three months, and in this city a fortnight, employed by an English oil company. It was not the first time he had been out of England, and he was prepared to find here aspects of what he had known in Italy and Spain: among them the volubility and good will of the poor.

'A pity we're going to Jardim Florida tonight,' the man said. 'It isn't my night for Jardim Florida.'

'I don't understand.'

'On Thursdays I go to Jardim Texas. I have a girl there. Jardim Florida – that's for Saturdays and Sundays. It's a good place, too. I've had some grand times there.'

In the evenings, at the gates of big houses the Negro and German servants stood silent with shining eyes. Later on, each would withdraw into the shrubbery with a man leaning on her.

'Only fun-and-games, mind you,' the driver went on. 'Besides, I have to be careful, a married man with four children.'

'Naturally.' Because he was married, or because he was so obviously fertile?

When the taxi stopped at some traffic lights, the driver started fumbling under the dashboard. He handed over a tattered photograph: three little girls in ringlets and white party dresses, and a little boy with a bow-tie and flat hair held down by a slide.

'Very nice.'

The driver put his children back under the dashboard and out of mind. 'Sometimes, of course, we get one who wants to go further.'

He braked loudly, rounding a corner, and shouted: 'Clown! Assassin!' at a large car that was jutting out into the road.

'It's tricky for us drivers, though, with the police always

against us. They can cop you if there's a woman in the front seat, even.'

Now the taxi had left the centre of the city. Looking out, the Englishman saw houses with lawns surrounded by trees. He knew the Fonsecas must live somewhere near here. His feelings of apprehension returned to him, and now he wished he had time for another drink at the hotel.

'We go out beyond the airport. There are some eucalyptus woods there, it's quite safe. The little one I have in Jardim Texas likes that. What road did you say?'

The other repeated the address.

'She's a grand one, that little one. *Mulata*, of course, but I like that.'

The car stopped at a big gate. The driver switched on the inside light, for the Englishman to see into his wallet.

'Thank you. Always at your disposal.' He looked quickly up at the other, standing on the pavement waiting for his change. 'Sometimes I have a client who asks me to get a little one for him too.'

Dr Oswaldo slid back the glass door of the bookcase.

'It was the first time that modernistic ideas had been introduced in South America. We thought it very important,' he said. 'I published three books of lyrical verses. I was greatly influenced by Guillaume Apollinaire. Wait, I will show you.'

'I don't think I would understand them yet.'

'One of them has been translated by a man of the British Council that was here. Wait, Mr Morris, I will show you.'

Dr Oswaldo pulled a leather-bound book from the shelf and handed it to the young Englishman.

The book fell open at the front page. Stuck to it was a newspaper cutting of a poem.

But Morris could hardly read the poem. His attention was rivetted by the photograph that served as a frontispiece. At the age of nineteen or twenty, Oswaldo wore a straw boater and a striped cravat. His hands were covered with rings. The photographer had caught in him a stare of complacent sensuality that time had made absurd. Yet, as he lolled backwards, the young Oswaldo still seemed to exude, like a character from Colette, the atmosphere of prestigeful beds: those of Italian divas, perhaps, or well-preserved stars of the Comédie Française, on their visits to the capital.

'What do you think of it?'

'Yes, I see.'

'Of course it does not appear modern to you now.' The old man snatched the book away and slid it into its place on the shelf. He seemed bristling with anger as he went on: 'You are young, and nowadays everyone writes like that. But in those days we were the true revolutionaries, I assure you.'

'Have you – are you writing any more?'

The other shook his head impatiently. 'I have no time nowadays. My work keeps me entirely occupied.'

'I see.' The work might be law, or medicine, or political intrigue – nearly everyone in this country was 'Dr'.

'Hullo there.'

'Oh, Mrs Fonseca.'

She still wore tinted spectacles, but she had changed them. The new pair was extravagantly tilted, and ornamented with gold. Her dress she had bought in Paris, during the last congress that she and Oswaldo had attended there.

'Well, this is grand, isn't it?' Betty's remark indicated everything: Morris himself, the company they were expecting, and the long low room, which ended in a jungle of potted plants and trees.

'Why, Oswaldo, you've let his glass get empty.'

Her husband slammed the glass door of the bookcase. 'And Celina?' he asked fiercely.

'She'll be right down. I'm crazy for you to meet my step-daughter. She's a truly lovely person.'

Oswaldo crossed the room and returned with the cocktail shaker. His wife's praise of his daughter seemed to appease him.

'My dear Celina, this is Mr Morris.'

She was suddenly beside them in a swirl of white lace. Her skin was golden brown, her eyes green. She looked at Morris in such a way that for a moment he thought she must have mistaken him for someone else; she seemed to be expecting more than the hand he held out to her. The two older people were watching them.

'I think you have not met before' – Oswaldo came through behind him. 'My daughter has not' – he handed her a drink and seemed to observe her coldly – 'She has not been present in my house recently.'

This statement caused a precarious interval during which glances were exchanged. The greatest effect was on Betty, who gulped at her highball, her rings clicking against the glass.

'For heaven's sake, do you think those Newtons will be able to find the way?'

'Mr Hadleigh will bring the Newtons.'

'Isn't that grand, just think, all our guests being British-ers? And I've never even visited in your country.'

'Mrs Newton is not English,' Dr Oswaldo said. 'She is from Chile, or perhaps Peru.'

'And Ronald Hadleigh's a Canadian,' Celina added.

Mrs Fonseca looked squashed, but she grabbed Robin Morris's arm and swung it to and fro. 'Well, this at any rate is the genuine article. Eton and Oxford I presume?'

'Well, almost.' He gave an interior groan of embarrass-ment.

Celina said: 'My father is always trying to know English people. He was educated in England.' Morris guardedly watched her, admiring the bright brown shoulders against the white lace that covered her body. Already he thought he identified something original about her, an element that set her apart from the convent-bred sweetness of her country-women.

'Yes, I was at Stonyhurst, a Jesuit school. I think you have heard of it. I used to spend my holidays at Pinner. Do you know Pinner?'

'I'm sorry, I don't.'

'I expect it has changed very much now. Mr Newton knows Pinner and he will tell you all about it. I have the impression that he was born there.'

They dropped into silence. There was the sound of people arriving.

Ronald Hadleigh had a level gliding walk. It seemed as if he was treading on something softer than the floor.

'My dear Betty.' He kissed her hand. 'Simply no taxi. One telephoned and telephoned.'

There was a relaxing of tension. Hadleigh separated from the Newtons at once – seeing them, one realized that the whole idea of bringing them here appeared to him as something of an imposition. He went on talking, in a largely English voice. His own personality deafened him to any but the most simple remarks of other people, and his conversation was of the sort that can be projected without discrimination at anyone who happens to be around.

Betty Fonseca gripped Mrs Newton's large bare arm. 'Welcome to our home. It's just grand to have you here.'

Professor Newton intervened. 'I'm afraid my wife hasn't learned to speak English. She understands, though, if you talk slowly.' He was a small red-faced man, and he seemed to regard the presentation of his wife as something that needed careful attention, like the backing of a large car into a small garage.

'I speak, Cecil,' Mrs Newton said majestically.

'I'm sure you do, my dear,' Mrs Fonseca said. 'We'll get along just fine.'

But there was trouble at once over what Mrs Newton would drink. She did not recognize the names of any of the drinks offered to her, there was one she knew she liked but she could not remember what it was called, and she giggled as if in any case this was an invitation to instant drunkenness. Celina and her father together managed to get the problem straightened out – Betty Fonseca merely stood in the background saying: 'The poor thing, let her have what she wants.' Finally Mrs Newton was calmed and settled on a sofa, where she sat smiling vaguely until Dr Oswaldo brought her a glass of sweet vermouth. She sipped it once and placed it on the low table beside her, where it remained untouched.

Morris felt his hostess's sharp clutch on his arm.

'Isn't it fine to have all these lovely people around? You know, I think I must be the genuine hostess type. I want everyone, simply everyone, to have fun. I say to Oswaldo,' – she drew out his name into three distinct words – ' "What's the point in having this truly beautiful home and all these lovely people if you don't ask them to come around?" '

Certainly the house was fine, with its areas of rough granite walls, its jungle of green plants, French pictures and North American furniture. If you wanted to change the décor, it would be necessary to tear the whole house down and start again. As it was, however, it seemed likely to outlast the present set-up.

'Don't you agree with me?' Mrs Fonseca was squinting up through the dark glasses at him.

'Of course.'

'Nobody more than I admires this wonderful country, but they just don't have any fun. You're laughing, you bad man!' His face had not moved. 'Well, I know what you mean. Celina's brother Jango, for instance, he's a lovely boy, glory, how I admire that boy, all the girls here are just crazy about him, they won't leave him alone. And you, a handsome young Britisher, I'm sure you'll have yourself a wonderful time in this country.'

She turned away to find her drink, and Morris could look at her again. He saw how precarious and brittle she looked, with the lime-white powder on her colourless skin, the dark red hair chalky at the roots.

'But I'm the original extrovert, I suppose. I can't live without my friends around me.' She looked round the room at the ill-assorted collection, and went on kneading Morris's arm. Her voice dropped: 'And I hope we'll see you around often and often.'

The words were conventional enough, but as she spoke her voice dropped. He looked at her eyes through the protective green glass, and knew at once that she was quite drunk, and that her friendliness towards him carried an element of danger. The fact that he hadn't been able to see her eyes had deceived him up to now. It must have been obvious to anyone who knew her, and had taken the trouble to watch them both – Oswaldo for instance, whom Morris had already unintentionally insulted about his abilities as a poet.

Suddenly he felt that whatever happened tonight would not really matter, since he would never be invited to the house again.

Morris found Mrs Newton beside him at dinner. She smiled at him but did not speak. There was an animal placidity about her, a detachment from what was going on, that made him wonder whether she might not be pregnant. Her wide dress of white-frilled purple satin looked like a lampshade. Above it her round shoulders moved up and down a little as she munched her shrimp cocktail.

On the other side, Mrs Fonseca sat at the end of the table.

'I put you next to me as a very special person.' Her long jewelled hand kept on stroking his arm. Morris wanted to draw in his sides to make himself narrower, though in fact there was plenty of room.

When the glasses had been filled with white wine, Mrs Fonseca suddenly gripped him more tightly, caressing his sleeve with her hard thumb.

'Don't drink, anyone,' she called out. 'I want to propose a toast.'

She pushed her table napkin against her mouth. There was silence and then her voice rang out: 'I want to drink to our British friends here tonight, far from home, and hope that they, too, as I have done, will be as lucky to find a wonderful home in this wonderful country.'

'Charming, Betty, charming,' Ronald Hadleigh said.

'But you're not drinking.' Her voice was still hoarse. 'You must drink to one another.' She herself had almost finished her glass and, letting go of Morris for a moment, she caught hold of the white coat of the servant who was passing and pulled it. 'Paulo, another bottle.' Then her hand came back on to Morris's arm. He already felt that the bone there had shrunk and the muscle was weak and thin. It was as if the woman had to be in physical contact, plugged in on to someone else like a radio or an electric fan.

Dr Oswaldo was translating the toast to Mrs Newton. Conversation had again become general by the time the claret glasses were filled, and Betty's second toast came as a surprise to everyone but Morris, whose forearm was gripped again and whose feet were being trampled under the table.

'There's a very personal toast I should like to make. It's to a family, a very fine and brilliant family, who have done so much for their country – a family to which I count it a privilege to belong. To the Soares de Fonsecas. To my dearest Oswaldo.' Again it was three distinct words, as she looked down the table at him, and her eyes creased in a smile. Her husband's face was impassive.

'To Jango, who could not be here tonight because he is serving his country.' Betty raised her glass again. 'And to Celina, to her I'd like to say,' – she dropped her voice meaningfully to almost a whisper – 'Welcome home, Celina.'

'Thank you, Betty, thank you.' Celina's voice seemed not merely kind, but sincere. Her face was still and a little sorrowful.

To his profound consternation Morris heard his own voice say 'Hear, hear.' At once Mrs Fonseca turned back to him. 'I knew you'd understand. May I tell you something ... something very personal? You're going to be very very happy in this country. I hope you will find, as I have done, so much love, as much ...' She broke down and was silent. Her arm, withdrawing from his, knocked against her glass. Red wine raced in long tongues across the table towards Professor Newton. Expressionlessly, he watched it approach. Up to now, he had hardly spoken at all.

3

In the drawing-room Celina had turned on the gramophone. Mrs Fonseca was selecting records with cries of enthusiasm. Mrs Newton was sitting on the sofa, rather upright with her massive white arms folded in her lap, and smiling.

Without speaking, Dr Oswaldo and his daughter began to dance.

Ill-at-ease, Morris moved out of one of the french-windows that opened on to the balcony. Two great danes were patrolling in the garden below. They paused to sniff by the wrought-iron gate. Beyond the gate was the empty road and a street lamp; against the wall of the garden opposite, a white man and a Negro maidservant were pressed together. Morris wondered if it was his taxi-driver.

A man smoking a cigarette came and stood beside him. Against the light he saw that it was Professor Newton.

'Miscegenation,' Morris said shyly.

'What does that mean?' Newton asked.

'Those two people against the wall.'

'I see.'

They stood in silence until Betty Fonseca came out to find them. Then Morris saw, in Newton's gesture of acceptance and the way he said 'Back to the fray,' then, a reflection of his own feelings.

'Just watch,' Betty said, as they stood in the doorway. 'This wonderful sense of rhythm. I'm sure we foreigners never get it.'

Though Celina was taller than her father, they danced well together, as if it were nothing they had been taught but part of their instinctive life. Oswaldo was neat in his movements and he seemed to have developed a sort of threatening energy to which Celina responded, her eyes flashing and her body moving with precise violence.

'Doesn't your wife dance, Professor Newton? Don't they dance like this in her country?'

'No – that is, I do not think she will.' He spoke as if things might get dangerously out of hand if his wife was allowed to perform.

'That's too bad.'

Betty went to put on some more records, but returned directly to the two Englishmen. Morris decided that he must ask her to dance.

'We'll show them, won't we?' she said, gripping him. Hadleigh had taken Oswaldo's place as Celina's partner. Her father and Professor Newton watched from the french-window.

Until now Betty had appeared more definite in speech and

action than in the dining-room. Dancing, however, seemed to stir up the alcohol in her veins. At first she was limp on Morris's arm, and then uncomfortably close. Her cheek fell, warm and nerveless, against his. He piloted her through the motions, trying to hold her upright and at a distance, but he was too bad a dancer to make the attempt appear convincing to anyone watching. She kept getting nearer to him and rubbing against him. His body grew resistant and clumsy with the effort to concentrate. But she must have been more conscious in her intentions than he thought, for suddenly he found that she had steered him out of the french-window. 'Cooler here. We can still get the music,' she whispered. Before he could reply, her wet mouth was on his, she was whimpering, and her hands were running down his body. He tore himself away.

He edged round the curtain into the room.

He was unobserved. They were watching Celina and Hadleigh.

There was something grotesque about Hadleigh's dancing. With his knock knees, broad buttocks, and splay feet springily treading the floor, he resembled a large domesticated bird. Celina was made a little ridiculous by being his partner.

When the record ended, she sat down.

'Won't you dance any more?' Morris asked her.

'I'm sorry, I'm too tired. I love dancing and usually I can go on all night.' She told him that she had driven from the capital today.

Morris accepted the whisky-and-soda that Oswaldo gave him. His knees were trembling and he still had a sensation of shock, of skinlessness. He sat down beside Celina.

'How long did it take you?'

'Seven hours. That was not the worst part. I saw something horrible on the road.'

He began to laugh but saw that it would be wrong. 'A motor accident?'

'No, this was cruelty.' She told him about the crowd by the locked railway carriage.

Celina looked up and saw Betty watching her from the other side of the room. She felt a momentary jab of anger.

'You see, whatever my stepmother may say, this isn't a wonderful country at all. I was educated largely in Europe and I find it difficult to be like the others here.' For a moment she looked down at her feet and was silent. When she spoke again she was still impersonal and dogmatic.

'South America is a tragedy really, or perhaps a farce. It began as Eldorado and now it's the most boring continent in the world. Everything looks all right and it all tastes flat. Everyone wants money, but only in order to be respectable and dull.' She lowered her voice as if there were a risk that Mrs Newton, sitting near them, might hear and understand. 'After that, they all become indifferent. It's a very cruel land, but they are not cruel like the Spanish. They are cruel because they are indifferent.'

'I'm sure – what you were saying about the pigs, for instance – isn't that due to lack of education?' His reasonable words seemed stupid to himself. In fact he agreed with everything she had said, but he was afraid she might not want him to agree. After all, he was a foreigner.

'I don't think education matters much. We all do the same things, whether we're intelligent or stupid. It's very monotonous.'

Morris found himself pleased by her melancholy, by the natural gravity of her clear features, which she did not try to hide with little smiles and affected grimaces. Their eyes met; for a moment he was glad that she had not noticed his departure with Betty.

Across the room Betty was talking to Ronald Hadleigh.

'No, you got it all balled up. At the cotillions we curtsy like this.'

With surprising neatness she moved her feet and sank

down, still holding her glass. The whisky slopped to and fro but did not spill. She rose to her feet again.

'You see.'

'My dear Betty, you mean like this.' Hadleigh performed a passable curtsy beside her.

'No, no, that's way out. Like *this*.'

Dr Oswaldo stepped quickly between them. He took the glass from her hand and placed it on the table.

Betty Fonseca's achievement this time was more precarious. Hadleigh watched her, holding his hands clasped in front of his face.

'Like that.'

'But, Betty, in London all the debs are taught like this.'

'No, no, no. Watch here.'

Something went wrong. She was sprawling on the floor, her legs outstretched, her skirts pulled up over her knees.

Oswaldo pulled her to her feet. Suddenly she hung her head in silence. It was a movement of despair and surrender. It seemed as if all the bones had gone from her neck. Celina moved swiftly across to help.

'No, no, quite all right,' Betty mumbled, as they steered her out of the room. 'Want to dance again. Where's that young man?'

After they had gone, there was a long silence. Hadleigh came over to Morris and whispered: 'Oswaldo's asked the chauffeur to take us home. You live in the centre?'

'Yes.'

'Excellent.'

The Newtons were sitting apart, talking quietly in Spanish, as though they wished no part in anything that might happen. They received Hadleigh's information with alacrity. The party had seemed to Newton for a long time to be not his wife's sort; he had intervened between her and what was going on. With his quiet neatness, he was more than ever like a little mechanic in charge of a large and unmanoeuvrable machine.

It was now learnt that Mrs Newton also was feeling unwell. This news made the two other men respectful. So much seemed to be latent in her formidable exterior that they stood back, expecting the indisposition to manifest itself in some violent way. But all that appeared was her smile, this time a little altered in its sweetness by physical discomfort.

'What's wrong with her?' Morris asked.

'Tummy,' Hadleigh said briefly.

Celina rejoined them and walked down the steps with Morris.

He was silent. He felt bruised and skinned, and even a little guilty.

He had known himself to commit this error before : when you were unaware of the tensions in a family circle, you might make yourself pleasant to a member of it who had long ago been dismissed by the others – the loutish elder son, for instance, who had been kicked on the head by his pony as a child, the neglected sister-in-law, the vulgar French grandmother with the wig. The gratitude these mistakes involved you in was like a sticky feather on the fingers. While you were trying to get rid of it, the rest of the family were watching with amusement. Afterwards you found it difficult to get on the right terms with any one of them again.

Celina, however, seemed unaffected. Her sad calmness, which he had already found awe-inspiring, was the same as before.

'I was so glad that you could come to our house. But you ought to see some more of the country, not only the city. The next time we are going for a drive, I will telephone you. Or to our *fazenda*, for instance.'

Morris was gratified.

But later he heard her repeat the invitation to the Newtons. He remembered that vague invitations, though frequently given in this country, were seldom followed up. For surely, he thought, Celina could not be interested in seeing Mrs Newton again?

The guests were almost silent during their drive back into the midnight city. There was only one interruption: Mrs Newton's malaise resolved itself into an attack of hiccups.

Morris looked out of the window at the lighted bars, the groups of men on street corners. He tried not to think about Mrs Newton, for her hiccups, like a child's, had a reverberating quality. Apparently her mind was incapable of grasping that one hiccup made the arrival of another probable, for each one seemed to take her completely by surprise, catching her when the stage of her breathing made its resonance most violent.

Newton said 'Darling!' in a deprecatory voice after each attack. Morris wrung his hands together between his knees; he wanted to shout out 'Thar she blows!' Hadleigh was silent, impatiently watching the centre of the city approach, the lights grow brighter and more frequent.

The hiccups were having their effect on the occupants of the car, and both Hadleigh and Morris were experiencing a similar reaction. The natural forces that shook Mrs Newton were making it increasingly difficult for either of them to accept her as anything more than a figure of farce. Later, for Morris at any rate, it would take a determined effort to overcome this first impression.

'I suggest, after all that, we have a drink somewhere.'

Hadleigh spoke, standing on the pavement after Oswaldo's car had driven away. The words 'after all that' might have referred to the entire evening or to Mrs Newton's indigestion.

'That's a wonderful idea.'

'I don't expect you know the town well.'

'I don't. You suggest somewhere.'

Hadleigh led the way down a side street. Morris wondered

why they did not stop at any one of the bars they passed, whose French names were scribbled in neon-lighted handwriting over their dimly-lit doorways. He wanted to suggest this to Hadleigh, but the other, apparently suddenly full of nervous energy, kept walking ahead of him. Morris followed the plump figure bouncing in crêpe soles, his slotted jacket flapping like a bird's tail. They pushed their way over traffic lights, between cars parked bumper to bumper, and across a public square, whose palm trees were alive with chattering birds, kept awake by advertisements flashing on the tall surrounding buildings.

When they arrived at the bar – it was called Chez Toi – Hadleigh sat down at one of the little tables and ordered whisky for them both. An elderly woman in a black velvet dress was playing the piano and there were some blond men in dark suits seated at the bar. They seemed to be West German businessmen. There was still no apparent reason why this bar should have been chosen.

The Canadian's bout of energy had subsided, but his hands trembled a little. The waiter brought the whisky, showing them the bottle, which itself was genuine, and measured out a small dose into each glass.

'Good health,' Hadleigh said.

Morris expected him to start talking at once with the same persistence that he had shown at the house. But the older man did not speak. He stared long and silently at Morris. A new meaning had come to his face. Morris looked away at the bar. When he turned back Hadleigh was still staring at him. He shifted his right foot under the table from where one of Hadleigh's was pressed against it.

The waiter brought toasted peanuts to the table. Nervously Hadleigh clutched a few and put them in his mouth. He coughed, and then spoke:

'Rather a tiring evening, all told.'

'I enjoyed it. I thought it was very funny.'

'Of course,' Hadleigh said, ignoring this, 'the Fonsecas are a charming family. I've known them for years. Oswaldo is among my oldest friends down here. In spite of everything, they are completely informal, as you saw for yourself. No pretension, like some of these people.'

'Why should they pretend?'

The Canadian's face expressed amused toleration.

'They are about the oldest family in the city. Five hundred years, and longer than that in Portugal.'

'I see.'

'Besides,' – Hadleigh, feeling his initial superiority in social gambits was now established, was prepared to be informative – 'Oswaldo is something of a national figure.'

'I thought he was a poet. He told me he was a poet.'

Hadleigh snorted. 'He was leader of the SDN. Exiled at the time of the *Ditadura*, of course. A rather comfortable exile in Manhattan, as a matter of fact. That was where he met Betty.'

'I see.' Morris was near the end of his whisky. He wondered whether to order more.

For a moment or two, Hadleigh stayed silent, glancing with quick searching eyes round the bar. He was rewarded in this, though not perhaps in a way that he expected. Two young men who had just come in from the street approached their table. Red faces and ill-growing hair announced them as English before they began to speak. Both wore light tropical suits which were cockled and fitted badly.

The taller of the two men put his hand on Hadleigh's shoulder. He had the smiling silence of contented drunkenness. Hadleigh's face showed a desire not to be caught at a loss.

'Heard the radio today, Ron?'

'I did have it on, yes,' Hadleigh said.

'Know who come top of the leagues?'

'I'm afraid I don't.'

'Plymouth City.'

'Oh yes.'

'We're celebrating,' the second man said to Morris. 'The funny part of it is, we're both from Yorkshire. But you got to have something to drink to. What's that you've got there, Scotch is it?'

He was a small compact young man who wore shell-rimmed spectacles. With whistles and fingers he ordered a round.

'It's the first time we've been out in town like this,' he said. 'We're finding it quite agreeable. We started out at the club, but there didn't seem to be much doing there, so we've been trying some of these what they call "boîtes".'

'I like this place,' he said later, meaning the city and the country. 'A lot of the lads say they're not satisfied, but I'm satisfied.'

'What is it you do?'

'We come out here to set up this factory. Branch of our place in Bradford. Now they've asked us to take over as managers. Can't get a local man. Haven't the experience.'

'Will you do that?'

'As I say, I like it here. Les is not so sure.'

Les, the taller one, had been silent up to now. Now, hearing himself spoken about, he leant over and whispered: 'Ken and I want to get hold of two of these Portuguese women. Happen to know where they hang out?'

'Keep your filthy thoughts to yourself, you filthy bastard,' the other said smoothly. 'Can't you see we're having a serious conversation?'

But once the subject had been broached, there was obviously no going back. Such are the perils of late-night conversations in foreign cities. The men grew quieter, seeming to see the distances that separated them from the places where they had felt at home, the beds where they had found comfort. They were respectfully silent for a moment or two; it

37

was as if they had doffed their hats in the presence of the goddess.

'There don't seem to be any of them in here,' Leslie said.

The bar was almost entirely filled with groups of men. 'You'd better ask Hadleigh,' Morris said. 'He's been in this city longer than I have.'

Hadleigh received the request calmly. He was informative and his ability to tell them what they wanted, and the way he spoke, gave him a certain kindliness, whose existence one might not have expected.

For a moment everyone's feet shifted a little with the desire to be going, but nobody stood up. Quieter now, they drank more whisky. It was half-past one when they finally made a move. Outside on the pavement, lit blue and orange by the signs above the doorways, the commissionaire called them a taxi. While he went whistling up the street, the men stood silent.

Morris was embarrassed by Hadleigh's presence. He hoped they would be able to detach themselves from him before entering the taxi. It was a relief therefore when he saw that Hadleigh was already saying good-bye to the two Yorkshiremen.

The taxi drew up beside them. Hadleigh turned to Morris and said: 'Well, I hope you sample the delights of the city. Ring me up at my office some time.'

'What office?' Morris asked.

But the other had already gone back into the bar. His evening was not yet over.

4

Before luncheon, Paulo brought in the telegram on a tray. It was for Celina, and Betty was watching her intently as she picked it up and slit open the envelope.

'It's from Jango,' Celina said, surprised.

'Jango! But –'

'He wants me to meet him at the military airfield.'

'Send the chauffeur, honey.'

'Of course not. I'll go myself.'

'Imagine Jango! Something must be going to happen,' Betty Fonseca said. 'It's all politics with him these days.'

And so that afternoon Celina left the city once more, to meet her brother. This time she drove out in a different direction, through residential suburbs. Here the middle-class houses – all painted dead white with red-tiled roofs and built in a variety of Spanish, Turkish and North American styles – were still isolated among half-made roads. Between them lay waste areas of castor-oil plants and banana thickets. Mules wandered loose. The car bumped in places where the road had never been finished, or the surface had been washed away by the summer rains.

For Celina, it was a relief to be outside the city again. Already after one week she was tired of the things there were for her to do there: the course of lectures at the French Institute; the Italian films in little air-conditioned cinemas, to which one crept from the afternoon heat; the official cock-tail parties for charitable causes, where she met her own contemporaries, somewhat scared of her now, since they had husbands who checked on all their movements. And in her father's house there was Betty, who wanted company as a dog wants it, ranging from room to room until she traced someone beside whom to park herself.

Celina came to a barbed-wire fence and a gate across the road. There was a shabby platoon of soldiers. All were young, almost childish. The round steel helmets seemed too heavy for their thin necks, and their faces, whether blond, Negro or Indian, still had the blank innocence of country bumpkins. Celina's arrival created confusion. A corporal appeared at the window of the car.

Celina explained. The corporal blushed and looked embarrassed; he did not know what to do. He looked round to see if any of the soldiers were in earshot. Then he waved her through.

Celina drove off, but at the same time something caused the corporal to change his mind. She heard shouting. In the mirror she could see him waving his arms and beckoning for her to stop or come back. A line of soldiers was spread across the red-dirt road. An officer came running out of a shed, buttoning his trousers.

The little scene dwindled away in the mirror. The car took five minutes to reach the main building. The airport had been built by the Americans during the war. Once it had been the best in the country and there had been talk of turning it over for civilian use. Now it looked shabby and deserted, surrounded by the dismal litter that an army creates, even in a continent where there can be no wars. The civilian airport had been built a few miles away across the same high plateau, and aeroplanes sank and rose from it as regularly as wasps visiting a nest.

Celina got out of the car. She asked a passing soldier to find out if her brother had arrived.

She walked up and down beside the car. She pulled her coat round her, for it was cold and the wind brought a few spots of rain. You could see for miles here : the reservoir, with stumps of submerged trees showing above the surface of the water; hills of dull-green eucalyptus; ink-blue mountains far away.

A different soldier, this time a Negro so black that he seemed to be the colour of an aubergine, told her that Tenente Fonseca's plane was preparing to land now. He asked her if she wished to come into the building.

Celina declined. In fact she was a little nervous with anticipation. She was uncertain about her present relationship with Jango, for in times of crisis they avoided one another. Even in ordinary times their eyes dodged away in the way that brothers and sisters have: it was as though each of them had done unforgiveable things to the other as children, and each was scared now of the other's grown-up judgement. If Jango wanted to talk to her – it was to her, not their father, that the telegram had been sent – she was sure that it would be about other people.

The Negro reappeared and said: 'You can see the Tenente's plane now.'

The low mass of clouds had opened a little; there was half a rainbow, and the tiny army aeroplane was working slowly across the middle of it. So Jango made his entrance, in a setting fitted to his slightly absurd romanticism. The plane came round, then vanished behind the roof of the building. After a moment's apprehension, Celina saw it come bouncing across the red earth of the airfield.

Jango came out on the steps with two other officers. He shook hands and embraced them.

He ran down the steps to her, followed by a soldier carrying a bright leather grip.

'Jango!'

He kissed her.

'Isn't that Clovis Amaral? Doesn't he want to come to the city with us?'

'He has to arrange this colonel here.'

Jango stretched out on the seat beside her. He was smaller than she was, and resembled her closely, though in him the family characteristics produced a less impressive result. His skin was fine and his hands small as a woman's. His hair was shaved down to the bare walls of his head. Even on this overcast day, because of myopia and vanity, he wore dark glasses.

Jango gave her an American cigarette. He pulled the lighter from the dashboard and lit hers and his own. 'I'm tired. Clovis had a hangover, so I piloted the plane.'

He swivelled to look at her, but she kept her eyes on the road ahead. Already there was something between them: she knew that he had not wanted her to meet Clovis, who had once been one of her greatest admirers.

'How is everything?'

'What?'

'The house. *Papai*. How's Sunset Boulevard?' His English was very bad and the last two words came out irrecoverably twisted. They were the nickname he had invented for his stepmother after seeing Gloria Swanson's film.

'You mustn't call her that.'

'Seriously, how is she?'

'We had one breakdown, when there were English people to dinner.'

'English people. Do I know them?'

'No. Finally, perhaps, if it had to be anyone, it was better that they were English people.'

Jango noticed that Celina was driving very fast.

'Did she say anything?'

'No. I think she tried to make love to one young man.'

Jango groaned. 'Did *papai* mind?'

'I don't think he minds any more. He's looking very well. I don't think he minds.'

'*Coitado de papai*.'

'Poor Betty.'

'That cow.' He spat hatred. He was automatically on his father's side. 'What does he think? You always knew.'

'Jango. I don't know what he thinks any more. I used to know –'

'Yes, yes.' He cut her short: she had touched a spot that they both winced away from. He looked out of the window, whistling through his teeth. But a few moments later she felt him staring at her again. She knew that one part of him admired her still, and she was glad. Perhaps, in that part, he was proud of her and thought of her as someone rather international and chic, outside his understanding. But, of course, she had a life, and that was terrible. Women couldn't have lives. In his language the very expression 'to start life', when applied to a woman, meant to become a prostitute.

Worse, at that time and afterwards, there had really been nobody to go and fight. She was discreet, and the only evidence was her unhappiness.

Jango's puritanism, violent and uncertain, had been precipitated by his new political friends. In the Party there were priests among the soldiers and journalists, all of whom referred to their opponents by the names of their sins: a politician who had been a doctor of medicine was 'the abortionist', a brigadier 'the cuckold', another 'the —'. The word 'whore' was used coldly and technically by them to refer to the wives of their enemies.

Celina knew of these people in the Party, they were friends of her father's as well as Jango's. She also knew where they were wrong – not because they were hypocrites, though some were, but because they confused sin and crime, and attacked the sins that were ingrained in Man, rather than the curable evils of injustice, corruption and hunger. These barely interested them at all. For this reason she was against the interference of the Church in politics.

She had attempted to explain this to her father once. Suddenly, however, she had seen a detached knowing look in his eyes, a look which meant 'You in your position, of course, would think that'.

She had stopped short, hating him at that moment with all the strength of her love for him. Inside her head she had heard far off people saying: '*Coitado*, his daughter is a whore.'

Jango spoke again beside her. The approach to home saddened and disquietened him a little; political problems were easy, compared with coming back to where you had always lived. His voice was small and strained.

'Oh God, what am I supposed to say to her?' he asked, like a little boy.

'Will you be in the house much? Surely you have a lot of things to do?'

'Yes, of course.' She had made him feel more important again. 'Yes, I have a great many people to visit. The brigadier commanding the area. Some state deputies. Possibly the governor.'

'Well, then.'

He was retreating safely into his man's world. He was secure there. Celina had heard once that the wife of the French military attaché was Jango's mistress. But this had been a feather in his cap rather than an attack at his heart. Emotionally, he felt better off in the army among his friends.

That evening, as a matter of fact, he treated Betty very much as he had always done. With a flourish copied from the Latin-American lovers in Hollywood, he kept jabbering away at her :

'How is the beauty queen of North America? My second Marileen Monroy?'

'Celina, tell me what this dreadful man is saying.'

'It's his nonsense.'

'How are you, Jango darling?' Betty said. 'You look fine.'

'I am very well,' he said in English. 'Very busy. Making a lot of politic. Very exciting. I will bring you the president's head?'

'Fix me a cocktail, honey, will you? I'd like that much better.'

Celina stood apart, ashamed of him when he was like this. She thought broken English vulgar, as vulgar as the broken Italian they spoke in the factory areas of the city. It was vulgar not to do a thing properly.

Then Oswaldo appeared, his arms open, waiting for the embrace that was his tribute. Father and son walked out of the room in silence. Betty saw little more of Jango. He spent a long time telephoning, and that evening there was a political reunion at the house: a couple of colonels in uniform, and four or five state deputies, among whom was Father Albuquerque, the little Jesuit with grizzled hair and deeply sunken eyes.

5

Morris moved out of his hotel into a furnished flat in one of the residential suburbs. The flat was the upper floor of a small house; you reached it by an outside staircase. In the garden there were two servants' rooms.

The owners of the house lived downstairs. On the first morning that he was there, they invited him in for a drink.

His landlord, wearing sandals and a flesh-pink sports shirt, led Morris into the darkened sitting-room.

'My darling, it is Mr Morris.'

Mrs Kochen came forward. She was larger than her husband; she was dressed in a dark-brown linen suit of masculine cut, a white-netting turban tied on her hair. For as long as Morris knew her she was to be dressed in this way. Her white wedge shoes made clapping noises on the polished wood floor.

'If there is anything you wish, you will please ask,' Mrs Kochen said. 'We like to give good value.'

Her husband lifted his shoulders and squeezed his eyes shut. 'My darling, already we are talking business. Mr Morris is here on a friendly visit.'

'I wish him to know.' Mrs Kochen sat down temporarily, as if grudging the chair her presence in the middle of a busy day. She was clumsily built, and her scarlet nails were already scratching at her muscular bare legs.

'The boy is not back from school. He is at the English school.'

'Oh, yes.'

'To you he will be speaking English, but he is native of this country,' Mr Kochen said. 'He is speaking the language better than I myself.'

Mrs Kochen said: 'The boy was born here when we were coming in 1939. So he is native and we have always right to return here. After the war we went to Israel, but then we could come back because of the boy.'

'Thank you.' Morris took the small glass from Mr Kochen.

'Chin chin.'

'Chin chin.'

'Chin chin.'

'I did not wish to come back,' Mrs Kochen went on. 'We were thinking of the boy's future. I do not like this country, Mr Morris, but I live here because of my boy.'

'I see.'

'Now, my darling, let us let Mr Morris talk. These are our affairs. You think you will be happy here, Mr Morris?'

'Yes, I do.'

'Your firm is certainly greatly known. Though not greatly popular among the politicians, ha! ha!'

'They tell me that.'

'It is an interesting economic problem, this conflict between nationalism and self interest . . .'

The sitting-room was crowded with orchids in blossom and tanks of tropical fish. It was obvious that these decorations had not been chosen or arranged for their beauty. They were a hobby and, being in such numbers that they almost completely concealed the heavy black furniture, they took on the power of an obsession. In the world indicated by Mr Kochen's financial survey, they were like the canaries kept by the boss of a concentration camp.

Suddenly Mrs Kochen leant forward. 'Let me speak, Rachmel.'

With a little gesture of resignation her husband gave up his discourse in mid-sentence. Mrs Kochen turned to Morris.

'You are finding yet a servant?'

'Yes.'

'She is good? You have the references?'

'Yes I have. She used to be with English people.'

'With English people?'

'Yes.'

'That is good. Then she will not be a nigger.'

'But she is.'

'With English people!' Mrs Kochen frankly did not believe him. He had been duped. The references were obviously false. 'It is possible? Mr Morris, I am sorry, I think you will not be contented wtih this black woman. I think you will have trouble.'

'Oh, surely not. Why?'

'My wife is very sensitive.'

'Sensitive! We shall see if Mr Morris is not also sensitive. Mr Morris has not been here a long time like us. He will learn, as all foreigners learn.'

'I am afraid you will think my wife –'

'It is no good, that race. They hate us.' The whole appearance of Mrs Kochen had changed. She was white-faced and shrill. 'Mr Morris, you will learn. But you must forgive me if I do not permit her to come near my part of the house.'

'But really, my darling –'

'Rachmel, I shall keep everything locked, I shall so.'

Morris was furious. The woman seemed to be making a deliberate attempt to interfere with and control his life. Worse, she was a polluter, a creator of neurotic evil. Here, among the labelled orchids and the fancy fish, was a little stagnant corner of hatred. When Mrs Kochen left the room, Morris stood up to go.

'My wife is very nervous. You see, before the war she suffered greatly in Germany. Since then she has always worked very hard. She has worked far more than I, I am afraid, at our factory. I was brought up in a cultured atmosphere. My father, who was a Doctor of Medicine, knew very well Alfred Adler. This world here is my wife's world. Her father and mother are living here. I am afraid it is not mine. Some more cocktail?'

'No thank you. I must go.'

'We hope you will be happy here.' The wish seemed futile. There wasn't any happiness in the house. 'If there is anything you want, please ask.'

Morris had signed a year's lease. He had to stay, whatever happened. They both knew it.

'I will. Thank you.'

Mr Kochen shook hands warmly. He put his hand on Morris's shoulder. Radiant good nature shone out of him.

Morris walked out into the sunlight. He climbed the stairs and unlocked the door of his flat. He walked along the corridor into the main room. The sun came in blurred with green from the leaves outside. He opened the window and looked down into the garden.

Everything was thickly green with summer, and there were pink trumpets of hibiscus on the wall under the window. A flock of parakeets was screeching in the palm trees overhead. He felt very contented. He would have liked to spend the afternoon in the flat, but he had to go out for lunch. The servant would not arrive till evening.

He opened a bottle of gin and mixed some of it with water.

Outside, someone was summoning him with the clapping of hands.

'Mr Morris. Mr Morris.'

He went along the corridor to the front door. Mrs Kochen was standing at the foot of the steps. His heart sank when he saw her. He had the feeling of evil, battering round the tired face of the world, falling on everyone in turn.

'Mr Morris, you will forgive me to disturb you. I was not wanting to speak this before my husband.'

'Yes, what is it?'

'I hope you will watch your servant very closely, Mr Morris. Please, I beg you.'

Her obsession was back, and she was pleading with him now.

'All right,' he said curtly, turning to go.

'You see, it is my boy. You understand why I am not wanting to speak this before Rachmel.'

'Your boy?'

'Our son. He was born here, I think I tell you. But we are always careful. Always German and English school. At first I was not wanting for him to have contact with the low people here. Even the language. But the boys pick that up at school, among themselves.'

She gripped the balustrade and stared up at him. She was a tortured woman, a woman who had suffered, but he could feel no pity.

'I am afraid for my boy, Mr Morris. The other day, out with him walking, there was a wall and there were words – bad words. I did not of course understand them. But he understood them. I was watching his face and I could see that. And he is talking with children, dirty black children in the road, and I am not understanding what he is saying. It is so difficult for me, Mr Morris. You must help me.'

He had rarely met anyone whom he less wanted to help, with whom he felt less sympathy, than Mrs Kochen.

'How can I help you?'

'You see, this black woman. She will talk to him. He is only fourteen, Mr Morris, but that will not prevent her. You will watch and I will watch.'

'I'm sorry. I don't understand.'

'Mr Morris, she will try to do things with him.'

He stared at her. He could think of nothing adequate to say.

Mrs Kochen was looking away from him now. 'It is this country. We had to come back here to make a future for our boy. But I hate it, I hate it. They mutter things as I go past in the road. Once a nigger followed me home; he was drunk.'

He wondered how he could get rid of her. He wanted to escape from her hatred, which was everywhere, like the clinging affection of Betty Fonseca. But Mrs Kochen wasn't concerned with him. She didn't mind if she bored or infuriated.

'In Tel Aviv we were trying to get visas to the United States. You British did not want us to stay in Israel. I wished to go to the States; my sister is there. There my boy would have healthy life, with nothing of trouble like this. They know how to treat black people there.' She laughed her dreadful hurt laugh.

He turned away and went back into the house, slamming the door.

'We shall see, Mr Morris. We shall see which of us is right.'

He heard her wedge shoes clapping against the concrete. His feelings began to subside. A ready flow of emotions and a thick skin – that was Mrs Kochen. He hoped that he would not have to see a great deal of her. She depressed him already, because of her treachery to the only hopes there are in the world.

The taxi-driver, an elderly white man, unloaded the six cardboard suitcases. He was wearing an expression of patient irony, mingled with sexual appreciation. Expedita was very smartly dressed, with gold-rimmed spectacles and a frilly parasol. She carried a potted plant and a cage of little birds.

Morris paid off the taxi.

Half an hour later she came up to the flat in a blue overall with a handkerchief round her head. The spectacles were gone. He gave her some money and she went out shopping. She returned with two carrier-bags weighed down with food and cleaning materials.

'Everything's far too expensive round here,' she said.

He spent the earlier part of the evening playing the gramophone and mixing himself gin fizzes. In the kitchen the refrigerator hummed, with its belly full of food. There was a noise of the elaborate preparations for dinner. The atmosphere was entirely peaceful; Mrs Kochen could be forgotten.

When Morris went out later, he found a tall well-dressed Negro standing at the gate.

'Excuse me, does Dona Expedita live here?'

'Yes, she does. Why don't you go in?'

'I'll wait here.'

On succeeding nights when he came home later, the same man was standing there, half-hidden in the shadow of the hibiscus trees.

'Oh, that one,' Expedita said, when Morris told her. She giggled. 'He wants to marry me.'

'Why don't you marry him?'

'Oh, I couldn't do that,' she said deprecatingly.

'Why not?'

'Oh, I couldn't possibly.' She giggled. 'He's far too black.'

6

At first Ronald Hadleigh did not notice Celina. He was being busy and official: it was the inauguration of an exhibition of Italian lithographs at the Museum of Contemporary Art. Ronald was talking to a tall man whose face seemed vaguely familiar.

She waited a moment. Someone handed her a cocktail. She knew that, if Ronald was being exceedingly official, he sometimes forgot to recognize one. But she was always ready to talk to him. He knew everyone and it was through him one kept in touch with what was going on in the city.

Celina was amused to see that, in this case, it was Ronald who was at a social disadvantage. His companion, whose head was beaked and bald like a vulture's, was not giving him his full attention. He peered here and there, not at the lithographs, which were on separate screens, but as though searching for someone who might be hiding behind them.

Then Hadleigh saw Celina. He introduced Prince Koronski. The prince began speaking English.

'We meet before. I remember we speak much of England.'

'I was there, three or four years ago now.'

'I am knowing well your country. When I am in England in the Polish Army, I receive much attention from English aristocracy.'

'Oh, yes.'

'You are long in this country?'

'I was born here,' Celina said. 'I'm not English. It is rather confusing. You see, my mother –' She realized that he was not listening any more. His vulture's eyes had unhooded and were glaring away over her shoulder. Sipping at her cocktail, she watched him. He had a military appearance, and he held his back as straight as a fencer's foil. He stood a head taller than the crowd that surrounded them, the art critics and the fat women with feathered hats.

'The prince's company is filming on the coast,' Ronald Hadleigh said to her.

Celina now knew where she had met this man before. But at that moment the Pole made a dive, quick as a heron, and returned from behind a screen with a young man secured by one arm. The young man was gabbling excitedly: 'No, *bem*, I was only speaking to Minna Rabinowicz. When we are on the coast, she wants me to visit her beach-house. It's a beautiful place!'

'You will not go,' the other hissed. 'I know Minna Rabinowicz. Her father was a tailor on our estate in Poland. Also I know Moshe Rabinowicz, her son, your friend who calls himself a sculptor. I do not wish you to visit them.'

'But, *meu bem* ...'

'How is Betty?' Ronald asked Celina.

'She is better. The doctor says she must be careful, though.'

Celina's directness confused Ronald. His question had been purely formal; he had forgotten what had happened at their last meeting.

'And how are you yourself?'

'Oh, I'm rather miserable, Ronald. Some time I will tell you.'

'Poor Celina.'

The subject had ceased to interest her. She turned away to look at the young man who now stood beside the prince. He was certainly something to look at. His dark suit was tight-fitting, he wore a tie of silk brocade and black suède moccasins.

The prince said: 'This young man is called Nelson Vasconcelos. He is working in my company.'

The young man's hair was a skull-cap of black fur. His face was flat and symmetrical and he had hardly any eyebrows. Celina remembered that she had already heard about him. He was a full-blooded Karajá Indian; three years before, he had been brought back from the Amazon region by a Danish ethnologist. Since then, he had adapted himself quickly. The long jungle stare he gave Celina was mixed with a competitive pertness. While she watched him, he preened himself a little, like a wild bird.

After intently observing the effect the young man made, the other dismissed him by talking English again.

'You must come to visit our location. We will make one great film. One great film.'

'I should love to. When do you start?'

'Last week. Already we have our English cameramen down there. Fortunately there is one excellent hotel, managed by Austrian people.'

The Indian Nelson Vasconcelos watched them both closely. His eyes moved like a spectator's at a tennis match. He seemed to be observing the talk emerge from their mouths.

'Will you be there long?'

'Three weeks. For myself, on the production side, it is only to observe.'

By this time the prince again appeared distracted. Celina was preoccupied with her own thoughts. The conversation lapsed, and suddenly he was saying good-bye.

'Forgive me. It is a great pleasure.'

As he left, Celina and Ronald could hear him whispering in his thick accent: 'Finally, you are not going to Minna's beach-house.'

'Oh, *meu bem*, I promised.'

'I gave no permission.' Propelled by an iron arm, Nelson Vasconcelos disappeared into the crowd. Only the other's head could be seen, its sharp beak like a prow cutting a path among the golden floating feathers of the women's hats.

When Celina turned, she saw that Ronald Hadleigh was watching her attentively.

'What is his name again?'

Ronald told her. 'He seemed to think that you had a previous acquaintanceship.'

'I have met him, yes.'

Ronald waited, his features tense with curiosity.

But a moment later, she was rescued from his scrutiny by four young women, married contemporaries of hers. Overdressed and over-made-up, they flashed and rustled like a wave of silk and brilliants. They embraced her and drew her away to one of the leather sofas with which the gallery was furnished. There Celina sat, safe from interruption, with the young women talking and laughing across her. Their conversation was harmless and inane, and she enjoyed the relaxation of their little excited world.

7

At the gate the Packard stopped, a shining mass the length of the front garden. It slid back, and hooted.

Expedita looked crossly down the outside staircase. Then, leaving her broom, she went indoors. Morris had finished breakfast and was waiting impatiently.

'Yes?'

She stared him slowly up and down. This was a gambit that always unnerved him.

'There are people,' she said.

He picked up his bathing things. In the doorway she merely shifted from one foot to the other. Her hips swayed aside but he could not avoid touching her. As he pushed by, her improbably thin eyebrows were arched.

'I'll be back tonight,' he said.

Expedita scratched her cheek with a crimson claw and patted the wiry cushion of her hair. 'For dinner?'

'Not for dinner.'

She shrugged shoulders and her eyebrows went higher. Morris ran down the steps two at a time.

A minute later Expedita burst into wild booming song: longings, what longings she had for her love! He had gone away and her heart was broken because he would not return! She got out the hose and began sluicing down the steps and the concrete drive.

'Hullo. Good morning. This is wonderful.' He was hot already, and over-shaved. He scrambled in beside Celina on the long pillowy front seat of the car.

Celina said: 'You've brought your bathing things? Good, you will need them.'

They whirled down tree-lined streets to a part of the town which Morris had never visited. He watched Celina out of the corners of his eyes; a small figure in a T-shirt and blue jeans. Her bare brown arms were raised and he noticed the patches of fur under them. He decided that she kept them because somebody had asked her to; he wondered who he was, and whether Celina's air of sadness came from the same origin. Certainly it was nobody he had met at her father's house. Already Morris liked her much better than he had then: she seemed to him as light and glittering as the morning that opened out in front of them, the white houses among azaleas and the streets wet with the night's rain.

'This is most awfully kind of you,' he said. 'Where are we going?'

'To the sea. There is no one at the *fazenda*. I hope you do not mind?'

'Of course not. But I mean now.'

'To pick up the others.' She glanced at him curiously. Of course there would be others.

'Who are they?'

'A Mr and Mrs Newton. You met them at our house, you remember.'

He was sharply disappointed.

The first appearance of the Newtons fulfilled his gloomiest predictions. Indeed, as the couple came out of their *pension* the spectacle was so lamentable that he wondered if he knew Celina well enough to exchange a commiserating glance. But the Newtons were her guests and the choice was hers. The *pension* was built in a German Gothic style, and under the arched doorway the couple reminded him of an English country wedding: the stout woman, probably past child-bearing, dominating her brick-red and embarrassed husband. Mrs Newton seemed even larger, in a flowered print and high shoes, than she had done before. Her husband was wearing a dark suit and tie.

Once in the car Mrs Newton began talking. She talked all the time, pausing only to demand answers to her questions. Morris saw Celina grow tense as the car descended the winding road through the mountains.

Celina parked the car in the shade of a tree.

Morris walked over to some rocks, where he put on his bathing trunks. A few moments later he was swimming out in the warm bay. On either side, the mountainous islands seemed to hang in air, cut off from the sea by a band of haze. As the day grew hotter the haze thinned in front of solid objects: here and there you could see roofs of houses, half-screened by thickets of bamboo.

Morris came inshore and walked up to the car.

Newton was wearing scoutmaster's shorts, but the two women were as he had last seen them. Celina was trying to persuade Mrs Newton to shed some of her clothes and to sunbathe.

'What is she saying?'

'She says she doesn't like the sun,' Celina answered. 'What is the good of coming here unless you make the most of it?'

In the part where the car and the tree combined to give deepest shade, Mrs Newton sat smiling quietly.

'You'll come and bathe, won't you?'

'As soon as I can. I'll change in the car,' Celina said.

The two men went down the shore together. Newton returned to fetch some cigarettes. Morris made for a point in the middle of the bay and then looked back. The car stood under the tree with Mrs Newton still in its shadow.

Morris swam to the rocks, to search for a place to dive. Newton was already sitting there, smoking.

'Thank you.' Morris took a cigarette. He threw the match away and a fish splashed at it. 'Your wife won't bathe at all?'

'No. She's really frightened of the sun.'

'Isn't all that thing about sunstroke out of date? I mean, if you eat salt and drink enough.'

Newton laughed unhappily. 'It isn't that at all. She's frightened of getting too brown.'

Morris was silent.

'It's the same in all the equatorial countries. My wife comes from a distinguished family, but some of her cousins are mulattoes, that's all.'

'I see.' Morris couldn't think of any comment to make. 'What were you doing there? When you met Mrs Newton, I mean?'

'In the university. Mercedes was a doctor; she ran a clinic for children. As a matter of fact it was the first one they had like that up there. It was entirely free – her family put up the money.'

'Does she work here?'

'She can't. Her degree is not accepted. Anyway, I stopped all that when I came along.'

Morris looked at the swaying weeds just under the surface of the water. He heard Newton say: 'I was very grateful to Mercedes. I think she saved my life.'

It turned out that Mrs Newton's assistance had been psychological. Newton's first wife and their child had been killed by a flying-bomb while he was in the army. He had no near relatives, and he had spoken Spanish in his child-hood: as soon as he was demobilized he came to South America. Mercedes was the wife of a university colleague, the Professor of Political Geography, a peasant who looked like a butcher and devoted a large part of his time and salary to women. Naturally he was shocked and horrified at becoming a cuckold.

There was no divorce in the country; instead, a tremendous row. Mercedes hadn't wanted to go with Newton. Legally separated from her husband, she might have been able to continue with her clinic. Newton, however, resigned his chair, and he persuaded her to leave the country with him.

He lit another cigarette and said: 'I wanted to accept the full responsibility for what I'd done. After all, I'd deprived her of everything. She had lost her life's work and she was not even divorced.'

He paused and looked at Morris. 'We got one of those Mexican ones later. And we were married in Uruguay.'

'I see.'

The morning sun detached itself from the hump of an island. It glared in front of them. Morris began to feel burnt and sweaty. He stood up.

Beside him Newton shifted, uncomfortable with his past and his future.

'Yes, we're married all right. The trouble is that now I hate her guts.'

At that moment, Morris dived. Underwater he opened his eyes. The sea was clear as gin. He could see little smoke puffs of animals scattering on the sand below. When he came to the surface he swam back to the shore and the noise of water and the sense of movement filled his head.

He was a little appalled at the series of disasters Newton had narrated to him. Perhaps such mistakes were inevitable; the fact that he himself had failed to make them meant that he was too detached, insufficiently enlisted in life.

He came up beside Celina.

'It's very good.' She was wearing a bathing-cap and shouted louder than was necessary.

'What about her?' He jerked his head in the direction of the shore.

'She's quite happy.' He saw that Celina was uninterested. 'When we were children we had a house down here, on the other beach. We used to spend the whole summer here. There was no bridge then, you had to come by boat. One of my uncles had a yacht. He lent it to the government and it was sunk by the Germans when we came into the war in 1943.' She ran her hands across the sleek surface of the water. 'I think I've been happier here than almost anywhere. I hope you like it. I want everybody to like it.'

'I think it's wonderful.' All his senses were quivering and alive. He stared at her, with his heart thudding.

Celina plunged through an approaching wave and struck out for the rocks where Newton was sitting.

Morris walked up the sand to the car. Mercedes Newton was patiently sitting on a camp stool, with her hands folded in her lap like a woman at the door of a cottage. She was not doing anything. She smiled at Morris.

'Cold?' she asked.

'No, the sea is warm.'

She smiled again. He felt sorry for her now, an isolated and pathetic figure, her natural talents unused. Heavy make-up diminished her eyebrows and concealed the moustache-shadow on her lip; in the same way the flowery dresses and refined gestures were a disguise for physical strength.

Even if Morris had found it easy to speak to her, there was something in her appearance that made conversation impossible. Now she was looking past him, towards her husband and Celina.

'No, it seems we cannot make your wife happy.'

'Please don't worry about it. She always does what she likes.'

'I'm not worried.' Celina sat down beside him on the rock. 'It is always difficult when everyone does not speak the same language.'

'It's my wife's own fault. She had plenty of opportunity to learn.'

'Have you tried to teach her yourself?'

Newton looked across the water. Mercedes had left the shade and was walking fretfully up and down the edge of the sea. Her high heels dug into the sand and made her totter. She was trailing a long fichu handkerchief, like a signal of distress.

He turned to Celina and said violently: 'Mercedes will never learn English.' Celina said: 'My English grandmother lived here for forty years without learning the language. But in those days everyone had French.'

Newton wondered if his wife could ever have been included among those Celina called 'everyone'.

Celina stood up, a small brown figure in a white bathing-suit, against the sea and sky. She dived and he watched her body silvered with bubbles in the clear water below.

He walked slowly back along the top of the sand. By now both Celina and Mercedes had arrived back at the car. He knew that they would not talk easily. Whenever he left his wife alone with other people, there was an uncomfortable atmosphere on his return. He was used to it; he accepted it as a part of his life.

Beside him, a man and a small boy emerged suddenly from the undergrowth. They were Japanese, and the man was carrying a swordfish he had caught: a long strip of dusty aluminium, with the frayed tail dragging in the sand.

'Good day. Foreigner?'

'*Ingles.*'

'You are making a film?'

'No.' Newton pointed to the car in front of him.

'Picnic?' The Japanese indicated his son. 'I will bring him to see it. But a lot of them here are making a film. It's a great thing.' He smiled with two fangs. 'Yesterday they photographed me and the boy.'

Celina had spread out a cloth in front of the car; she had brought a sliced chicken, salad, some ham, a bottle of Portuguese wine and various fruits. In the middle of all this, Mrs Newton's battered sandwiches waited for someone to come to a decision about them.

Morris asked: 'Who are your friends?'

'They want to come and watch us eat.'

The Japanese knew he was being spoken about and smiled. The child stepped forward and stared at Mrs Newton. For him, she was by far the most interesting and extraordinary of the group. He had chosen rightly, for she welcomed him with open arms. In a moment she had begun a game with him, which he watched with fascination, his eyes full of laughter. She was overwhelmingly successful; it seemed that she could not fail to please him.

'He thought we were making a film. Apparently some foreigners are making a film here.'

'Yes,' Morris said. 'They're English. I know some of them.'

Celina looked up quickly. 'You know some of them?'

Morris told her about some men he had met at the English Club: three Londoners with lizard-like faces and elderly blonde wives – Spike Ditch, Len Bagoban and Cocky Bird.

'No, no,' Celina shook her head. 'You don't remember the name of the company?'

'I'm afraid not.'

Celina began questioning the fisherman. After a time, she looked round for something to give him. The first thing at hand was Mrs Newton's packet of sandwiches. The Japanese and the child bowed their thanks and went away. Celina was preoccupied during lunch. Beside her, Mercedes Newton, silent and furious, displayed the maximum of refinement with paper plates and serviettes.

Morris walked over to another tree and lay down. He had been there five minutes when Newton settled beside him.

'What's up?'

'What do you mean?'

'I mean, what's biting the ladies?'

'You've noticed they don't get on together? My wife always dislikes any woman that I might be attracted by.'

Morris felt again the touch of the other man's obsession. 'Celina, though. I thought one of us must have made a blob.'

Newton looked puzzled.

'Or perhaps it's something to do with the Japanese,' the other went on. 'You must have understood what she was saying to him.'

'I didn't listen.'

Morris broke up his cigarette in the cool sand. He continued meditatively: 'I find her a confusing person. It isn't merely that she's not European. She doesn't really seem to belong anywhere, let alone here. I mean, what's the idea of us coming here today? I've been asked out on these expeditions before, but somehow in this country it never comes off. There's one woman who keeps inviting me to her *fazenda* every time I meet her. Only she never quite fixes the day. It's got to such a state that I avoided her, cut her even, every time I see her approaching. I just can't stand it any more.'

He looked up and saw now that Newton's face was closed and his lips prim. Morris realized what at first had been difficult to assess – that Newton came from a class in England that left discussions about other people to women. Newton was one of those men who, if they are lucky, can go through life without finding it necessary to judge their fellows at all.

'All I know is that she'd make some man a wonderful wife.'

'Who?'

'Celina.'

'Do you think so? She seems so absent, somehow. I had a feeling that perhaps she might be Lesbian.'

Newton looked horrified. Morris rolled over and fell asleep.

When Newton returned to the car he found Celina carrying the knives and glasses they had used at lunch. 'There's a spring among the rocks near here. I'm going to wash these.'

She walked off into the scrub, along a path beaten by the naked feet of fishermen, and washed the things in the green water of the spring. She left them for a moment on the warm rock to dry, and then carried them back towards the car. She had reached the edge of the scrub, and had come out into the open behind some trees, when she heard a howling sound ahead of her. It was Mrs Newton.

Celina halted, unwilling to share in a domestic scene. She could not retreat without the risk of being observed. Newton was trying to calm his wife. 'My darling, it was a mistake. She was preoccupied. You know very well she did not do it on purpose.'

'It was on purpose. It was to shame me.'

'Please stop this. She or that young man will be returning here.'

'I do not care. I hate them. I hate all your English. Mother of God, why cannot I have my own people! Almighty God is punishing me for what I have done!'

There was a silence of paroxysm, and then she began again: 'My sandwiches! The sandwiches I made with such great trouble! She gave my sandwiches to the Japanese!'

After a time, Newton said: 'There, that is better. See if you cannot smile. Perhaps it was a bad idea to come, but we are guests. They are trying to be friendly. I want you to make friends with people here.'

'How can I be asked to make friends with such people? What manners! What lack of education!'

A sound of whispering followed. Bargains and promises

were being made. Newton again had sold his soul for a few hours of peace.

Celina gave them two minutes more and then she walked towards the car. Mrs Newton was turned away, sulking in silence. 'My wife is feeling the heat a little,' Newton said.

'Surely it is much hotter than this in her country?' Celina said. She was furious. She swore to herself not to change any of her plans for Mercedes Newton's sake. 'Why on earth doesn't she sit in the car? If the windows are all open she will be cool there, and it's completely in the shade.'

Surprisingly the suggestion was accepted. In long-suffering silence Mrs Newton resumed her place in the back seat of the Packard, where she sat upright, with flustered dignity. Celina left her and lay down on the hot sand, and later she again went into the sea.

An hour had passed by the time she returned to the car. Mercedes Newton was still sitting in exactly the same position, but now her eyes were shut. Perhaps it was only a sense of *amour propre* which forced her to pretend to be dozing, for when Celina had got into the front seat and had begun to change into her dress, she suddenly became conscious of the intense scrutiny of the older woman on her neck, her sunburnt arms and the exposed parts of her body.

When he awoke he felt something on his shoulder. It was Newton's hand. He was standing over him, fully dressed.

'We're going. It's four o'clock. They asked me to wake you.'

Morris stretched enormously, smiled, and crossed his hands on his belly. He felt warm and curiously content. During his sleep his attitude to the other seemed to have undergone a change. It was as though, by going to sleep in Newton's presence, he had given him something – a token of trust perhaps.

'Did I snore?'

'No. I slept as well.'

Morris stood up and yawned. 'What's happening?'

Newton was watching him paternally. 'We're going to some hotel along the coast.'

'Why does she want to go there?'

'She didn't explain why.'

They grinned at each other.

Half an hour later they were settled at an iron table outside a bar. Celina had gone to park the car in the shade and had not returned.

A truck pursued by a crowd of ragged children came bouncing and lurching down the dusty road. In the back two men in overalls were steadying a camera on a trolley. The faces in the driver's cabin were European. The truck turned in a cloud of red dust and disappeared behind the hotel.

'There are your film experts,' Newton said.

'I didn't recognize any of them.' Morris got up. 'I wonder if it requires great courage to go to the loo here. I'm going to try.'

A waiter pointed the way to him. The place fulfilled his worst expectations. Damp flies clouded up and settled on the dripping walls and then on his face and hands.

Suddenly he heard Celina, somewhere near.

'But I must take them back. They can't go by bus, can they?'

Her voice was entirely changed. There was a note of nervous desperation: she sounded like someone who might soon burst into tears.

The reply was English, a plushy university voice: 'I don't really see why not.'

Piqued and apprehensive, Morris walked out into the sunlight.

'How was it?' Newton asked.

'What?'

'The jakes.'

'Average,' Morris said briefly.

When the English voice came again, he did not look round. He could hear it drawing nearer between the tables, louder than any of the others, talking bad Spanish to the waiters, and breaking into laughter. And its confidence in itself seemed to be justified, because you could hear the waiters laughing too.

Celina appeared beside them.

'Mrs Newton. Professor Newton. Mr Morris. This is Gregory Cowan.'

Standing there, the man was enormous. His head was bald, his nose aggressive; he wore a brown suède coat and thick sandals. It was the voice, however, that still hung on to Morris's perception: in this out-of-the-way context, its recognizability was appalling. To the others it probably sounded very like his own. The moment, in fact, that he opened his mouth, there would immediately be overtones of 'Dr Livingstone, I presume'. And sooner or later they would find, all too soon, a mutual stamping-ground, somewhere in London, known girls, known writers, known pubs.

8

The newcomer sat down at the table and looked at each of them in turn. Though his smile appeared good-natured, his eyes were without benevolence.

'We've been down here for a week now, doing continuity shots. And now we've heard that the company has run out of money again.'

'What will happen?' Celina asked.

He laughed. 'They won't be able to finish the film at all.'

Morris watched him lean across to light her cigarette. The whole time Celina's eyes were looking up at Cowan's face, not down at the flame. Suddenly it became obvious who this man was. Morris's earlier sensation of pique increased. It was now the sharp prong of jealousy.

Cowan gave him the same smile again. It seemed less good-natured now. Undoubtedly it was faintly superior: 'How did poor you,' it asked, 'manage to get mixed up in such an intolerable and boring situation?'

He said: 'I've got to get back to the city as soon as possible. We haven't been paid for the work here. I shall have to try and extort the money from them.'

Celina fingered her glass. She did not look at him when he spoke about money.

In Morris, the man aroused confusion and apprehension. Already he dominated so much that the others, the Newtons, were silent, pushed aside, out of the picture. The moment of friendship that Morris had experienced with Newton on the shore this afternoon was past and forgotten. But with Cowan apprehension was always there – it was this sensation that, remembered later, would make Morris think that he had guessed all about Gregory Cowan from the first. At present he knew he would go on seeing him and he knew why.

It was not only the voice, but a question of dialect. In the English Club, for instance, they always asked 'Where are you from?' and Morris answered: 'I suppose Wiltshire' – his grandmother lived in Wiltshire. 'You'd better meet Bill Ferris,' they said, 'Bill's from Swindon.' Thus he would go on meeting Cowan, perhaps from friendship, but perhaps only for the sake of hearing words ring out with the special connotations of a group of Londoners – a floating 'Upper Bohemia' no longer anchored to or identified with any postal district there.

Having begun as impressively as this, Cowan became more purposeful. They were at the end of a day whose object had been attained, and were tired. It seemed easy for him to impose himself further.

'Why don't we drive back to the city now? We can intoxicate ourselves when we get there.'

'No. I want to rest for a little,' Celina said.

He was so large, so ebullient and full-throated with his actor's voice, that her small firm objection was unexpected.

'Let me drive you. Then you needn't rest.'

Celina was still. She stared at him and surprisingly he became confused. Then she drained her glass. 'All right,' she said. 'If I am not going to drive, I can have another drink.'

This disturbed Cowan even more. He tried to control his impatience, which already exposed his desire to make use of her car. There was nothing for him to do but submit. For the next quarter of an hour he sulked in silence, tilting the iron chair uncomfortably and shifting his long legs. When Mrs Newton attempted conversation, he glared at her in blank amazement, then looked round him as though asking for witnesses to the fact that such a person should exist, or that he should be expected to meet her.

Finally, Morris paid the bill, and the five of them returned, without speaking, to the car.

When he was at the controls of the Packard, Gregory Cowan was able to reinforce his initial impact. At the beginning the road was narrow and rutted, but they soon emerged into the state highway which led up the mountains to the city. Cowan drove well and extremely fast. Celina sat between him and Morris on the front seat; in the back, the Newtons seemed grieved and neglected. Once or twice, as the car began the series of hairpin turns that were to bring them to the top of the range, Mrs Newton gasped and fell forward. Otherwise they were both silent.

Morris felt uncomfortable, as though he had betrayed the little man who had this morning chosen him for his confidences. He guessed that it was Newton's fate only to find

69

friends on rare occasions – occasions that his wife's attitude would make as furtive as another husband's visit to a brothel.

At the top the impression of power was easy to give. There were twenty kilometres of straight highway. They arrived in the city before the street lamps were even lit.

The streets were full of loitering crowds. 'Where shall we go?' Celina asked.

But there was no question about where they were going. It was to the Newtons' *pension*. Morris opened the back door of the car for Mrs Newton. He watched the two of them go up the steps between the potted plants.

They looked beaten.

Book Two

I

Already Morris had tried to escape three times, but they had insisted on his staying. Perhaps each of them wanted an intermediary, to delay facing the other alone.

They were at a café table in the middle of the city. Around them were groups of men in palm-beach or tropical suits, drinking beer or tonic water and munching peanuts, laughing and shouting from table to table. The men picked their teeth and sat astraddle, scratching where they pleased, on blue bristly chins or damp armpits, or sending an exploratory finger between the flies. Now and then a new arrival was applauded, embraced and patted, and, after he'd blown on the seat of an empty chair, was settled among them. The German waiter went scurrying for another glass.

In the darkening street beyond, groups of girls wandered, with arms linked for protection. They were not prostitutes, nor did they wish to strike up acquaintanceships among the men at the tables. But they teased and excited themselves by dabbling a little at the edges of this encampment of masculinity, which was as strident and raucous as a rookery of bull seals.

Celina had been home to change and now wore a linen suit. An element of aggression in her seemed aroused by the surroundings; her movements were sharp and cautious; she kept her eyes close to their table. She chain-smoked as consciously as a woman on the stage. Morris could not understand the loud voices nearby, but he could watch what they said having an effect on her. Though she was listening to

Cowan and himself, half her attention was away. She could not enjoy being here. He wondered why she had agreed to come. He remembered that it had been Cowan who chose the café.

'Let's go somewhere a bit quieter.'

Cowan said: 'No, don't let's. I like it here.'

'Why? Because it looks like Paris?'

Cowan did not answer. A moment later he said: 'We're seeing life, that's what we're doing. Look at that.'

Morris looked behind him. There was a disturbance a few tables away. Iron chairs shrieked against the pavement. Five or six little men with umbrellas were jumping up and down. A glass rolled over and smashed. The group, surrounded by waiters waving napkins, disentangled itself from among the tables. Now they moved into the lit area under the palm trees between the café and the roadway. Voices called out: 'Indecent!' 'Abnormal!' 'Great dog!'. Everyone but Celina stood up to look.

'Long live the foreigners,' Cowan said. 'Wouldn't they be scared if their chums stopped holding them!'

'I don't know. Would they?'

Now the two principals had revealed themselves. Each one had two others in attendance who, clutching either arm, were half-heartedly trying to push him to safety. One lot moved obliquely towards the street corner, with the central figure gesticulating his protest, and disappeared. The others came back to the table: their participant jabbered hysterically for a time, then fell into a seething silence.

Morris and Cowan sat down.

'God, what a country, isn't it?' Cowan said, looking at Celina. 'As soon as I can rake up enough money, I'm going to Spain.'

Celina trembled, still silent. Morris said: 'Why wouldn't you watch?'

'I am so ashamed.'

Before Morris could ask her why, the three men who had disappeared were in front of them again. The middle one must have been strong, or his friends, enjoying the scene, were not seriously attempting to restrain him.

Everything began again: the two groups were out on the pavement, threatening and flinching from one another. Someone ran for a policeman.

'I got into a fight on the ship coming here. It was about a poker game. Most extraordinary people. Most extraordinary behaviour.'

'What happened?'

'It was all very boring really,' Cowan said. 'They made a complaint to the captain.' He giggled.

They waited, but he did not say any more. Cowan gave his own pointlessness to everything that had happened to him.

'I think this sort of fighting only happens in Latin countries,' Celina said. 'For you it is amusing but for us it is a serious thing. It makes everyone think how immature we are, how irresponsible.'

'It doesn't make me think that,' Morris said.

'It doesn't?'

'Why should it? Perhaps we oughtn't to have lost our natural pugnacity.'

By now the café proprietor had come out to join the waiters. Two policemen arrived: one had already been slipped some money. The whole situation became too confused for the spectator to understand, and finally the waving shouting crowd inched its way, like an animal with many legs, to the street corner, where it broke up among the passers-by.

Morris went on: 'English people can't be insulted nowadays. We accept too few criticisms as insults. We cheerfully admit ourselves dishonest about love or money, or cowardly. So when other people tell us what we are, we're merely irritated. Or even pleased.'

'But this fight wasn't about that.'

'What was it about, then?'

'It was not about any of the things you said.'

'Well, what *was* it about?'

There was a fraction's pause. 'No,' Celina said. 'It is a natural weakness. It is what makes foreigners despise us.'

Morris pushed ahead: 'In our most civilized periods all men carried swords.'

'But this thing here is childishness. It is because we are an immature and emotional people.'

Gregory Cowan was whistling between his teeth. He had turned to Celina and looked at her emptily for some time, before he suddenly said: 'You know you're a bore, old thing. Isn't she a bore? Shut up, old thing, you're a bore.'

For a moment Morris was wildly angry. After all, he thought, one had dragged on with this tedious conversation from a desire to be kind – a desire that would never have arisen if Cowan had treated the woman with anything resembling good manners.

Celina was terribly hurt. She was silent, her hand jabbing a cigarette.

Morris looked at the other man, enormous, pacific, the whole mass balanced on the tilted iron chair. He was appeased by his inanity, by the grin on the round face. In the end you would accept Gregory Cowan, and might even despise yourself for not doing so. You had seen him so often before, known his self-destruction, his almost suicidal tactlessness, the whole story of his failure. 'His *curriculum vitae*,' you had heard the office-holders and the members of selection boards say, 'was appallingly weak.' But Gregory Cowan would make you see his endless calamities as an attempt at rebellion; you would end up by liking him because of his own indifference to being liked.

'Go on, don't listen to him,' Morris said to Celina, in an amused voice.

But her face was blind with worry, and she couldn't respond to anything he said to help her.

'There, there, old thing. Don't get all upset now.' Gregory Cowan leant over and patted her shoulder. His hand lay there, large, and soft. An English girl would have turned on him and cursed him, but she was of her own country in this, fundamentally fearing rejection in all her attitudes to men. Besides, it was the first time today he had touched her; she trembled and was silent, and only after a minute or two did she try to pull herself away.

He tightened his grasp to restrain her. The table jarred. The tall glass rolled over into Celina's lap. A slice of lemon, dark sticky Coca-Cola and rum ornamented the front of her white suit.

'Silly girl. Now go and clean yourself up.'

'Please, will you come with me?'

'Why on earth?' Cowan asked, laughing.

She was quite desperate now, physically affected, without pride, and he was teasing her. She turned to Morris.

'Would you mind? I don't like to go through to the back alone.'

When Celina stood up the patch of damp had a humiliating look. Now she had lost all poise, she seemed older and rather drunk. Morris stood up, steering her through into the café. She was certainly right to have demanded an escort, for the eyes of all the drinkers swivelled on to her. Their voices rose, and quietened only when they saw Morris following.

'I hope to God,' he thought, 'they don't say anything I can understand.'

Celina disappeared. Standing alone at the back of the café, he began to reflect on the relations between his two companions. Cowan's tortures may have been performed half-unconsciously: they consisted merely in treating Celina in the same way that an Englishman of his type would have treated the quiet urchin-cut girls of Notting Hill and Battersea, who regard it as a point of honour to follow their men wherever they go, though it may be through the brothels of Marseilles or Naples.

There was more to it than this, but Morris began to tire of the subject. He was feeling rather undignified. He remembered that rich people always made use of you, and he felt he had been made use of. With an idea of protest against this, as well as in order to have something to do under the eyes of the male crowd in the bar, he asked for the telephone.

As he dialled the number, he felt clearer and more definite. Celina and Gregory Cowan were making claims on him already: their unhappiness was inviting him in. He himself had claims to make too, but, since he was not yet unhappy, the things he claimed were more easily granted him.

The receiver was picked up. His heart jumped with excitement.

'Who is speaking?'

'Is that Maria Aparecida?'

'Who is it?'

'The Englishman, Robin. Do you have a programme for tonight?'

'Robin!' The name came back at him, knocked out of shape. Then a clatter of words: she seemed excited, pleased like a child. Finally they got it straight: he arranged to go round to her flat as soon as he could get away.

He felt his insides churn with anticipation; he had joined a conspiracy against unhappiness. Now when he accompanied Celina back to the table, her troubles were no longer important to him.

Morris looked at his watch. It was a quarter to eleven. He told the two of them that he was going. They hardly noticed. When he thanked Celina for the day by the sea, his words seemed slightly absurd, as though referring to a remote period in both their lives. He took about a quarter of an hour to get to the block of flats. The building seemed meant to depress him at once. It was about twenty years old, modern-istic and dark grey, with a fringe of potted plants on each concrete balcony. Inside, everything was dingy, the lift smelt like breath, its gates jerked and clanged erratically. At last he stood in front of a dark-stained door, from which a peep-hole looked sharply at him, like the meaningless eye of a bird. This was too cold-blooded. He refused to despise what he was doing, but that did not prevent him from being unsure whether he wanted to do it or not.

There was a scuffling sound at the lock. For a moment he was violently jealous of Gregory Cowan. He wanted love, not prowess. He wanted some of the love that women devote to the futile and the desperate. Then the door opened.

Maria Aparecida was younger than he remembered her, and her skin was darker. He cheered up immensely as he followed her into the room. He was no longer the one who got the worse bargain; physical beauty, he thought, is never a bad bargain. He sat down on the bed and kissed her politely. She was obviously not expecting this – he remembered someone saying: 'In this country the average man sleeps with his first woman at fourteen, and kisses his first girl at twenty.'

In spite of their conversation on the telephone, Aparecida seemed again to have decided that he could not understand her. With her hands, she told him to wait and watch her. She switched on the wireless and began to dance. She was wearing a dress of red gauze with gold strands on it.

'Look, *meu filho*.' It was strange to hear her calling him her son. She must have been four or five years younger than he was.

She lifted her skirts and showed a scarlet silk petticoat.

'Look!' A white cotton petticoat with frills.

'Look!' Her thighs were perfect, a young girl's, gapped at the top.

'Oh, my God.' She fell beside him, and he sat with her,

holding on to her firm body and letting his face sink against her throat. 'I want to stay the whole night,' he whispered. She nodded.

He sat upright again. Confident, he began to feel himself at home. It was now he remembered he had not eaten since the picnic on the beach. This evening he had drunk slowly, wary of Gregory and Celina. He decided to suggest to Aparecida that they went out together to eat. He told himself he was hungry, but in fact he was trying to give an air of reality to the proceedings, to find a final escape from that cold-blooded moment at the door.

Maria Aparecida sat on a high stool beside him and drank a sweet chemical drink, while the barman grilled steak for sandwiches. They all knew her in the bar: the two Civil Guards with their white belts, holsters and short swords; the drunken Slav in the corner; the group of smart mulattoes talking about football. They shouted and spoke very fast to her, up and down the bar. Morris could not understand a word they said. At one moment, Aparecida put her arms round him and said 'No! No!'

He blushed and was confused, but there was nothing for him to do but continue eating. It was the old problem of the young traveller: were the natives friendly and, if they weren't, how soon could you tell? When handing over two more sandwiches, the barman pinched an ear lobe between finger and thumb: a gesture of approbation, but was it for the girl or the sandwiches? The writers of travel books always seemed so certain, and yet one was as confused as a child that has wandered out for the first time alone. In ten minutes' time it would make no difference anyway.

He was relieved when the moment came to pay for what they had eaten. He walked along the broken pavement with the girl picking her way beside him. In the lift he put his hands on the polished wood on either side of her head.

'Careful, *filho*,' she said, turning her head away. He was surprised and a little offended.

They arrived back at the apartment and he made her sit down on the bed. But the moment he touched her, she broke free.

'No, no, you cannot!'

She was looking down at him with a worried expression on her face. It became quite obvious to him that everything in the situation had changed. What on earth had gone wrong? He began to be nervous again, the blurting undergraduate, tremulous and unsure of himself.

With an effort of will, he stood up and caught hold of her. 'No, no.' She struggled to get away. 'You must not do that.'

What was the matter with her? Did she think he wouldn't pay enough? By her expression and gestures, she seemed to want to help him. It was as though she were soothing him and exciting him, brushing him off and at the same time insisting that he stayed. But he was angry and worried. All his ecstatic cockiness of beforehand had vanished, and his mind flooded with suspicions. Perhaps she was ill, perhaps she had a disease. It was unjust of her to invite him here, then, to excite him as she had done before they went down to the bar together. Perhaps she had been going to steal his wallet, and had decided not to. Disgusted and miserable he reached for his coat.

Again she came beside him, pleading to him to wait, but when he tried to assert himself once more, she began sobbing. Then, quite suddenly, a word she kept repeating came clear in his mind. 'A congestion, *filho*, a congestion.'

'The sandwiches?'

She nodded. 'Yes, the sandwiches.'

The weight of his anxiety left him. His heart leapt and the blood sang in his ears. He was so relieved that he wanted to burst out laughing.

'That's all nonsense,' he said.

'It isn't nonsense.' She still twisted about in his arms. 'You'll die. I don't want you to die.' He saw then that her tears were genuine : she was really afraid.

While he sat quiet, she gravely explained to him what had happened to a federal senator who had visited a girl-friend of hers too soon following an official dinner. When she had finished offering this final proof, his good humour was entirely restored.

'But it is nonsense.'

'How can you say it is nonsense?' She asked scornfully. 'My girl-friend –'

He had an inspiration. 'I am a doctor. A medical student. I know well.'

At once Maria Aparecida was silent. She examined him as if she were seeing him for the first time, her round eyes searching his face. He looked deep into her eyes and was moved by the admiration he saw there, the admiration of an innocent soul. At the same time her quick dark hand began undoing her dress. She had the poor person's almost religious respect for doctors of medicine; for her, to be a doctor was an infallible sign of distinction.

'Oh well,' she said. 'In that case –'

A few minutes afterwards they were together, and Maria Aparecida was calling on her saints.

2

Soon after Morris had left, Celina got into her car. She waited to see if Gregory Cowan would follow her. But he stayed on the pavement. He looked directly at her and said nothing.

Unavoidably, her hand lifted in a small gesture from the

wheel, and fluttered down again. Then she started the car.

Celina turned down a long avenue into the suburbs. Her throat hurt and her arms were trembling. She passed silent factories, twice bumped over railway lines, and crossed the river, whose warm stink rose up through the darkness. Now the car slid out into the empty night, into the interior of the state. Driving always calmed her; her few tears had gone, leaving only a dry stiffness round the eyes. She had looked back only once, when the car swooped first on to the wide concrete highway. Then the red glare of the city took up half the sky. She would drive on until the glare was gone, and then she would feel that she had escaped from all of it.

Much later, Celina stopped. She had seen only night wanderers, wild dogs and stumbling men. She thought she had been driving for about four hours. She had no idea of the time, for the car clock was not working, and when her life was running fast she did not wind her watch. Whenever she turned round, though, the light was still there. At last she realized that it was no longer from the city; it was the light of morning.

The Packard bumped on to the unmade side of the road, and she stopped the engine. Silence surrounded her. Almost immediately she fell asleep. When she awoke, the light had advanced and a chain of hills planted with eucalyptus had sprung up in front of her. Cocks were crowing at various distances. On the banks of red earth beside the car, the tussocks of grass were wet with dew and heavily scented – *capim*: it was one of the smells of her childhood. But, in this sad remote continent, the morning brought only a few moments of freshness. The coils of mist along the road died away and the woods of eucalyptus were completely silent, for no insect can live in them, and thus they are deserted by the few singing birds that remain.

Celina opened the car windows, and the air, still cold with night, blew in against her. Her eyes ached and her brain felt tainted with alcohol. She looked at the speedometer, a little horrified at the distance she had driven during the night. Had it mattered so much? Had her desire to escape been so exaggerated? Suddenly it seemed an enormous effort, more than her will could give, to turn back once more to the city. She switched on the engine to see the gauge: the car was almost out of petrol.

Footsteps sounded on the road behind her, hesitated and stopped. Celina put her head out, and saw a string of Japanese children, wooden-faced and prickly-haired, staring back at her. She called to them, but they kept an unmoved silence; in all probability they still only understood Japanese. The round heads gazed blankly, as owls do, and exchanged no look of comprehension with her. They live here, she thought, where I have lived all my life, and I know nothing about them, nothing whatever. This idea gave her a feeling of complete alienation, of belonging to a world so broken up that no relationship existed at all, each person wading ahead alone through the mess until death. A moment of horror at her own loneliness took control of her. Then she remembered Mrs Newton on the beach of the day before. That absurd idiotic woman possessed some power of attraction, some animal magnetism which had brought the Japanese child to her. Celina herself had none. She thought of Gregory Cowan and was sure that she had none.

She lit a cigarette, but put it out. Her mouth was dead dry and now by itself it began trembling. She felt her whole face start to work under the muscles tired with sleep, and realized that she was about to cry.

Celina wept for about five minutes, then looked up at herself in the car mirror, thinking about death. She remembered a friend from the distant past, Ecilda, a girl from a rich family, who had eloped to New York with a married man. After three months he had deserted her – had, in fact, flown back to a great welcome from his wife and children.

The girl, who was pregnant, returned alone. When the liner put in at Rio de Janeiro, she hired a taxi to Copacabana. There she entered a new block, asking to inspect one of the apartments. The doors were unlocked and the porter allowed her to go up by herself. A few minutes later she fell from the highest balcony into the street.

Yes, this was a country where one died for love. With her hands over her eyes, Celina felt again Ecilda's journey in the elevator to her death. But the girl had a weak personality, sensual and sentimental, a lightning-conductor for disaster. Then Celina remembered the little Negro girls who, when they had lost their virginity and could no longer get married, poured kerosene on their clothes and set themselves on fire. Why kerosene? She had always wondered. Was it to purge their poor small souls with fire and keep them from Hell?

Celina turned the car violently, the wheels screeching in the loose earth, and began to drive back along the highway. At the first petrol station she stopped, had the tank filled, and drank a lot of black coffee. More Japanese were in the bar, but only the live chickens and turkeys they carried under their arms showed any interest in the newcomer. After this Celina drove fast, almost triumphantly. Soon she was passing cars and market carts on their way to the city, and the big dust-caked buses that came in, with loads of sleeping unshaven men, from remote towns she had scarcely heard of – towns with the names of Indian tribes or nineteenth-century senators. She felt more than ever the contrast between the enormous spaces around her and the tiny arena, under four eyes, in which a woman's life is played out.

It was early morning when she arrived in the city. The streets glittered, still wet from the watercarts. She parked her car near the cathedral, then went round to the flowerstalls in the market.

Towards dawn, Maria Aparecida awoke Morris and began

myself. Have I failed in my duty some place? Lord, what parried them as best he could. Then he had to confess his ignorance.

'But you told me you were a doctor.'

'I had to. Otherwise –'

'Last night, then, you didn't know?'

He shook his head. 'I was right, wasn't I? I'm still alive.'

To his surprise she began to laugh. '*Filho*, you must have wanted to make love very much.' She embraced him with enthusiasm after this, and he became very happy.

When Morris awoke again, the soft elastic tangle of her hair was against his face. The room was already light, and, while he lay listening to her sleep, he stared inquisitively around him. The flat was carefully looked after: there were sprays of white flowers on one table, and a collection of the little pottery animals you could buy in the market – he-goats, dogs, and humped Indian bulls, each with a '*figa*' – a lucky clenched fist – tied by ribbon round its neck. Above the bed was a crucifix, and a print of the Last Supper, all ringleted beards and uprolling eyes. He was delighted by the presence of another picture on the opposite wall. It was divided into two parts. On one side, a thin ragged man was sitting on an iron bed; on the other, a stout man in kneebreeches with a napkin tied round his neck was tucking into a meal which included a ham and a turkey. The first picture was titled 'I gave credit', the second 'I took cash'. All the same, he reflected, Maria Aparecida was a kindly girl; it was quite possible that she gave credit at one time or another.

Morris sat up on the bed. He could see himself in the distorted glass of the wardrobe, a white English figure against the brown shoulders behind him. She had slept as they all did, with the sheet tight over her face, doped by her own carbon dioxide. Now she was moving, she yawned brilliant teeth and without opening her eyes pulled back the sheet, up over her dark pointed breasts and her head. He lay beside her again and hid his face against her. She was quite asleep. He could feel the tug of her sleepiness, pulling him back to her. But he kept wide awake, and soon he was violently bored by her silence. He pulled her elbow. 'I must go,' he said.

Two eyes woke up in the still sleeping face and looked at him with unnerving indifference.

He patted her. 'I must go.' And now he was really anxious to be gone. He pulled on his shirt and trousers and stuffed his tie into a coat pocket. Still wrapped in the sheet, Maria Aparecida padded after him to the door. In spite of its being early morning, her mouth tasted fresh, but she was only half there, asleep on her feet. She locked the door after him.

He had been inhibited in the presence of this brown sleepwalker. Now he could express his animal content by running down eight flights of stairs into the street. It was only seven o'clock in the morning but, smartly dressed and with shining shoes, the mulattoes had already taken up position outside last night's bar, and were watching the day go past. The barbers' shops were open and the white-smocked barbers were shaving themselves, leaning against their mirrors. Morris rejoiced in them and in everything else. He thought he had found something in the night, a sensuality that was complete and final. Knowing that, one wouldn't have to worry any more, hardly even to think. It was always there, he believed, not knowing at this moment how quickly he would tire of it, how he would return to his thoughts outside the door last night, and be jealous of Gregory Cowan for the love he extorted.

He was in a street of garages. Backs of cars jutted across the pavement, and half-naked figures were clattering round on wooden shoes with torrential hoses, He skipped between the floods of water and came out in front of the cathedral.

At the corner of the flower-market he stopped short, and,

before he knew why, he had retreated into the shadow. Celina was a few yards away from him. She was still wearing the white linen suit with the Coca-Cola stain, the sign of damage. She looked strange, rather battered but attractive. He knew she was beautiful and now this fact no longer scared him. This, together with the sensuality of the night, made him realize, more violently than he had ever done in England, the enormous possibilities of human passion.

He wondered whether she had spent the night with her lover. Whatever had happened, she was now calm, preoccupied, conversing quietly with the old woman from whom she was buying flowers.

Flowers for that big pudgy man, her lover? Flowers for herself? Or for a grave?

'Betty, you're still awake?'

The bedside table was covered with boxes of sleeping-pills, a silver flask, a biscuit tin – equipment for the campaign against the night. But the night had won. The campaigner herself lay exhausted among pillows, her eyes wobbling unfocused in the early light. Outside the broad glass doors on to the balcony, you could see the tops of palm trees in the garden and beyond them the towers of the optimistic city, already splashed with sunshine.

'Couldn't you sleep?'

'I slept a little, honey. I usually sleep a little at the beginning of the night.' The words 'sleep' and 'night' encouraged some overtone of emotion, and Betty Fonseca's rough tired voice gave them the throb of tragedy. 'What are those?'

The flowers Celina had brought with her were like big white irises, with yellow stamens and dark-green leaves like wild garlic. Their scent was already heavy in the room. 'I don't know what they are called. I bought them in the market just now.'

The long succulent stems squeaked a little as Celina disentangled one of them to show her stepmother. The flower twirling at the end shed pollen on to the silk eiderdown.

Both at once, the women saw that it was crawling with black ants. 'Ah!' Betty screamed. 'Take them away! Throw them out, honey.'

Celina crushed together the sheaf of flowers and bore them away quickly. She pushed wide open the sliding glass door, and went out on to the balcony. She flung the flowers away from her and they fell like a green-and-white parachute on to the lawn of the shadowed garden.

A crash came from the shrubbery. One of the great danes broke through and ran grumbling towards the flowers. 'Claudius,' Celina called, and he began swinging his tail, gazing from side to side but forgetting, like all dogs, to look upwards. But he was soothed by her voice and loped away into the shadow.

She turned back to the room. 'Why don't you try and sleep now? It's still early.'

'I've already had my sleep, darling. I told you how I usually sleep a little at the beginning of the night. I get tired so easily these days. Sometimes when Oswaldo's busy I come up quite early and oh, I'm just so tired, if that Terezinha isn't on hand to help me undress, I just fall on this bed and sleep, right here, with all my clothes on.'

Her hand crawled across the eiderdown to take Celina's. But Celina was silent. She saw too well the meaning of this curious account.

'This is not too happy a home for you to come back to, Celina.'

Celina let her hand be fondled. 'Why do you say that?'

'I know I must always be a foreigner to you, but it is my home now too, dear. I gave up everything I had in America to come down here with your father. I even sold my securities. Now with you and Jango away it isn't a home any more. I don't know what to do. Have I done wrong? I keep asking myself. Have I failed in my duty some place? Lord, what have I done? Almighty God, help me, I don't know what to do!'

She began to heave with dry sobs on the bed, and to cough her terrible smoker's cough.

'Just give me the flask, honey – helps me – Dr Conant in New York said – to always –'

Celina gave the flask. A golden trickle coursed down the sagging chin. She was calm again.

'Maybe I should go back to Philadelphia. There's Patty there. She loves me. And Aunt Bedwell, who I haven't seen in years. Not since twelve years. Twelve years we came back. It was the war in Europe, you remember. You and Jango were just kids then. I loved you both so. I had such hopes, such wonderful dreams.'

Her voice drained away. The tide was right out now and the woman could see only mud-flats of despair.

Then the tide turned. Betty grabbed Celina's hand.

'And you, sugar, where is this cruel life leading you? I get so sad seeing you like this.'

'How, Betty?'

'You know, Celina. This man.'

Celina was silent.

'I don't want to interfere, surely. But I worry all the same.'

Celina gave an amused laugh. 'But why should you worry?'

'I don't hear any good of him, not at all. The British want to get him – he took a new British car to Spain and sold it. They don't let you do that over there. That was how he got here.'

Celina guessed that this information came from Ronald Hadleigh. She said: 'He explained all that to me. It doesn't concern anyone else.'

'And his wife's looking for him – they say he took her

money when he left England. He abandoned her, honey, with three children.'

'He explained that, too.'

'But, darling, what does it all mean? We've never had anyone like that in *my* family. Nor in your father's. What does it all mean? You've had such bad luck, Celina, with Raimundo turning out no good. Oh, you know I always took your side in that, even against my own dearest Os-wald-o.'

'I know you did.'

She had taken Celina's side too strongly, with her American clubwoman's attitude. She had harangued Oswaldo, but he had not understood. He yawned at things he didn't understand – the polite Latin yawn of someone righteously content with his own limitations. Because of this, Celina thought, because of me, Betty lost him. But I cannot blame myself, for she would have lost him anyway.

'Now I feel perhaps I was wrong. Ah, honey, can't you help us to help you?'

Celina left this question unanswered. She stood up, tired beyond all feeling. She felt now that she could sleep.

'Can't you explain, honey?'

'Does there have to be an explanation? Can't we let it go on as it is?'

3

When Celina came down to lunch that day, she found Jango in full dress uniform with a black brassard. Their father wore a black suit and tie.

'What has happened?'

'Paulo Alcantara died last night,' Jango said. 'The funeral is this afternoon.'

'I am sorry. He was not old, was he?'

'It was cancer.' They looked at each other without speaking: the world was heavy between them, because of their mother's death.

'There are getting to be fewer of us,' Oswaldo said sententiously.

The word did not make him remember their mother. Celina saw that he had been weeping; from time to time he still dabbed his eyes with a cream silk handkerchief. On his black suit he was wearing the badge of the 1930 revolution. Paulo Alcantara Mendes had been one of the leaders; he had gone into exile with Oswaldo, but had stayed the whole time in Portugal. Celina remembered now that her father had never been intimate with Paulo; he had considered him something of a charlatan, and when all their women had surrendered jewellery, including their wedding-rings, to help the revolutionary cause, there had been some doubt over Paulo Alcantara's disposal of the funds. But now the man had died. His burial would take place this afternoon with all the hurry that the tropical climate demanded, and his name again had become important and symbolic. In his honour Oswaldo had opened a bottle of Portuguese wine, the strong wine they had drunk in exile together. Perhaps it was fortunate that Betty had not appeared for lunch. Without the problem of two languages the family was more united. The Fonsecas belonged once again to their own country and their history.

'It's twenty-three years,' Oswaldo said, 'since Paulo and I left the country together.'

'I can hardly remember,' Celina said.

'We had sent you to the *fazenda*. Your mother was too ill to travel.'

Their mother had died a year later, without seeing her husband again. The children joined him in New York, where Jango suffered from homesickness. They returned to live with their aunts and to go to school.

Celina noticed how well her father was looking today. A feeling of importance had returned to him. He seemed to be looking forward to the ceremony this afternoon. She could imagine how crowded the cemetery would be: there would be no room around the Alcantara vault, and most of the crowd would be hidden among the cypress trees and the other big shed-like tombs of white and grey marble. Huge wreaths would be brought up, all made of arum lilies, with a revolutionary badge in the centre. The lilies were always already withered and their juglike blossoms had the texture of dirty kid gloves. The cardinal would be present, and some of the reactionary generals, and many of Jango's accomplices, including Clovis Amoral, who was believed to be the cardinal's son. For once in their lives at the centre of attention, those two dull girls Nelly and Lourdes Alcantara would be there, snuffed out under black veils.

All these people considered themselves the local aristocracy. Most of them were still retired from public life, but now it was no longer because of the dictatorship. They told each other that they would not dirty their hands with political corruption, and so the Syrians, the Italians and the Jews, who now controlled the optimistic city, had left them out of consideration. Only when they were all together was the myth that they formed an aristocracy a compelling one; it died out when they separated to their various lives.

'Paulo's decease' – Oswaldo avoided the sonorous word '*morte*' – 'marks something, the end of an age and perhaps the end of our class.' He was half-way through the bottle of wine.

Celina said nothing. The end of what? There was nothing in this house that showed tradition, little that was more than ten years old. All trace of their mother, even, had gone. This may have been due to Betty, who in those enthusiastic months after her arrival had paid for the building and decoration of the new house. A block of apartments stood on the site of the old mansion where Celina and Jango were born. Oswaldo had never raised the slightest objection to the destruction of evidence of the past.

It was true that the family had travelled and that, except for Jango, they spoke foreign languages with fluency. But Celina thought of her father's library: not the expensively bound editions that he had displayed to Cecil Newton and Robin Morris, but the true arcana, as carefully chosen as another man's set of Restif and Sade. These books were 'philosophical' and most of them were in English. They included *The Art of Happiness, The Function of the Orgasm, The Importance of Living,* and *On Being a Real Person.* A new acquisition was *The Power of Positive Thinking.*

It was as though her father was endlessly preparing to be interviewed for some unimportant executive position.

Afterwards, Celina was alone with Jango.

He paced up and down the room whistling and swinging his arms, like a boxer warming up for a fight. He was pleased with himself and full of self-confidence. He'd have a fine time this afternoon, the young military hero playing up to the tearful old gentlemen, giving the deepest embraces and hinting at significant developments. During the past weeks he had swelled in importance, for in the capital he had been a mere henchman, a hanger-on of the rightist politicians, whereas here he was a connecting link with them.

He lit a cigarette and gazed at Celina.

'I may tell you that this afternoon will be important for us. We shall be together for the first time in many years.'

Celina picked up a newspaper. Paulo Alcantara was not to be avoided: his photograph stared back at her, under solid headlines.

'Don't you agree with me?'

'No, I don't,' she said angrily. She could not endure his smugness any longer. 'It is not important. What you are doing is mere Latin-Americanism. This might be Costa Rica or Honduras. Your politics don't mean anything, except possibly something for us all to be ashamed of.'

Jango frowned. He was abashed, and she felt sorry for him. His sister was far more intelligent than he was. It was all wrong, it was impossible, it was a break in the law of nature, for Jango was the son of the house. But they both knew that she was the more intelligent and the better-educated.

'Jango, if you are involved in this because you want to act in some way, because you find life insupportable here where there can be no wars, no nobility of action and no great art, where nothing of importance can happen in the history of man – then you must go ahead. Not because you think it will do any good. Because it will not. This is not the politics of civilized countries.'

He was really worried now, a child whose game had been spoilt by his elder sister's interference.

To answer her, he had recourse to inside information, to his own male world which she knew nothing about. 'I have been spending a lot of time at the house of Jacinto Moreira. He has told me everything he knows. He has evidence – naturally I cannot tell you what it is – that will bring down the whole régime. You realize what this means?'

He waited, his eyes glistening with excitement. Celina could find nothing to say. Indeed, she had a moment's qualms about her indifference. She knew it came from Europe, and probably it derived from Gregory Cowan.

In this country's past there had been other gestures towards honesty and political justice; perhaps, even though they were hopeless, for a young man like Jango they were the only way of attaining dignity and nobility in his life. It is through such gestures, Celina thought, that we become civilized, and maybe they will make us, like the Europeans, proud and dignified, beautiful and not ugly when we are old.

Her father was handsome, but he was not yet sixty. All his older friends were hideous, the men no different from Portuguese milkmen, the women out of Dali – toads with blued hair.

'But, of course,' Jango went on, 'it is not as simple as that. They know at the palace what Jacinto is doing. Whenever I go to see him I take a platoon of my command to see him. And he is protected. He never goes out without the escort I have provided.'

He broke off. He was again aware of a look of irony on her face.

'It is important, I tell you. It is vitally important. And today will be an important day.'

But his confidence had been badly shaken. He buckled his belt, straightened his shoulders and began walking up and down again. Celina still watched him; she was enjoying her small revenge on masculinity.

When Jango spoke again, he appeared to have changed the subject.

'How is Sunset Boulevard today?'

'She told me that she did not sleep. She suffers from insomnia.'

Jango laughed without mirth. 'Is she asleep now?'

'I don't think so. She is resting. I called in on my way down to lunch. She says she has trouble with her eyes.'

'I see.' Jango nodded emphaticaly several times. This was all significant evidence that he must understand and remember. 'You will see that she stays all right, won't you?'

'I?'

'No, of course, you have your own life.' He rocked on his heels and blew out cigarette smoke. 'Nevertheless, you must know more than I do. How do you think she feels about everything?'

'Jango, you know I have not been here for several months.'

At this, their eyes began dodging again.

She hated him wildly at that moment. She realized what he was getting at, with his ham-acting and his native tortuousness. How could he be the son of his mother?

'If there was something seriously wrong with her, would you mind?'

He did not answer this. Instead he said: 'The Unity of the Family – you know that's one of our fundamental beliefs.'

The easy slogan enraged her still further. He really was a stupid young man.

'If you think that Betty –' She stopped. 'If you think either of us is going to cause scandal, you need not worry. Though, for your selfishness and insensitivity, you would well deserve it.'

With this she walked out of the room, only to find, as so often happened, that she had nowhere in particular to go.

She decided to drive out to the *fazenda* for the weekend. She telephoned to Gregory Cowan to inform him of this decision.

The line was a bad one. Once again it was impossible for her to tell what he was thinking or feeling.

4

The July sun was shining through trees bare with winter on to the terrace of a café. Girls in tapered black trousers were walking past; young men in sports cars followed them along the kerb. The scene was pleasant, but Morris had a slight hankering after the English Sunday papers. Instead, he had Gregory Cowan on his war experiences.

' ... That one's family was terribly rich, too. After the war they wanted me to go back to Italy and marry her. But I gave them the slip. Anyway, I'd decided to become an actor.'

'I think you said you were at Oxford, weren't you?'

'Ha! ha! I always say that out here, it impresses them so. As a matter of fact the only time I was at Oxford was with this C.E.M.A. company. Then I got married and we emigrated to Canada. That was my wife's idea, not mine. Two of her children are Canadian – my children too, I suppose. At least, those two are mine.'

He munched a mouthful of peanuts from the table.

'This one that was born two months ago, though. That doesn't look like mine. Probably belongs to Peter Whitton-Tracy, the man who lived upstairs in Hampstead.'

'I was at school with him.'

'Were you at that place too? He wasn't very nice, was he? He's in the Home Office now. Tanya would have liked me to be in the Home Office. Well, anyway, her parents bought this house for us and split it into flats. I spent the whole time shovelling anthracite and Tanya planted pot-herbs in the garden. I was supposed really to be reading for the Bar.'

'You got around.'

'Her parents said they'd support us while I was doing it. It would have been much better for Tanya to be the barrister, instead of having babies in Vancouver and doing Mediterranean cookery in Hampstead. Shall we have another of these?'

Morris called the waiter. As he turned back, he noticed Ronald Hadleigh walking springily down the pavement in the sunlight. Hadleigh saw him and smiled; for a moment Morris thought that he intended joining them. On his way to the table, however, the Canadian appeared to change his mind. His smile faded, he gave a little bow and walked on. Morris sat back, somewhat relieved.

'Tanya *was* a bore. Always wanting people to be different things. It was a stupendous relief when I heard from old Koronski.'

'Koronski?'

'My present boss. An old lady who knows a lot about the cinema. He was with UFA, then British documentaries, Ealing Studios, all that. I met him first when I was acting at Oxford, but then he had to leave England, all because of something that happened in Leicester Square. The London police wanted to push him back behind the Iron Curtain, so he sold his jewellery and hopped over here.'

Morris wondered why the conversation of this man seemed gently to knock away at the props which upheld the world. When he imposed his statements, he produced a convincing picture of a life where strength and a thick skin had enabled him to get almost everything he wanted. But a moral deficiency prevented him from enjoying or following up his victories. Gregory Cowan was continually in retreat.

'This is really the only place you can still escape from things like that. Things like Tanya and the London police.'

A lottery-ticket seller approached the table and Cowan bought two tickets.

'I won quite a lot in last week's draw,' he said.

Was it true or not? In spite of their shared knowledge of England, Morris had no real evidence to go by. Perhaps everything about the man was an imposture – his appearance as well, the too-round head, the glittering eyes and the meaningless grin on the soft mouth.

The big body rose and lurched away into the bar behind them. He looked like a Germanic fool-friar, dressed up in a stiff corduroy suit and sandals, and perhaps there really was something lunatic about the back of his head, with its thin covering like rook's down.

Morris was alone for a moment only, then a hand fell, cupping his shoulder.

'Robby. How's the boy?'

He looked up. A round English face, behind spectacles.

He placed it as that of the smaller of the two Yorkshiremen he had encountered on his evening with Hadleigh.

'Sit down. Have something to drink.'

'Thanks, lad. Singing hymns gives you a thirst. I've been to the English church. I used to be chapel at home and here I go to the church. It's funny how people change.'

During the past weeks Morris had almost forgotten about this man. He had last seen him borne away on the arm of a determined girl with a dead-white face and black straight hair down to her shoulders. There had been something pathetic there – the provincial Englishman, far from home comforts, going to pieces in the tropics.

But the pieces had come together again. Kenneth Towner was fatter in the face, and his features had lost the dead look of the dark slum city where he had been born. He wore a neat chestnut-coloured suit, a pearl-pinned silk tie. He settled himself comfortably and gazed at Robin Morris with the ruminant internal laughter of someone remembering past indiscretions that he is pleased about.

'You been back there again – where we was that night?'

'My one gave me her telephone number. I've been to her flat once or twice.'

Ken nodded appreciatively. 'Heard about Les?'

'No.' Leslie too had remained a name, a visiting-card in his wallet which he vaguely wondered how he had acquired.

'No more, my friends, no more.' It was a quotation from nowhere special. 'All prim and proper. Holy Matrimony next month.'

'Who to? An English girl?'

'That's right. Her dad's important in the colony. Chairman of the British Chamber of Commerce.'

The waiter brought more gin. Ken asked to look at the bottle; he studied the seal top, read the label and examined the bottom of the bottle with a professional air. The waiter looked angry. For him, waiters would always look angry and he would never care.

'O.K. That seems genuine, all right.'

The tots of gin gurgled out of the bottle up to the marks on the glasses.

'Cheers.'

'Er – cheers.'

A group of young girls was passing, and Ken gave them all the same careful examination that he had given to the gin bottle. 'Lovely, lovely,' he chuckled, delighted. 'Did you see the little dark one? She looked back at me.'

He sighed deeply, then returned to the subject of his friend's fiancée. 'She's a really nice girl, too, Daphne is. Really nice.' His changed tone of voice seemed to imply that she was not pretty, but that probably she was a lady.

'What about yourself? Do you still share your flat?'

'Ah – ah.' Ken wagged his index finger from side to side. This new gesture fitted in with his Latinized appearance. 'I moved out two weeks ago. Came to an arrangement.'

'That sounds interesting.'

'Got her all fixed up, little flat, place to cook.'

'Wonderful.'

'Daytime I keep the key,' Ken said, twirling it round his finger. 'Just so as I know I'm the only one.'

'What about your work?'

'Gave us a bonus last month. Came in handy for the new arrangement,' Ken replied. 'I made the initial payment on a bit of beach property, too. The main road's coming right alongside it in two years' time.'

Morris was impressed to see this man being painlessly taken over by a different civilization. Ken Towner's career seemed settled. After he had tired of 'arrangements', perhaps he would marry the rich daughter of a local family. In that way he'd get to know the *politicos*, he would join the Automobile Club, the Jockey Club. At the same time he would attend the English Church, belong to the British Legion and the Freemasons, and make the biggest contribution to the charities of the British community. He was all set for the luxury suite on the liner going to England; there would be seats at the captain's table, and he'd throw a private party for the company directors and conservative M.P.s travelling with him. You could imagine, too, quick furious conversations with his wife in her own language, while she stood beside him in black taffeta, tight lipped and neglected, all her beauty gone.

Morris shook himself out of this reverie to listen to what Kenneth was saying.

'She's happy there all day, keeping the flat tidy. Always has a big welcome for me.'

'And you?'

'Me, I'm putting on weight. I like this place, I truly like it.'

They were both pleased with each other. There was no doubt that, if you tackled low enough, you could control your life in the city. Failure was due to personal scruples. Morris suddenly remembered Professor and Mrs Newton; he wondered how that situation was progressing.

Gregory Cowan reappeared. He pulled up a chair and sat down.

'Pleased to meet you. Kenneth Towner,' Ken said. 'You out here long then?'

'One year, lad.'

Morris looked up quickly.

Ken grinned with delight. 'You from North too?'

'That's right.'

'Where you from? I'm from Hull myself.'

'Isn't that strange us meeting up? My sister lives in Hull,' Gregory said. His accent was only a little exaggerated.

Ken was excited. 'Where've you been hiding all this time? How come we don't see you at club? There's quite a gang of us Yorkshire lads there. You don't come there much, do you?'

'I'm fixed up with a girl.'

'One of these Portuguese tarts?'

'That's right,' Gregory said.

'Grand. We've a hobby in common, then. I was just telling Rob here.'

Gregory's face had an oafish grin and his eyes were glittering. The situation was by now inextricable, Morris realized. He himself was always a prey to class prudery: encounters like these set him squirming with anger and embarrassment, beyond anything he felt for the people involved. He stopped listening to what the others were saying, disliking them both now – Ken, for being such a fool as to be taken in.

A few minutes later he was aroused by Ken's hand thrust towards him in the handshake of the country.

'I must get going, lad. Solange will be all worried about me. Told her I was only going to church. That's her name – Solange – comic, isn't it?'

He handed Cowan his business card. 'It's a real pleasure to meet somebody from home once in a while,' he said. They watched him hurry off along the street.

They sat in silence for three or four minutes.

Finally Morris said: 'I think that was absolutely bloody of you.'

Gregory Cowan roared with laughter. He was immensely pleased with himself. 'But he loved it. I made him ever so happy. Didn't you see how he was taking it?'

'That's all very well, but –'

'Well, then.'

'It makes no difference. I happen to worry about things like that. Besides, he's a nice man.'

'But he didn't guess at all. He was loving every –' Gregory broke off short. He had just seen Ken Towner coming back towards them.

'Just thinking,' he called out. 'The lads are giving a party next Saturday for Leslie's engagement. Care to come? You got the address, haven't you?'

'Yes, I have,' Morris said. 'I'd love to come.' He was smitten with a desire to make amends.

'That's champion, lad,' Gregory burst out.

This time it was all wrong, blatantly false. Kenneth's expression changed. Puzzled, he looked from one to the other in silence. Morris avoided his gaze.

'Well, nine p.m. then, Saturday.' His voice was refined and careful. He turned to Gregory.

'Don't bother about the white tie, old boy,' he said, in a ghastly music-hall-toff accent.

When he had gone, Morris said: 'He knows now all right.'

'Oh dear, I'm slipping. I could never change quickly from one to the other.'

Looking at him, Morris thought this was more of an admission than Gregory Cowan realized. He had one of those actor's voices that made it almost impossible to determine where he had started. All that seemed certain was that he had been in the R.A.F. on the ground, and later had for a time worn a beard. No one was likely to confess falsely to either of these accomplishments. Apart from that, Cowan wasn't even a creator of fantasies: he himself was the unreal shadow – the round head and the pair of unconvincing eyes. He came from nowhere and lived anywhere.

Morris, however, remembered the opposite of this, the final proof of the reality of the man who was sitting with him. He was loved, possibly desperately, by a violently attractive woman. The thought of this was confusing and worrying enough. Morris found that he no longer wanted to stay with him.

'I must go.'

'Go then. Good-bye.'

On his way home he decided not to see Cowan again; and

yet, at the same time, he was afraid of loneliness, the lack of someone who spoke the same dialect.

5

Kochen was watering his garden. As he usually did, he looked plump and well.

'How are things?'

'Horrible. My wife and I are exhausted. I am telling her: look, listen, or things get better soon or we sell out and go back to Tel Aviv.'

'That sounds bad.'

'Strikes. Protests. The Labour decrees. I am telling her it is the greatest mistake to come back to this country. Always there are some troubles with these people. She agrees, but she has here her mother and father, and there is the boy.'

'*Paciencia!*'

'Listen. We work Sunday shifts. We pay more money. Do they come?'

'Do they?'

'My wife is out there now with the boy. She is wishing him to learn about these people. I know what she finds. She finds the foreman is not there. He is spending the day at home. Since we start working Sunday, I am sacking three foremen.'

The water from the hose drummed down on to the thickly-spreading leaves called 'elephant's ears'. Insects fluttered upwards and the damp earth gave off a warm smell. In spite of the dry winter, the vegetation here was thick and lush.

'And how are you getting on, Mr Morris? My wife, I am afraid, is still nervous with your servant.'

'I am sorry about that.'

'It does not matter. You will not change and my wife will not change either.'

While Morris was wondering how to take this, Kochen screwed up the nozzle of the hose and it trickled back silver. He turned and the other saw for the first time that the spectacles he was wearing were polarized. The effect was disconcerting: were there any eyes behind those flat blackish mirror plates? Kochen grinned, all false teeth.

'Why do I water this garden? I do not know. Perhaps I am a little crazy.'

Morris walked up the steps to his flat.

Expedita brought lunch in complete silence. When he looked at her, she turned her head away. Her eyes were puffy and bruised-looking, and her hair completely hidden under a scarf. He had no interest in inquiring into her private life. But it was there in the room, damaging the atmosphere, and the taste of it seemed to have got mixed into the food.

During the afternoon he slept hotly and heavily, and he awoke covered in sweat. Later he wrote letters. At a quarter to seven Expedita came to set the table for dinner. During the past weeks, dinner on Saturday evenings had been getting earlier and earlier; he knew that she was in a hurry to go dancing and he had not objected. But today was Sunday: this heightened his feeling that there was something untoward in the air.

Before she had time to put the soup on the table, the doorbell rang.

Expedita came back, sulky and furious.

'There is someone.'

Along the corridor beyond the kitchen, he could make out the looming form of Gregory Cowan.

Still concerned by the attitude of the servant, Morris forgot about his last meeting with this man. 'Come in. Sit down. Have something to drink?'

He looked up at him and looked away. There was something ominous about Cowan's appearance here; he was troubled. He began to make conversation.

'What did you do this afternoon?'

'I went to the cinema.' Cowan laughed away this attempt. 'Actually, I came to ask you something.'

'What?' There was a silence.

'Will you lend me ten thousand cruzeiros?'

The question now hung in a frame of silence. Morris felt deaf, as though his eardrums had blushed. They did not look at one another.

He turned away and poured himself a drink. 'Why, are you in a mess?' His voice was cramped.

'It's absurd, really. The company refuse to pay up until next month, when we're supposed to complete the film. I simply have to have my last month's rent.'

'But when will the company pay?'

'In three weeks' time.' His voice did not bother to sound convincing.

'You're sure of that?'

'As much as one can be.'

'You need ten thousand cruzeiros right now?'

'Yes.'

Morris waited, trying to put his thoughts in order. This short cross-examination had not made him master of the situation.

'Will you?'

'I suppose so.'

The words seemed to have been spoken for him. At the same instant he knew that he would never see his money again. It was like this, then, that one learned.

'I'm not rich, you know.'

'You'll have it back in three weeks. It's a certainty!'

Morris now could hardly bear to listen to this. 'Well,' he said heavily, 'after that, let's have a drink.' He turned away and began clattering the glasses and the lemon squeezer. When he went out to fetch a lemon, he found Expedita sitting inanimate in the kitchen, her face a mask of sadness. One of the saucepans was boiling over.

When he returned, Cowan was standing up.

'Could you let me have it now?'

'Now?'

'Yes.'

'I'm not sure I have it.' He felt the man was intimidating him, and successfully. 'Would a cheque do?'

'No, I want cash.' Cowan was staring down at him, smiling with his usual empty gaze.

Pure weakness flooded through the young man, like a rush of bile. He was on the operating-table and his insides were being removed. For the first time, too, he realized how far the indifference of exile had taken him. He could no longer find any reason not to accept whatever was happening.

'I suppose I can do that.' Morris went into his bedroom and unlocked the drawer where he kept his money. The ten new notes – he looked at them with regret and nostalgia – seemed beautiful, with their idyllic eighteenth-century panorama of colonists and naked Indian women. He pushed them into Cowan's hand.

'Thank you. Actually, I've a taxi waiting outside. I'll have the drink another time.' He was gone.

Morris quivered with fury and impotence. It was a bruising of the consciousness against life. There is some part of every exile which must become battered and hard as a schoolboy's knees.

Expedita came in and put the food on the table. The door slammed after her. After a quarter of an hour, he waited for coffee. He called two or three times, but she did not come. Out in the kitchen he found the coffee drying on the metal round the gas-jet. He went to the front door and looked out. There was no light in her bedroom. At that moment the front gate clanged, and he heard quick foot-steps going away down the street.

'You are looking for your servant?'

He jumped. The voice came from just below the steps. In the darkness he made out Mrs Kochen standing there in her brown-linen suit. She had probably been spying on him, but scorn and triumph had brought her out into the open.

'You are too late, Mr Morris. She is already going. Now I think you learn. They are all like this. They do not want to work.'

Without answering Morris closed his front door. In the corridor he put his forehead against the cold plaster of the wall, and stayed there for about five minutes.

6

Ronald Hadleigh stared into the small mirror in his office lavatory. From downstairs in the committee rooms, he could hear the noise of the *coquetel*, now nearing its end.

It had been a stifling day, exhausting to the nerves. The alcohol he had consumed this evening was already blazing hotly in his face. Now he rubbed his cheeks with cologne and dabbed on some talcum. He decided to wait for a few moments before returning to the party: Iracema, his social secretary, would have everything in hand. He lit a cigarette and sat down on the closed seat.

This afternoon the governor of the state had arranged to visit the headquarters of the Inter-American Aid Program. It was the fifth anniversary of the Program's initiation. Whisky, journalists, press attachés, newsreel and television cameras had all been assembled. Iracema Kfouri, a stately Lebanese with a complexion like smooth sour yogurt, had decorated the rooms with the flags of unidentifiable Central and South American countries. Everything was prepared; they waited.

The photographers refused to waste their flashes on the minor celebrities who were present. The journalists and television men drank all the available whisky. Ronald Hadleigh got one of his headaches.

An hour later the governor's second deputy official representative arrived. He was a small stout army captain with exceedingly wide epaulettes of gold braid. He had shaved recently, though not today.

Ronald Hadleigh's gestures had been growing slightly extravagant. Usually he disliked the ritual embrace with which public officials greeted one another; now, however, he managed to seize the captain in his arms and beat him soundly and fraternally on the small of the back. The moment was photogenic. All the flash bulbs popped at once. Now the arc-lights were blazing down, and the news and television cameras were whirring. Like sheep in the presence of a crouching dog, the guests in the front row edged and backed against those behind, while the captain read out the governor's usual speech. It lasted twenty minutes and was inaudible. Hadleigh replied in English. He mentioned the crusade the Program was making against communism. By the few present who understood it, the speech was regarded as typical but tactless: it made them momentarily a little more sympathetic to communism. They nodded, not at what he said, but at each other. When he had finished, there was a tiny rattle of applause.

Iracema produced the whisky she had kept hidden from the journalists and the waiters. She managed to make the captain drink as much as possible. Leaning over him, tactically unapproachable in her Lebanese fastness of eternal snow, she began to flirt. Hadleigh watched with gratitude. In spite of two years of complete lack of intimacy they knew a great deal about each other. The party was a success and the press notices would be favourable.

That evening Hadleigh was dining with Oswaldo and Betty Fonseca, to meet a young Canadian couple who had just arrived in the city. He thought with pleasure of the rich and comfortable atmosphere that would shortly be engulfing him. One more drink here, and he would feel less tired, and ready to go.

'Honey,' he told himself in the mirror, 'you've got to take it easy. Relax, let up. You owe it to your subordinates.'

To himself, he used a mixture of his two vocabularies: the platitudes of his official position, and the astringent slang of his intimate life.

Hadleigh had a great admiration for the very rich. Even if their company was not very amusing, their money made it tolerable, in the same way that poor jokes are helped by being attributed to Voltaire or Louis XIV. In fact what he worshipped was the façade. Too often, however, among North and South Americans you found purely domestic skeletons protruding, often without any serious attempt to hide them. It was a lack of manners, an absence of social standards, for the rich to believe their feelings were important or interesting. Hadleigh, a fugitive from domestic life and from profound emotions, found it shocking. He had to confess his preference for the British: they never gave the show away.

When he arrived at Jardim Florida, he found that the Canadian couple who had been invited to meet him had cried off at the last moment. Celina had gone to the *fazenda* to rest. Throughout dinner Oswaldo was heavily silent; shortly afterwards he disappeared without apology. Poor Hadleigh found this as distressing as anything: it was as though the hospitable side of the house was only Betty's. Oswaldo, like all his countrymen, never invited foreigners. Hadleigh had been left, therefore, with the coffee, a bottle of kirsch, and Betty.

The thick make-up she was using tonight increased the chalky mineral look of her face. Although the short evening dress was particularly sumptuous – it was dark crimson and cut low on her gaunt shoulders – Hadleigh recognized in it a signal of inner discontent. Behind the façade, things were becoming unstuck. As usual, a fantastic pair of tinted spectacles shut away Betty's eyes. Her nodding head turned on him the blank stare of the praying mantis.

Hadleigh soon found that he had come in long after the rise of the curtain. The story she was attempting to tell him had gone on before, to other people, perhaps not today but on some other occasion when her alcoholic content had reached an equal point. She slopped some more kirsch into her glass.

'Jango's fault too. He wants her to talk to that priest. Look, I adore that boy, but he's not fair to his sister. It's politics. He wants to stop scandal. We had the same thing in Philadelphia with Cousin Lou's divorce. Poor Lou, she cried and cried when Poppy told her she'd have to stick to Ham until after the Primaries.' Her mind wandered back into the past and her head recommenced its frightening blind nodding.

Ronald Hadleigh tried to keep detached. He had known Betty for two years now, but he didn't want to know her like this. Socially these confidences did him no honour. She was being a bore; he was dog-tired and liqueurs always made him sick.

'A woman's happiness doesn't count down here. I know. I've suffered, darling. Dear God knows I've suffered. But I can hold my head high. I've done nothing shameful. That poor child – why can't she have her own life?'

As far as Ronald knew, Celina was having her own life.

But Betty's passion was American and abstract. She was concerned with rights, not with situations.

'She's a fine girl, but she's proud, proud. It's the Scotch blood. I have Scotch blood, do you have Scotch blood, Ronald? All you Canadians have Scotch blood. I have Scotch blood and I'm proud. I hold my head high.'

One of her gestures appeared to have dislodged some lipstick to above her left eyebrow. He had fancied it at first to be same terrible scar, hidden under cosmetics, that only appeared when she was mentally distressed. Perhaps it was. He did not wish to examine more closely. He couldn't feel any sympathy at all, only a tetchy irritation because he himself had been undervalued.

Betty stumbled for the bottle. 'I admire Celina. I drink to her for her progressive attitude.' Doubts, however, followed quickly. 'The young man, though. They say he was an R.A.F. hero. They say. Can't someone find out? If he's an R.A.F. hero or not? Celina won't answer me when I ask her. She says it's not important.'

Out of the corner of his eye, Hadleigh became aware of presences beyond the tropical plants and the glass doors. He turned to look : they were being watched.

The two great danes were sitting in silent judgement on them. They did not move. They expressed no comment. They were merely handsome, dignified and expensive, and they were separated by a wall of glass from the squalid situation of the drunk woman and the bored embarrassed man in the room. Though Hadleigh did not like animals, his heart went out to these. They were gentlemen, all right. This was how things should be done, as things were among the British.

Hadleigh's experience of the British ruling class was limited. He summoned up a memory of Sir Roderick and Lady Drummond-Bates in their Kensington flat. He had dined there on horrible food from a trolley, and had been insufficiently supplied with drink. But the vision of the Drummond-

Bateses and their son from Wellington remained. There had been no blurting there, no uncertainty of tone. They were pedigree, like the dogs beyond the glass.

It was this vision he held with him, until Betty finally became speechless. Hadleigh tiptoed across the wide floor and rang the bell. Before Paulo arrived, however, he had walked swiftly and quietly out of the house, down the granite steps and into the night air. The two dogs turned to see him go, and then their interest was again held by what was going on inside the house. They watched the manservant and Betty's maid pull the clumsy unwilling figure towards the staircase. The room and the lower part of the house became quiet. The dogs whined and yawned briefly, then returned in silence, like a couple leaving the cinema after a disappointing film, to sleep in the garden.

7

The memory of the Drummond-Bateses stayed with Hadleigh until later that night. It made him welcome the only Englishman in the city who might possibly be said to belong to their world. Standing in the doorway, Robin Morris, small and with the snub face of a scrum half, could have been Andy Drummond-Bates from Wellington five years later. Hadleigh slid off the bar-stool, leaving the people he was talking to: they were merely the stage properties of the bar, its imitation of life.

'Let's sit down,' he said. 'What are you drinking?'

Morris looked surprised.

Hadleigh brought his drink to the table. 'How is the world?'

'Fairly well, thank you.'

'Well, most of us could say that.' He smiled charmingly.

'Of course, I shouldn't expect this place resembles anything you've previously been accustomed to. It takes some time to make the necessary reorientation.'

'I've lived abroad before.'

'Oh?'

'France and Italy.'

Hadleigh shook his head dismissingly. 'All that' – he waved his hand – 'means nothing down here.'

'But I like it here. One lives comfortably. Besides, one makes a lot of money. Far more than one could in London.'

Hadleigh grinned to a couple of men who were going out, and Morris felt he had not been listening.

But when he turned back he said with feeling: 'How different we are!'

'In what way?'

'About our aims. You see, I'm not doing that at all.'

'Not?'

'Oh, glory, no.' Hadleigh laughed, leaned forward, looked the younger man insincerely in the eyes, and began to speak with more intensity. 'Before we go any further' – where are we going? the other wondered – 'you must understand this: I have been entrusted with a mission down here. I cannot fail that trust. I am not ashamed to say it: I have a mission to help these people.'

Morris had not seen this transatlantic aspect of Hadleigh before. 'But in what way? I mean, they seem to know what they are doing.'

'You're in business, aren't you? Well, I expect that's all very well. But I see beyond that.'

'Beyond what?'

'Don't mistake me. I am not merely speaking in terms of our organization. Inter-American Aid is a great organization. I feel privileged to be a member of it, and proud of the confidence they have played in me. These boys I have on my staff down here are as grand a lot as you'll find anywhere.

Fine Canadian and American boys from sound families – magnificent physical specimens, too, some of them. Er. These boys are setting an example of fairness and fine treatment. And the local boys who come in, they notice. They say, Why can't we enjoy these great privileges of democratic free enterprise? And that counts, I tell you. That counts.'

'I suppose so.'

'I am the first to admit a great future for this country. But firstly, there must be a process of readaption.'

'I'm sorry?'

'Readaption.' A tic of doubt stayed on Hadleigh's face. 'let me explain further. Take my case – as you know, I was not educated in Canada.'

'No?'

'No. I was educated at a great English public school.' He gave the name but Morris had not heard it.

'I needn't tell you,' Hadleigh laughed, 'as an Englishman, what a fine school that is. I feel myself privileged to have attended it. But, after, when I returned to Canada, I had a problem on my hands. A problem of readaption.'

Morris stared at him.

'Readaptation,' Hadleigh said quickly. He passed a nervous hand across his forehead. 'Shall we have another of these?'

'Yes, but this is mine.'

'Then came the war. Of course, with my qualifications they snapped me up at once. Canadian Navy, educational division. Hundreds of officers passed through my hands. And in doing that I achieved integration.'

'That was your finest hour.'

Hadleigh was about to nod, then his face stiffened.

'It's so easy to mock, isn't it? So difficult to do anything fine and true.'

'Forgive me.'

Hadleigh smiled; now it was like a man examining his teeth in a looking-glass. 'Your criticism is of no importance.

You have a lot to learn. You will learn. Everyone learns that there is one thing.'

Morris did not answer. He waited.

'Faith. I have faith.'

The young man felt desolate. This ageing joker might after all be sincere. Now he himself was unsure of his attack: he wished there was someone else to witness it and support him.

Hadleigh's jowly face was already darkened by a bad heart condition, and now his eyelids took on a great weariness. His sentimentality had been aroused, he had believed himself dominant and convincing. Suddenly this young man had hurt him. He felt thrown out of gear, over-used, ready for scrap. People today were conspiring to disappoint him. The *coquetel* at the headquarters of the Program had been unsatisfactory enough and dinner with Betty had been worse. Greeting Robin Morris with a burst of confidence, Hadleigh had rushed ahead, and been tripped. It was as if Andy Drummond-Bates – even Britain herself – had let him down.

When he began to speak again, it was in an entirely different tone of voice.

'I fancy that was Gregory Cowan you were with this morning, wasn't it?'

'Yes, it was.'

'I didn't know you knew him.'

'I know him quite well.'

'Quite well. I take it that means you have known him for a considerable time?'

Morris looked up, surprised. 'Yes, I have.'

'For some considerable time. Of course, then, you may think me old-fashioned, but I see the other side of these things. Also, as you know, I am devoted to Oswaldo and Betty. They are lovely people. I count them among my dearest friends.'

Hadleigh was coming back fast. Morris was getting

ready to defend Cowan, whom he considered indefensible.

'I didn't know any English people knew him,' Hadleigh said.

'I'm afraid I don't mix much with the English colony.'

'One hears a lot in an official position like mine. I've heard some things that are not very creditable.'

'Well, after all, we're in a South American city. Most people here must have left their countries for curious reasons.'

Hadleigh did not flicker. 'These things to which I make reference happened in England.'

After this, he dropped into silence. It was long past midnight but the bar was still full of people. Hadleigh waved to some more of them. He was a great waver. It was his certificate of popularity. Feeling better, he turned back to the table.

'He hasn't tried to borrow any money, has he?'

'No.' A bad liar, Morris was caught completely off guard.

Hadleigh settled in his chair with satisfaction. 'When you've lived abroad as much as I have, you get to recognize that type. I'm not snobbish, mind you. There are many people in poor social conditions, both here and in Canada, whom I think I can truly name my friends. But there's a type of Englishman down here who's just not wanted.' Hadleigh planted a small flag on the corpse of Andy Drummond-Bates.

Looking at him, Morris decided that it was best to let him race ahead. He ordered another drink. Hadleigh refused, but when the waiter came back with the bottle, he changed his mind: he pointed to his glass without a word.

'Here, of course, people are not socially experienced. You know who I mean. She's a lovely person, too. But like them all she lacks the standards people like myself have been accustomed to demand in private and public life. It was the same before, with Raimundo. They were both spoilt children. Neither of them made an attempt to reach adjustment.'

'Who was Raimundo?'

Hadleigh became charming again. 'Do forgive me. I was forgetting that you hardly know these people. Raimundo was Celina's husband.'

Morris flushed.

'I suppose you didn't know she had been married? She still is, of course. No divorce here.'

Hadleigh beat on the table in time with the piano. He was ebullient; he seemed to have increased in size.

'Raimundo is very special. So gay and intelligent. He's really one of my favourite people.'

Morris was no longer ashamed about asking questions. 'Where is he now?'

'In Paris. They gave him a job at their embassy. The whole thing broke Oswaldo. It was Celina who insisted on the separation. We none of us could imagine why. He never minded what she did.'

'What do you mean?'

'Gregory Cowan. Lots of them. A bit nympho.'

'People like you always say that,' the young man shouted suddenly. Unidentifiable feelings filled him to the throat. He knew that Hadleigh's aggression was not only a social one: it was the aggression of a man who is jealous of women, who speaks evil of them and is believed.

For Morris accepted what Hadleigh had told him as being the truth. But while he drank the rest of his whisky, the compass needles of his mind swung clear. It pointed away from all this imposition and to his own experience and values. He remembered the sad early-morning face of Celina in the flower-market, the dark stain on the linen suit, and the great sheaf of flowers she had been holding.

When still a child, Morris had several times heard his parents and their friends discuss some young girl of the neighbourhood, a brigadier's daughter or the grand-daughter of a rich widow, with remarks like 'She's turned out quite

117

impossible', 'She's making her parents miserable,' 'It's killing her father.' Awakened, he would seek out the girl and shyly admire her; at the same time he would feel her contempt, because he was too timid to declare himself and she still associated him with his parents and hers. For her, he was still allied to those who were trying to punish her for her attempt at happiness inside their chicken-run of a world.

Nothing of this could be explained to a man as deafly and blindly competitive as Hadleigh. He was at the opposite end of the scale: in spite of his delusions of grandeur, he remained from the dark side, an agent of damage.

Venomously the two men divided the bill, neither granting the other a *cruzeiro*. Then Morris got up and hurried away.

Book Three

I

The British colony in the city is not large. Those known to the consulate or the English chaplain must number about two thousand. Of course the figure leaves out many who have disappeared and are still disappearing into the seething population. Though it probably includes many refugees from Israel who wish to retain British passports, and most of the old ladies who teach English in remote suburbs, it does not take into account, for instance, the Scots girls who married Poles and disappeared from official knowledge.

The visible part of the colony, small as it is, is composed of several social strata, deposits from various waves of immigration. First there are the railway people. It was they who built the Anglican church and the British Club. Those who resigned when the last dictator took over the railways are rich; those who stayed on are very poor. Thus there is no longer any social contact between them. The rich still attend the church, and the poor inhabit the club. There are also the survivors of the coffee-boom, some still lost in the interior of the state, but many in more or less reputable businesses in the city. There are the employees of the banks and the big international firms, a migratory population. They join whatever stratum fits their accent or their income level. Their lives are centred on the British Club.

In a general way it is only the lost or the educated who, outside their work, communicate much with the inhabitants of the country. The rest live in a small village world, where the women meet to play Canasta and the men bowls. The

British colony is rather short of young girls. The younger men, the 'lads', devote themselves feverishly to games. Not football, though it is the game of the country, because this would identify them too closely with the class from which they originated in England. But tennis, cricket and even rugger.

Four of these 'lads' who shared a flat were giving a party to celebrate the secession of another of their number, Les Machin, who was getting married. Kenneth Towner had already moved out to his 'arrangement' in the city. This, however, had provoked no celebration. Envious, the other lads had warned him against 'catching something'. 'More likely to have half a dozen khaki kids,' Sidney Camargo remarked. Already another lad had moved in to take Kenneth's place. Les Machin's successor was undecided.

Sidney Camargo, a small dark hairy man, was the only one who was a permanency. It was he who arranged the finances of the apartment; he had the casting vote about who was to be allowed to replace those who seceded. Like his club membership, his place in the cricket and rugger teams, it was part of his precarious foothold in the England that his mother had left forty years before.

Mrs Camargo was a well-known figure in the city. What little money she had to live on she made from giving private English lessons, but she circulated in foreign colony society a good deal, playing bridge and Canasta, listening to people's troubles and cheering them up. She spoke several languages fluently, and Sidney was a little ashamed of her.

Though the lads were giving the party, their actual contribution was limited to the drinks. What were called the 'eats' were provided by Les Machin's fiancée.

'Leslie, I've left the taxi waiting. Get the other parcels and pay him off, will you?'

Daphne, an English girl of twenty who had been born out here, moved in with a swirl of silk. She produced a flowered apron which she tied round her, switched on the gramophone and commandeered all the plates.

'I don't think much of your servant. That kitchen doesn't look as if it's been cleaned in a month.'

She began undoing her parcels. 'Mind now, Leslie, you mustn't eat all my stuffed olives.'

'I wasn't going to, no fear.' Les's voice went down deep, as though trying to duck out below his accent. 'Who likes those things anyway? I'm sure the lads won't touch them.'

'One simply must have olives. You don't know about these things, ducky.'

Leslie looked at her with admiration, watching her take over with her ladylike ways, as he hoped she would take over large empty areas of his life. Daphne was a thoroughly nice girl, from railway people. Her father had got out in time and was rich. She was the plain second daughter – the elder was repenting marriage to a 'Russian prince'. After the convent, she had attended a domestic-science course in London : the cocktail delicacies she was now producing from her parcels were a proof of this. She had a Kensington voice which contrasted rather strangely with her parents' honest Lancashire. If Ken was doing well with his arrangements and his beach property, Leslie, unconsciously, for he was deeply in love, was laying even more solid foundations for his career.

'Where did I put that tin of anchovies? Leslie, open them for me, will you? I'm dead scared of them spurtling.'

To be the efficient mechanic was Les's chosen role. The other lads, brought up in this country, couldn't put their hands to anything, but Les had already fixed the radio with a loudspeaker so that they could dance in three rooms. The other bedroom would be used for the ladies' coats and handbags. He had tickled up the refrigerator so that it made ice in half the time. Daphne however had stopped him putting a notice, 'Ye Olde Pumpe Shippe', on the bathroom door.

'The lads like that sort of thing,' he protested.

'No,' Daphne said firmly. 'No.'

He accepted her ruling at once. In fact, he himself had been a little shocked by the idea when Sidney Camargo had insisted on it.

Leslie knew that Daphne wanted to help him, but he did not know how perfectly he fulfilled a long secret desire of hers. Brought up outside England, she had been, intimately, deeply disappointed at the middle-class young men she had met on her arrival there. But she had had a crush on the man who came to mend the gas ovens at the domestic-science school, and she had enjoyed many interesting conversations on long train journeys. Leslie, opening the anchovies in a jiffy, fitted in with her private longings: he was handsome, healthy and things obeyed him. Where people were concerned, she was at hand. She did not yet know that his social insecurity required pleasant compensations: that he would be a passionate lover after a party where he had used the wrong fork.

Standing together at the sideboard, they were extremely happy and they kept bumping into each other.

Daphne found Bill Ferris, the other lad of the apartment, trying to press a pair of trousers in his bedroom.

'Here, you men, you don't know a thing, do you? Let Daph take over.'

He accepted with alacrity, liking her bustling about their male domain. But Sid Camargo, who was taking a long time about pushing an electric razor over his bristly blue jowl, was less enthusiastic about the whole thing. These secessions, he felt, were in some way un-English. Les, as a husband, would be less likely to turn up on the rugger field. As a cricketer, he was obviously scratched from the team that would play the British Clubs of 'Monte' and Buenos Aires.

'What heavenly canapés. Do let me guzzle.'

'No, Tinka, you mustn't. They're special.'

'Special who for?'

'Well, you know what I mean.'

'I've no idea. Not with this crowd.'

Daphne frowned. Tinka was her best friend, the pretty one of a two-girl alliance, but she was in all innocence a snob. She was eighteen years old, blonde and child-like. She was wearing a dress that Daphne thought was too old for her.

'There are lots more people coming. Including some of my *chic*-est friends from Les Oiseaux.'

'Convent girls? Which ones?'

'Maria Cecilia and Aracy and Lourdes.'

'All your old gang from Mère Hélène's class. You know as well as I do they won't touch a thing. I'm going to have another canapé. What about the drinks?'

'The lads are seeing to that. But I've arranged iced punch for the girls. I got the recipe from the *Ladies' Home Journal*.'

'I bet the one I saw in *Vogue* was much better.' Tinka saw Les watching her as she licked her fingers carefully. 'Where's the loo here?' she asked. 'I'm bursting.'

Les giggled and looked down quickly at the drink he was mixing.

'Second door on the right,' Daphne said. Now Tinka was here, how glad she was that the carefully prepared Gothic script had been taken down from the door! But she loved him all the more for making such a blob. It made him seem more real, somehow.

Daphne's convent friends, Maria Cecilia, Aracy and Lourdes, arrived with English punctuality. Tea-rose-petal beauties, with clear-skinned pouting faces, they wore little caps of red and yellow feathers, and tight black dresses over their wide hips. They clustered in innocent dismay to see the room arranged for dancing. As Tinka had prophesied, they refused food and drink, but declared everything wonderful all the same. Daphne, who went over to chat with them, found them an excellent audience. Inertia was what these girls expected of the world, and to them it seemed continually surprising and astonishing that anything should happen at all. 'Não diga!' they exclaimed, again and again. 'You don't say!' When she left them, they retired to a sofa in a corner to jabber among themselves.

The lads of the British colony entered the flat warily. They smoothed their hair and glanced round them, fidgeting with their cuffs. One of them, Reg Putnam, while still on the stairs outside, began a quick pep-talk to himself under his breath: 'Good show, just the job. Well, why not? Absolutely on the line.' This trailed away when he came into the presence of the others. Soft-footed and wry-shouldered with self-consciousness, he stepped across the room to join Bill Ferris and Sidney Camargo at the bar. Reg Putnam hoped to be invited to take Les's place in the apartment. Tonight he would show an exaggerated and muscle-bound virility.

Most of the lads left their coats in the bedroom and appeared in shirt-sleeves. Though Daphne disapproved of this – it seemed a falling-off from the high standards she had set for the party – there was no doubt that Les looked his best in a white shirt, with his tanned skin and blond curls falling on his forehead. He stood behind the bar, glowing, shy and silent – his silences were another thing she loved. Excited and pleased about this, Daphne went to the door to greet her other guests, leaving the lads to discuss the British Legion dinner. Their conversation fossilized many popular expressions of the war years, and these were adopted even by the younger ones who had never been to England.

2

The day before, Kenneth Towner had telephoned to Robin Morris at his office in the city. He suggested calling to fetch him in his car.

Morris was surprised; he had hoped that Ken had forgotten all about his invitation. He still remembered their last encounter with something like horrified embarrassment. He felt that they had all come out of it badly, and Ken especially would be unwilling to revive the subject.

But when he appeared tonight in the dark street outside the house, Ken seemed as placid and as definite as ever. The moment Morris had writhed his way beside him into the new Volkswagen, he began:

'And your chum?'

'Which one?'

'Our Yorkshire lad.'

'I haven't seen him.'

'He fair tricked me. What is he, an actor or something?'

'Something.'

Ken chuckled. He stared steadily at the road in front of him and went on laughing. 'He had me beat talking about Hull like that.'

He became silent for a time, and then he said: 'You certainly do get a strange lot here. Not that I go about in what you might call social life. I leave that to the gang now. You might say I have other interests.'

For the rest of the journey and on the way up the staircase, he entertained Morris with an account of his adventures. He was without guilt or furtiveness, and seemed to be entirely pleased with himself. And he still read the lesson in the English church every Sunday.

'You know the lads, don't you?' Ken said.

'I'm quite lost. I'm afraid I don't know anyone.'

But Daphne had already greeted them. It was the first time she had seen Robin Morris. When, however, she had given a brief calculating glance right down to his shoes, she guessed without regret that he was for Tinka.

Tinka thought so too. She looked very young and turned slightly pink. She pushed a bowl of olives at him and soon began throwing questions after them.

'You're with *them*, are you? How jolly good. Then you must know ...' And she reeled off a list of the names of his colleagues.

'You know them better than I do.'

'Well, you see Daddy's in I.C.I. He's their top man here. So naturally we see an awful lot of your people. Have you been out here long?'

From her, he could take the standard questions easily, and like them. He could hear, as if it were a final truth, that 'Daddy finds the country frightfully interesting, but Mommy hates the black servants.'

Her face was pale and English, her hair not entirely successful. There was none of the easy achievement of Maria Cecilia, Aracy and Lourdes on the sofa, but for Morris she was somewhere he had not been for a long time. She was part of something he had disdained when he had known it, but to which he now seemed to return battered, an old warrior from the optimistic city. He drank Tinka in, conscious of all her gestures, her pinkness and her clumsinesses.

'Are Mom – are your parents here?'

'Heavens, no. This is Daph's do. It's her thing absolutely.'

'You sound terribly superior.'

'Oh I'm not, don't say such horrid things. Everyone's always saying I'm such a snob. They do, really. I do try my best, but you know I do just naturally like people who do things properly. I mean, don't you?'

'I expect so. Like what?'

'I mean like the Oliviers. And that man who takes photographs in Vogue.'

'My God.'

Daphne pushed a plate furiously forward. 'You might help a bit, Tinka. The lads haven't got anything to eat.'

Tinka made a wry face at Robin Morris. 'I'll be back,' she said. He watched her go over to the crowd at the bar.

Reg Putnam looked her up and down. 'Well, why not?' he said.

'Who's the attraction?'

'Not bad.'

They clustered round Tinka, but she did not look at any of them. She hummed a little, as if her mind was occupied with other thoughts. The lads took the canapés to attract her attention, but she pulled the plate away so quickly that their arms were crossed and entangled over it. When Bill Ferris spoke to her, she did not answer. She pushed him firmly aside and carried the empty plate back to Morris. The lads followed her with their gaze.

'Ho ho!' they hooted.

To Morris, Tinka pretended exhaustion. 'I've done my stuff for Daphers,' she said. 'I've fed her blokes for her. Now I'm on strike. Let me get you a drink.'

From the doorway a silence was spreading round the room. Two people were standing in the middle of it, and nobody seemed to know who they were.

Though obviously English, the man was wearing a corduroy suit and a tie of coarse orange wool; tall and stout, he seemed to be trying to belong to a different race from the other Englishmen in the room. They in their turn were at once hostile and wary of him, of his huge bald head, his beak of a nose and the glittering eyes that looked at them all over scornfully.

The woman appeared to be a little more accessible. She was small, with sunbleached hair. Her eyes were greenish-blue, the white part very white against the tanned skin. From the dress she was wearing, the girls guessed her to be very rich. About the man, they were unsure.

'We're looking for a Yorkshireman,' he boomed.

When Morris heard that cultivated 'Robert Morley' voice, his heart sank with apprehension. He realized that there was hardly anyone he less wanted to see than Gregory Cowan. The presence of someone who has lied to and intimidated you, even though the wrong is all on his side, is bound to make you sorely ashamed of yourself.

Kenneth Towner had been summoned from another room. 'The Yorkshireman!' he shouted. 'How are things in Hull? Come and meet the gang.'

'Does one have to do that? I would prefer a drink.'

'Anything you say, lad. Drinks at the bar.'

Sidney was mixing the drinks now. 'The name's Camargo,' he said.

'What name?' Gregory asked.

'What are you taking?'

'I'd like some gin, please.'

Reg Putnam remarked: 'I say, old boy, your lovely in blue certainly livens up the old festivities.'

'Forgive me, I don't see how the woman I bring can interest you.'

Putnam took a moment or two to digest this. 'Well, I like that,' he said. 'I like that very much –' But these, the vaguest of threats, he delivered alone, because Daphne had already gained the newcomer's attention.

Daphne was not looking her best. She had been going at the party hard, a sense of insecurity making her over-attentive to her guests. She smiled at Cowan a little too enthusiastically. 'You've just come, haven't you? You're not too late to try one of my canapés. They're my own very specials.'

'Delicious. My wife makes these, too.'

'Oh, does she? How funny! I wonder if she uses my recipe. I must make her taste them.'

Gregory looked at her for a moment in frank astonishment. Embarrassed, she dropped her eyes. Then he burst out laughing.

'That's not my wife over there. My wife's in England with our children. In Hampstead, to be clinically precise.'

'Oh, I *am* sorry.'

'That one there is – is – wait a moment, I know the word –' He held up his finger and thumb as if trying to grasp it from the air. 'My "*companheira*"! I got it right, didn't I? Ha ha!'

'I see.'

When Morris saw Celina, he felt a little shock. He had not seen them together since the first evening, Gregory Cowan never spoke about her, and so he had subconsciously separated them. He had almost forgotten that Celina's remoteness, her slightly boring mysteriousness, was due to her passion for this man.

Tinka came up, innocently excited. 'Do look, who are those marvellous people? How on earth did they get here?'

'I know them. Perhaps in a way it was my fault.'

Celina was standing alone. Someone had given her a glass but no one had plucked up sufficient courage to speak to her. But the three on the sofa, Maria Cecilia, Aracy and Lourdes, established her identity. She had been at Les Oiseaux with their elder sisters. One of them was a cousin of Raimundo's. They called Daphne over, and through her the information crossed the language barrier and leaked round the room.

'Please excuse me. I must go and talk to her.'

'Do go. She looks fascinating,' Tinka said.

He found that his susceptibilities were heightened, not only by the drink, but also by the rather desperate atmosphere of the party. Whatever you knew about Celina, he felt, in spite of Hadleigh and Raimundo and Gregory Cowan, the personal physical impression she gave would always remain the same; she charged the surrounding atmosphere; she seemed to carry invisible wings of air with her, that brushed lightly against you; she brought you beside her in any room she might be in.

But for the first moments that he stood with her, he was conscious of the same slight disappointment. She was detached, preoccupied, glowing but not warm.

'Robin, how wonderful to see you.'

'I'm surprised to find you here.'

'Yes?' Celina looked round her. 'It is certainly not very exciting. Why are you here?'

'I like the man who brought me.'

'Is it the fat one with the spectacles? Yes, he does look rather nice. What does he do?'

'He's a professional Yorkshireman.'

'What? Oh, I see.'

She was silent a moment. 'Let's move back a little, shall we? I think I'd like to lean on something.'

They walked over into a corner where they were out of earshot of Gregory Cowan. Morris had a suspicion that Celina might be keeping him away from Gregory on purpose: perhaps she did not want again to confront a possible friend with a lover so difficult to answer for.

But when they were alone, she began to speak with great intensity.

'It was I who insisted on coming here, as a matter of fact. I felt I simply had to see some other people, I did not mind who or what they were.'

'I see.'

'I find it does not help, after all,' she said desolately.

'I'm sorry.'

'Not you, of course, Robin. But it is not any good.'

He saw a gleam of tears in one of her eyes. It seemed that she was going to break down.

'Do you want me to stay here?'

'Yes, please do.' She paused, making up her mind, and then said: 'We have been driving all day. We went out into the country, but it was no use. He hardly spoke to me the whole time.'

'Let me get you a drink.'

'Thank you. But please come back here, won't you?'

'Of course I will.'

He felt excited and nervous, and also awed and respectful, as one always feels in the presence of strong emotion. He carried back the drink as though it were a life-saving vaccine. Celina took it gratefully.

'It's funny, this particular situation has never happened to me before.' Now she sounded off guard, a little hysterical. 'Always the opposite, I think.'

'How do you mean?'

'Well, for me it is very serious indeed. In fact it is final. And for him, just *brincadeira*. How do you say that?'

'Fun and games. Slap and tickle. I'm sorry, those words sound dreadful.'

'They cannot sound dreadful enough for what I mean. You do not mind me telling you all this?'

'Of course not.'

'You see, I thought at one time you might be the sort of person who might help me.' She looked at him inquiringly, but she saw him stiffen, remembering to be cautious.

'I don't know. Please ask me, anyway. Then I can tell you if I can.'

This did not satisfy Celina. Her face saddened. 'No, I will not bother you, Robin. Perhaps I shall not need to, anyway.'

'Please do.'

He realized now that he must have failed her in some way that she considered important.

'Let's talk about something else. I was wondering when

I should see you again. Some friends asked after you the other day. Cecil Newton. Do you remember?'

He accepted the retreat into conventional conversation.

'Of course I do. I liked him. He's a nice man. I must say I found his wife simply petrifying, though.'

'Mercedes is really a very remarkable woman.'

'That finishes her. Why did they move away?'

'Mercedes did not like it here. Her health was becoming affected.'

'And she was a doctor! She bullies him, that's all.'

'Perhaps you are right. Anyway he seemed very fond of you, Robin. He asked me to tell you to go and see him any time you were in the capital.'

'That's nice of him. I'd like to. I shall be going there quite soon.'

'I'll give you his number. Have you a pencil?'

'No.'

During the last minutes he had been concentrating all his attention on Celina. Because he was a little drunk, it seemed as if they both were completely walled off from the rest of the room. Now he looked round, without thinking, to find someone from whom to borrow a pencil. He received a slight shock. The lads – Sidney Camargo, Reg Putnam, Bill Ferris and one or two others – were watching him intently. Morris felt confused. At first it was the insolence of their stare that disconcerted him; then, as he looked closer, he came against tight knobs of hatred in the eyes of Sidney Camargo. What was this all about? At his direct gaze, one or two dropped their eyes. But Sidney Camargo didn't stop staring.

Hatred can be a stimulant and exciting: a sniff of it from the wind makes you plunge ahead. But sooner or later, it always demands questions. If the lads resented Celina's, Gregory Cowan's and his own presence, was it because they believed them to be happier and more successful than themselves? Perhaps their dislike was centred more on Celina. The women in their scope were unexciting; attractiveness was associated with social superiority or with prostitution. In either case it could be jeered at: for the lads, the cult of social unpretentiousness was as serious as the cult of rugger.

Morris looked at Celina with concern. People here must know who she was, and perhaps the situation was more tricky than he had thought. To make things ugly, it waited for one or two jovial remarks from a lad trying to keep ahead of the others in manly cynicism.

Morris walked over to Sidney Camargo and asked him for a pencil.

Sidney Camargo did not speak. After a moment of hesitation he shrugged his shoulders. He pulled a cheap propelling pencil from the hip pocket of his trousers.

Morris took it and went back to Celina. She told him Newton's telephone number and he wrote it down on a page of his diary. His hand was shaking; the lead snapped against the paper, but he managed to scratch the number down with the circular metal point.

He returned the pencil to Camargo. 'Thank you. Most kind of you.'

Someone said 'Haw haw' in the background.

He decided to ignore it. He returned to Celina but he could think of nothing to say to her. He picked up his glass off a table and spent a long time drinking the small amount of acid fluid that remained at the bottom.

Suddenly he heard a low groaning sound behind him. But this time none of the young men was looking in his direction. They were watching one of their number, who was humming.

The lads linked together with their arms on each other's shoulders. They were going to sing. The ceremony perhaps began as a ritual against strangers. But now the strangers were forgotten and, instead, they were trying to raise the spirit of those happy times that the leaders among them had known seven or eight years ago. In the war years, their unwelcome individuality as men had been disguised by uniforms and curly moustaches or 'wavy navy' beards; slang and technical jargon had fitted easily to their stiff tongues. Now, as works managers and bottom-of-the-ladder business men, exiled in a city on the underside of the world, they could only gather together in groups waiting for the spirit to descend. At a given moment an eye would catch another eye, an arm would go easily, without fear of cissiness, on to another's shoulder, and the tribal song rose from gravelled throats:

Roll me over

Roll me over

'Les,' Daphne called out. 'Do tell the lads to sing a bit quieter. We'll have the neighbours in on us.'

Roll me over

Roll me over ...

But Les was among them too, and when she caught his eye, it was strange and meaningless to her.

Celina moved to the other side of the room, away from the noise. Apart from this, she did not comment on it in any way. Morris followed her; suddenly he felt dog-tired and bored. Celina would not help any more. He knew that she was disappointed in him, but he believed he was right to be disappointing. Once recently he had let himself drift, had allowed himself to be pushed about, and he was still sore as a result. When that happened, you could not blame anyone but yourself. He had learned that he had to keep control of himself, or he would wag round like a puppy, trying to please.

Gregory Cowan appeared beside Celina.

'I've been talking to such a nice girl, darling.'

When Celina felt his massive hand on her shoulder, her whole expression changed; she moved in beside him, under his arm.

Gregory Cowan saw Morris watching him. 'Hullo,' he said. 'Ha ha!'

Morris turned away. Fury burned like acid in his throat and eyes. He knew the sudden discouragement of his shortness, his inability to make himself felt. Whatever happened, you always found yourself slipping out on to the margin like this. It was like a dream of running, where you lacked breath and your legs turned to water.

'I want to talk to you.' Gregory took Celina's arm and steered her in the direction of the other room.

The lads were raucous and deafening but their purpose was achieved. The spirit had descended, all trace of individuality was gone, and they were asserting themselves in their full power. Even Maria Cecilia, Aracy and Lourdes, the three girls on the sofa, had given up the attempt to talk among themselves, and were watching with respectful dismay, as though this were an exhibition of British folklore.

Morris found Tinka in the kitchen. She was stacking plates and was obviously pleased to see him.

'Your friend is heaven,' she said. 'He told me all about the films he is making.'

'I shouldn't believe a word of it.'

'You are horrid. Why do you always say such horrid things?'

'Do I?' Now rage and frustration had made him as gauche and boorish as any of the others, but unlike them he had no group to retreat into to restore his morale. He was alone.

Tinka shunted three sorts of canapés on to one plate; she put the two other plates in the sink. He gave her a cigarette. She puffed at it like a child in a potting-shed. Then she began in a small voice:

'You don't understand what it means to meet people like that. It's all right for you, you're a man, you can go where you like and meet who you like. But us girls get stuck with the colony. And the people in the colony are so – you know. And you can't go out alone. At least, you can, but everyone is shocked and men follow you in the street all the time. I used to think it was quite funny, until I could understand what they were saying.'

'Don't they say anything interesting?'

'No, they don't.'

'What do they say?'

'Oh, silly things. I couldn't possibly tell you.' She became pink again, and wandered off round the kitchen table. She put her hand on the corner of the table and whirled round it.

When she came back near him, she said: 'Anyway, it means an awful lot when you meet someone you can really talk to.' She looked down quickly. 'Like that man, I mean.'

He watched for her eyes until they arrived back at his face again.

'Does it, Tinka?'

'Yes it does. These are Daph's friends here. Not mine, never you fear.'

In his present mood he found her defiance and insecurity absurdly moving. He caught her hand, thin and rather damp, which was lying on the table, and gently lifted it towards him.

3

The lads had stopped singing half an hour ago, and were telling stories in low voices. Someone had switched on the gramophone; led by Daphne and Les, two or three couples were dancing. But when the stack of records was finished, nobody replaced it or turned it over.

A Negro in grey chauffeur's uniform appeared at the door of the apartment. He had called for the three girls on the sofa.

Lourdes, Aracy and Maria Cecilia had been silent for some time. Their minds, over-receptive rather than sensitive, seemed not to have recovered from the impact of the lads' singing. Now that the moment of departure was here, however, the girls encircled Daphne with their soft arms. They were moved to tears of sympathy by her forthcoming happiness. They laid their satiny cheeks against her, and bore her with them towards the door.

'But our handbags!'

'My scarf! In the bedroom!'

At once they dissolved in laughter. They were always like this, too excited and at the same time too relaxed. Everything in their upbringing had taught them that the expression of emotion was valuable in itself. Tears and laughter shook these girls frequently and to no purpose. Inside, they were trivial, humourless and rather cold.

Daphne accompanied them. She turned the handle of the bedroom door. It was locked. Behind her, the trio looked at one another, murmuring surprise.

'Wait a moment.' Daphne laughed, but they did not laugh with her. Humiliated by their eyes, she felt anger flare inside her. She pushed past into the kitchen, cast a furious glance in Morris's direction, and summoned Tinka.

With Tinka beside her, Daphne banged the door again. 'Would you kindly mind coming out? People want to get their things.' Her voice was at its highest social point.

'They've been in there half an hour.' Tinka said unwarily.

Throughout the party so far, Daphne had been trailed at a distance by a pale heavy girl, who seemed unhappy and afraid of being alone with strangers. Most of the time she sat enclosed in her own silence, only grinning passionately and pleadingly whenever Daphne spoke to her, or even came near her.

Now she had followed them to the door. Suddenly, with a little cry, she collapsed. She dropped her head and writhed away, stuffing a large greyish handkerchief into her mouth.

'Look after Molly, will you, Tinka?' Daphne said briskly, and battered again on the door.

Tinka dragged the girl into the kitchen, where Morris was still standing. He pushed up a chair and together they placed her on it. Tinka pulled off Molly's thick-lensed spectacles; they were the type with springy hooks, which scratched and tangled in the thick hair over the ears. She jerked them free and put them on the table.

'I told Daph not to invite her. It wasn't the sort of party for her and she's never allowed to go out. But Daph wanted to get her out of herself. Let her see life. Huh!'

'Who is she?'

'Her parents are Baptist missionaries. They lived for eighteen years in the interior among the Indians.'

Looking at the girl's thick smocked dress and flat shoes, he could believe this easily. His astonishment came when she quietened down. He saw that she was laughing.

'I thought she was crying.'

'Hysterics. Comes to much the same thing.'

'Shouldn't we give her anything?'

'I don't think so. Don't they say "no stimulants"?'

'Do they? She looks a bit young, anyway.'

'Young!' Tinka snorted. 'She's twenty-six.'

'My God! What made her behave like this?'

'I'll tell you later.' Tinka bent over the girl, who appeared to be recovering, though her face was still hidden in the handkerchief. Her neck, above the high-cut dress, looked long and weak and not clean. Now her blunt head was lifted; she stared myopically at Morris and burst into tears.

'That's better,' Tinka said. 'Let it all come. Take my hanky, Molly, yours is sopping.'

'I wish you'd tell me what is happening.'

Tinka looked at him. 'You were right, Robin. Your friend is simply horrid.'

'He's hardly my friend. At any rate, I'm glad you agree with me.'

Daphne returned to the first room. She asked Maria Cecilia, Lourdes and Aracy to sit down again; she gathered up a stack of records – anything, she did not look at the titles – and placed them on the record-player. She dispatched Kenneth to the girls on the sofa, grabbed Leslie and began to dance. Her party was doomed to go on.

By now several other people had had the intention of leaving and found themselves frustrated. Among the lads, someone said : 'Filthy behaviour.' Someone else, less realistically, said 'Throw him out. Who asked those types, anyway?'

'Who said Ken could ask who he liked?'

'Ken mixes with all sorts of types. No sense of responsibility.'

'No sense of decency, more like.'

When Morris appeared at the door the comments continued, for in their minds he was still associated with Gregory Cowan. One or two of the lads were drunk; in the colony there are never enough English girls to go round, and amatory frustration combined with an athletic disposition to make them pugnacious. Daphne made a quick sign to Morris, who asked one of the remaining girls on the sofa – it was Lourdes – to dance. He felt he was holding her firm supple body as a shield against further commentaries.

Now there were several couples on the floor. Morris and Kenneth Towner attempted to make conversation, but the young women were still stunned to silence, exchanging long looks over the shoulders of their partners. These looks expressed neither boredom nor shock nor even moral criticism. They were the looks of limited people, without ease, out of their setting. Though of 'good families', these girls had not been trained to attempt to hide this; like peasants in a city or soldiers billeted in a foreign country, their instinctive reaction in the presence of the unusual was to sulk.

When he passed him Morris saw that Ken Towner's mouth was quivering.

'What's the matter?'

'Our Yorkshireman.' His face was swollen even fatter with suppressed laughter. His voice bubbled. 'I just heard.'

Morris felt less able to see the joke. In the kitchen he had realized already that this was not a matter of Kenneth's bland adolescent Priapus; it was the manifestation of a god a good deal more destructive and agonizing. To feel this, however, you had to have his own estimation of Gregory Cowan and his own sense of the anxiety-state which the man liked to create wherever he moved.

At present, in the tiny surroundings of a British colony occasion, the situation might be humorous. The party seemed to be under way again, and the problem of the three girls and their chauffeur reverted to their own private concern. In the kitchen, Molly had stopped crying, though she was still weak and blotchy in the face. Tinka, enjoying worldliness and superiority, had finally dosed her with brandy. She now watched with detachment for it to take its effect. In a corner near the bar Reg Putnam was telling a long and surreptitious story; one or two of the lads guffawed too soon, but Sidney Camargo nodded approvingly without smiling. It was obvious that Reg was the right type to come and share the apartment.

Then Daphne's records came to an end and the murmured story was forgotten, because into the silence came the sound of the bedroom door being unlocked.

The voices of Tinka and Molly in the kitchen sounded light and far away. The lads put down their glasses. It was clear that not one of them could find an attitude adequate to the occasion : social unpretentiousness just didn't help. Those who had been dancing automatically made a lane. Daphne blushed smartingly, her two front teeth nipped into her lower lip. She wanted to cry out against the ruin of her party but instead she looked at the floor, and saw only the hem of the blue dress as it switched past. Les also looked at the floor and Morris was watching everybody else. Only Kenneth seemed unattackable. He was still quaking with subterranean laughter. Nobody spoke.

Sitting on the stairs outside, the Negro chauffeur stubbed out his cigarette. He sprang to his feet impatiently. He was disappointed.

'Good night, *senhores*,' he said.

He watched the two of them go silently down the stairs.

4

The night was very dark, with low clouds. Buds and fruits of the jacaranda trees pattered down on the pavements and the continual crowing of cocks was blown away by the wind. At the gate of the house, he was startled : a shadow moved and grunted. He recognized it as the night visitor who was always there. As he looked the visitor became a little darker than the darkness, and made indefinite noises like an animal. A large calm animal – you did not feel him dangerous.

Morris climbed the stairs to the flat. Without switching on the light he stumbled through the sitting-room and out on to the balcony. In the garden the bamboos and the lemon tree were being pulled about by the wind, which seemed low on the ground, as if it was trying to uproot things. Occasionally a large palm leaf fell from overhead with a flapping sound like cardboard.

His thoughts began to clear. On the way he had stopped at a bar for a little glass of *aguardiente*. He had not drunk enough at the party to quell the emotions he experienced. He felt tired and dirty and slightly revolted. He did not want to see any of the people again, even Tinka. As for Celina, he thought that this evening would be the end of her. Daphne's anger and the hysterical state of Molly – these would lead to the spreading of the story through the British colony. The three sofa girls would be guaranteed to tell it to local society. By now even Morris himself was beginning to think about Celina as something finished, someone he had known but would see no longer. He was surprised, slightly horrified at himself. This attitude made him realize how far he had come from England. About English morality, an American writer once complained that nowadays 'the abysses were so shallow'. But this was in another country. Celina lived on an Indian reservation near the Grand Canyon : the abyss was beside her.

His drunkenness led him to exaggerate the situation. Celina was gone, like the money he'd lent Gregory Cowan. It irritated him in much the same way.

During the time he had been standing on the balcony, he had gradually become aware of another sound, higher and more persistent than that of the wind tearing the palm fronds. It was regular and monotonous and at first it seemed mechanical, like the whine of metal against rubber or the gasp of a saw in wood. When he had traced it, he knew the sound to be human in origin. It came from the servant's bedroom. He had heard a similar noise before. Then, he had been deceived and embarrassed : he had mistaken the sob of ecstasy for that of grief. But now he couldn't be mistaken. The crying was as insistent and plaintive as a dog baying the moon. Expedita wept and wept, while her lover hung about, a pillar of darkness, at the front gate.

Morris leaned over the balcony. Spots of cold rain stung

his face. He listened to the soft hopeless sound rising and falling. Perhaps Mrs Kochen heard it too. Did her muscles stiffen into a rigor of hatred? Kochen would sleep innocently, like a gigantic baby. After a time Morris began to forget what the sound was. It became the waves roaring at a seaside hotel, the dynamo running at night outside a school dormitory. Then his thoughts came back to human feelings. He was ashamed; he felt inferior. Lack of feeling was the enemy. It was this that had produced the situation at the party. Perhaps you had to learn to feel all over again, because education had taken this capacity away from you. In this case, Expedita was still years ahead of him.

An Englishman might have thought that the abyss was ready to engulf Celina. But these things happen quite slowly. During the next few days she was at home, and for various reasons her family were too busy with themselves to be inquisitive.

Betty of course demanded Celina's presence, but she wanted company rather than confidences. Fortunately, perhaps, she was out of touch with the gossip of the city. She had only just heard the news of Ronald Hadleigh's sudden departure for Canada. This had shocked her and made her feel even more isolated. 'I can't understand it,' she kept saying. 'He never even told me good-bye.'

Chain-smoking, half-way between boredom and misery, she lay all afternoon on a chaise-longue outside the french-windows. Occasionally impressions and memories from the world outside impinged on her consciousness. They did not stay there but at once formed into sentences which dribbled past the cigarette at the corner of her mouth.

'I wonder when Jango'll be back. We hardly ever see that boy now. Do you think the army's up to something?'

Celina did not answer. She was leafing through old copies of French art magazines.

'My, the wind did pull the garden about. That night you were out, remember?'

Now the fine weather had returned and the sky was washed clean. On the calendar it was springtime; some of the flowers imported from the northern hemisphere were blossoming in the garden. The swimming-bath had been filled.

'Why don't we use the *piscina*, honey? Invite some people. Tell you the truth, I feel out of touch. Why don't we?'

Celina could not go on reading. She had been gazing at a reproduction of Cranach for five minutes and her hands were shaking. She was deeply grateful for the fact that Betty knew so few people. Luckily the American business colony was out of the question. Nearly all were from California or the Middle West, places where, as Betty said, she had never visited. There were also the religious groups: the Fellowship Community Church, the Southern Baptists, the United Baptists, the Mormons, the Interdenominational Missions, the Christian Scientists, Bahai, the Seventh Day Adventists and the Four Square Gospellers. All these had well-endowed foundations in the city. The reverends and their wives might have offered spiritual comradeship, but, back in Philadelphia, Betty had already experimented with the more fashionable of their cults. By now there were very few people for her to call by Christian names – and these, in the American fashion, she named her friends. Hadleigh had been one. The others seemed to be out of town.

Hadleigh's name came out several times that afternoon.

'Not a word. Didn't even call me up. I always declared his job was secret.'

'Whose job is secret, my darling?'

Betty started. She turned her head slowly and blinked up through the green glass at her husband, who was standing behind her.

'Ronald Hadleigh, honey.'

Oswaldo nodded. He was not interested. Like so many foreigners, that one had come to the city and gone. During the next six months, at the Jockey or Automobile Club, Oswaldo would, all innocently, repeat Hadleigh's name to other visiting Canadians, and perhaps some of them would have known him and would speak of him. But after that time Oswaldo would stop getting the name right. The Canadians would not recognize it, the subject could not be pursued. From then on, Ronald Hadleigh would have no further resurrection in the minds of men.

The political situation had changed during the past few weeks. The dictator had definitely made peace with the working classes, and there were no more strikes. Deprived of even the pretence of popular support, the speeches and articles of Jacinto Moreira became more and more hectic. He filled his own newspaper every day: the spirits of MacCarthy, Salazar and Franco pursued each other down the corridors of longer and longer sentences. Jacinto may have been right, but he was unreadable. Only the devoted stuck to him at all.

Among these was Jango. His peculiar radiance, which had irritated Celina on the day of Paulo Alcantara's funeral, had greatly increased. In his little Beechcraft aeroplane he was in and out of the city the whole time. He had become a liaison officer between Jacinto Moreira in the capital, and the group which centred on Father Albuquerque in this city. He was even fuller of other people's ideas than before, and his piety was noticeable. But above all he was changing with regard to his family. Previously he had felt himself rejected by his cosmopolitan father: his lack of intelligence, his mechanical gifts and his love of army life had increased this feeling. But now Oswaldo was in retreat, and he found his son once more. Welcomed back, Jango increased in moral certainty. He was no longer at a loss in the presence of his sister. When he arrived home that evening he embraced her fondly, patted her a little, looked inquiringly but kindly into her face, and put his arm round her.

Five days had passed since Daphne's party. Celina had heard nothing of Gregory Cowan. After two days, she had rung up the house where he lived; he had gone filming, they said. Celina knew this to be untrue. He himself had told her that the film he worked on had been abandoned for lack of money. Yesterday she had telephoned again: they said he had removed his luggage. Today her nerves felt like knife edges drawn across one another; beyond the range of the human ear, her whole body was screaming. The sense of loss was completely physical. Her mind had not begun thinking yet.

Jango squeezed her shoulder.

'I'm praying for you,' he said.

He had little feeling and no malice: it was merely an overflow of energy in the direction of other people. But the words were detonators.

She stood in front of him and cursed him soundly. In English, for in their own language the right words were too closely connected with sin and damnation.

Jango only half-understood. Untouched, he stared at her with an incredulous smirk.

'What is all this? I said I was praying for you. That is all.'

That night Father Albuquerque came to the house again.

He moved in swiftly, his big black boots banging their way across the polished floor directly to Oswaldo's study. There was nothing of El Greco's inquisitors about this man: he might have been a commissar, short and thick-set, with the mottled blunt hands of a peasant. Only his Spanish head, which had sharp grey eyes and grizzled hair, seemed aimed, like a lethal weapon, at everything he looked at; it gave some idea of the power of his ambitions.

Oswaldo sat near the window with one of the great danes at his feet. He looked tired and uninterested. Around him were the bookshelves filled with inspirational works – Norman Vincent Peale, Harry Emerson Fosdick – that had long ceased to inspire him. Above hung the framed political photographs: himself in a straw hat and carrying a rifle, standing in front of a sandbagged barricade; himself on board the Portuguese ship in 1930, going into exile among a crowd of his fellows. But now he was apart from all this and, though he had never had political power, he liked to consider himself an elder statesman above the turmoil of the present. If it had not been for his son, only curiosity would have kept him here.

Jango was in uniform, quivering with excitement. In spite of his moustache and his clipped skull, he looked extremely young. His face was pure, almost virginal. He took the paper with the list of names from his wallet and smoothed it out on the leather top of his father's desk. Father Albuquerque sat in the armchair opposite him, his hands on the lap of the soutane with all the points of the fingers touching.

Jango lit a cigarette, shook the match long after it was dead, and began: 'It's a matter of a list of names, Father. Jacinto gave them to me this morning. People in this city who are known to be supporters. Of course, as you know, he has not seen several of them for many years. That is why he wants our – your comments on them.'

'How many on the list?'

'Sixteen.'

'Do I know these people?'

'I think so, Father.' He could not imagine the Father not knowing anybody.

'Let me hear the names, my son.'

'General Olympio Cavalcanti. President of the Military Club. Member of Christian Democrat Party.'

Father Albuquerque put his fingertips against his forehead.

The general was an equation to be worked out: the lightning calculation of sins and merits, of weakness and strength, took about thirty seconds. Oswaldo and Jango watched; it seemed that they could almost hear the brain working.

The answer came: 'Yes.'

Jango waited for some comment. He was a little disappointed when there was none. The next two names were those of army officers. Father Albuquerque accepted both immediately. To the second name he added the comment: 'Yes, he is a good man.' For Jango the word for 'good' at that moment developed a precise and limited meaning, like a piece of technical vocabulary.

'Dr Alcibiades Medeiros. Director of the Faculty of Letters.'

'No, no, no,' the Father said at once. Jango looked up surprised. From the other's tone of voice, he thought he must have got the name wrong.

But the priest went on at once: 'You see, he has a bad personal history. His position in the university was obtained for him by his father-in-law, on condition of marriage. Within two years this man Alcibiades was living with another woman. I visited the house regularly. The wife died suddenly when I had not seen her for five days. She committed suicide, poor soul. Naturally, I demanded to inspect the death certificate. It was all in order – the doctor had been bribed. The family did not wish the facts known.'

'Then no?'

'No.' Jango put a line through the name.

'Dr Melo de Pombal, Secretary of the General Medical Council.'

'He was the doctor who signed the death certificate,' Father Albuquerque said simply.

Jango giggled and crossed the name out.

'Deputy Jose Vasconcelos.'

'Yes.'

'Deputy Washington Peixoto.'

'No.'

Father Albuquerque was a state deputy of the same party as these two last. The judgement seemed a guarantee of his disinterestedness.

'Dr Fairbanks Polastrini. Executive Director, Ministry of Education.'

'A political reappointment,' the priest mildly remarked. 'After dismissal for incompetence. I met him only once, years ago, when I was parish priest in the interior of the state, at S. Joaquim do Rio Vermelho. When I arrived there he had been principal of the state gymnasium for the past four years. Politically he was the most important man in the town. I had great trouble with him.'

He paused a moment. Jango was going to cross out the name.

'The fathers of two fourteen-year-old girls came to me and told the whole sad story. I went straight into the school and confronted him. I told him I would denounce him unless he left the town immediately. He took my advice. He came here and became an inspector of schools.'

'And the girls?'

'The father of one of them has a good job in the same department.'

Two more of the names on Jacinto's list had similar case-histories attached to them. The Father never moved from his chair, but his face became flushed and his voice was hot with emotion. There was no doubt that he was enjoying his task.

Once or twice Jango felt a horror-stricken suspicion that some of the information could only come from the confessional. He need not have worried for a second. News reached the Father in dozens of different ways. He already knew, as Oswaldo did not, that Oswaldo's daughter had behaved like a whore in public three or four nights ago. He knew about

Jango's affair with the wife of the French military attaché. Information was always there; it could be used when you wanted it, at other times ignored.

This, too, perplexed the young man. In one case the same sort of accusations could have been made against one of his own colleagues, an army colonel, as against Polastrini. Yet Father Albuquerque accepted his name at once, and obviously not from ignorance.

'Clovis Nascimento de Amaral.'

The young man looked up, questioningly. Everybody thought that Clovis was the cardinal's son. Here surely was a point of awkwardness. But difficulties like this resolved themselves with lightning clarity in the mechanical part of Father Albuquerque's brain. He was completely unembarrassed by the sins of man.

He aimed his burning eyes at Jango.

'Of course,' he said.

Jango put a tick beside the name.

In his seat by the window, Oswaldo was restive and annoyed. Several times this exhibition of *force majeur* had almost brought him to his feet. The Father's standards and sense of justice were completely alien to Oswaldo: all belief that politics were for limited human advantages was being dismissed as out of date.

Though Oswaldo would not have questioned the facts, Father Albuquerque's principles of selection seemed meaningless: of course everyone did things like that. A belief in humanity did not mean that you thought men innocent but that you counted fewer things bad. He suspected the priest of impelling his allies into a false position, of obliging them to be hypocrites so that he might have the moral advantage over them.

At the conclusion of the list, Oswaldo rang the bell for coffee. Jango glanced at the paper and saw that more than half the names had been struck out. He was appalled: wasn't this a reflection on Jacinto Moreira's judgement? Were there really so few who could be trusted, when the evil was so obvious? He looked up in despair, but the Father smiled reassuringly.

If Jango had been there a few months later, he would have been still more worried, for the names of Dr Alcibiades and Dr Melo de Pombal were to be included in the movement. The purpose of this evening's meeting was not entirely what Jango thought. Father Albuquerque knew that he needed distinguished supporters; he was not scrupulous in his choice of them. But there was something equally important. He knew that he would never get enough people to vote for his platform, but in this country they were used to dictatorships. If you could not get enough people to vote for you, then you need a certain number to die for you. Far fewer, in fact. Jango Fonseca was one of them.

The Father put his hand on the young man's arm.

'These are good men.' Again the precise technical term. 'All will be well.'

Jango brightened at once. He smiled at his father and Oswaldo's heart was filled with love for him. The old man had spent a lifetime on the fringes of the political world. He knew the score, he had no confidence in the priest, and by now he had little hope that anything would improve. But this present situation was another matter altogether. It was far more important, because it did not concern ideas, the well-worn ideas he had dragged through the decades with him, but a life, the life of his only son. A great many disappointments had brought Oswaldo back to this point. In the years of exile he had become indifferent, and indifference had made his family life without meaning. Jango, whom he had doubted on the proving grounds of adolescence, was now his only solace. He saw that his son had begun to live.

The servant brought coffee. Father Albuquerque stood up and gulped down his little cupful.

Jango stood between his father and the priest, and they both watched him affectionately.

'My son, all will be well,' Father Albuquerque said again. 'A little patience. Things are beginning to crack, and then –' He made the flapping gesture with his hands that indicates that something is of no more importance.

Jango grinned. For him, all was already well.

5

The following morning Celina telephoned Morris. It was early; she had to catch him before he went to his office.

The knocking at the door was certainly Mrs Kochen. He heard it from his bedroom. She was standing on the top step, and Expedita was beside her. Their faces were sullen and they were not looking at one another.

'Mr Morris, the telephone for you.'

'Thank you.'

She usually sent the servant when there were calls for him. Now, as he followed her down the steps, she hissed back at him: 'After, I would like to talk with you. Something very serious is happened, I must tell to you.'

'All right.' His heart shrank with boredom and apprehension. It was one of those hard bright dusty mornings that seem made to create small anxieties, and he had drunk too much black coffee.

He went into the Kochens' living-room. There seemed to be more potted plants than ever, and the tropical fish were still flitting round their tanks. Mrs Kochen's servant was on her hands and knees polishing the floor. He was stopped short, watching her fine strong legs and rounded buttocks with warm amazement. She was a Polish farm-girl, who had managed to keep the same clear skin that she would have had in Europe. She looked over her shoulder calmly at him, like a heifer over a gate.

Morris picked up the telephone receiver.

'Who is it?'

When he heard Celina's voice, his feelings of apprehension returned. There seemed to be too much of life around, too many people circulating.

'Yes?'

'I'm so sorry to bother you, Robin. Was Gregory there with you yesterday?'

'No, he wasn't.'

'Oh dear. It's only that he said he left something at your house.'

'That's not possible. He hasn't been here for a long time. In fact, I haven't seen him since – since that night.'

'What night?'

'The night of the party.'

'Oh. I see.' There was a silence.

'Hullo.'

'Hullo.' Celina's voice came back. 'Do you mind if I ask you a personal question, Robin?'

'Of course not.' His heart shrank again. 'Go ahead.'

'Did you lend him any money?'

'As a matter of fact, yes.'

'Oh God. I see.' Her voice dropped into a gulf of discouragement and sadness.

'Is there anything –'

'No, no thank you. Good-bye.' She had put the telephone down.

He replaced the receiver. The Polish girl looked back at him over her shoulder with calm speculation. She watched him out of the room and then went on polishing. Mrs Kochen stood at the front door, blocking the way.

'Please come with me, Mr Morris.'

She led him into the front garden, and near the gate pointed to the ground.

'Have you been told, Mr Morris, what such a thing means?'

'*Macumba* – voodoo, isn't it?'

'Your servant did this, Mr Morris.'

He thought for a moment. 'Why not somebody from your factory? You are always saying you have trouble there.'

'Only the manager knows our address. He is a German man. When he is not there, myself only and my husband.'

The Kochens expected hatred everywhere. Even when it manifested itself as now, out of the thin air, Mrs Kochen accepted it as her due. Morris looked at the *despacho* again. It had been carefully placed. The candles had been snuffed early but the black-feathered chicken with its throat cut still looked fresh. He saw the coins and the little packet of maize flour. He was surprised how meaningful the whole thing looked, in the bright morning sunlight. It meant that someone wished evil on Mrs Kochen.

'I've never examined one closely before,' he said, interested.

'It is a horrible thing. I sent the boy early to school, before speaking with you. I did not want him to see it.'

Morris turned back to the house. She followed after him, her voice hoarse behind his ear.

'I would never have a servant like yours, Mr Morris. These things are disgusting.'

'You mean you believe in it?' He looked more closely at her. He suspected that she was frightened.

'These blacks are savages. I will never have one in my house.' Her voice became shrill. 'Your servant had a man in her room the other night.'

'Not now. I think they quarrelled.'

'You see.'

'I don't see that it is any of my business. He did not come into the house.'

Mrs Kochen turned down her mouth with disgust and loathing. 'It is as you wish.' Her voice became heavily ironical. 'She must be a very good servant, Mr Morris.'

He looked at his watch, but she went on: 'If you keep her. She must look after everything very well, no?'

'She's all right.'

'All right. I know.' She laughed her hurt laugh. 'They start very well, but soon everything is very dirty. They do not want to work, only to impose themselves. They hate us, Mr Morris. Does not this horrible thing in the garden show this?'

She stopped, breathing heavily as though she had been running.

'I am not understanding, Mr Morris. I was thinking that Englishmen at least will know how to deal with niggers. I was wrong. The English Empire is finished. Now your soldiers want only to attack my country. I was wrong. Forgive me, please.'

'Please don't get excited, anyway. I will see what I can do.' He was as conscious as she was that this meant almost nothing. And he was beginning to feel less sure of himself. With all that lay behind her, which was most of the unhappiness of the world in this century, surely Mrs Kochen had a right to hate back? But she was not hating back. She was hating in an entirely new direction. In this city and in this country, she believed that at last she had found someone to despise, and she was making the most of it.

Under the bleak tubular lighting, the galleries of the Museum of Contemporary Art were deserted. The Italian lithographs had gone from the walls and screens, which were now hung with the canvases of an exiled Rumanian abstractionist. Celina wandered up and down, attempting to pay attention to the pictures, and listening to the sound of her feet on the polished floor. Then, with a moment of decision, she turned into the bar.

He was not there.

She had not really expected to find him. She had thought she might meet some of his acquaintances, and in this she was not disappointed.

The room was small, crowded by the large numbers of pictures on the walls. A gramophone was playing jazz behind the bar. On one of the upholstered seats, Koronski was holding court, an immense bird of rapine, bald even to the eyelashes. Beside him, in a polo-necked sweater, was the Amerindian boy Nelson; his features were sullen and unmoving, and his eyes showed only suspicion and gloom. The prince was devoting his attention to the two Italians who had the chairs opposite.

Nevertheless, he seemed delighted to see Celina. He greeted her effusively and insisted on speaking English. He dispatched one of the Italians to buy her a drink.

'And our friend Ronald?' he asked. 'How sad that his job was changed! I have a feeling that he liked very much to work here.'

'I heard nothing about him.'

Celina asked him about his film. He scratched his ear meditatively.

'Always money difficulty.'

'I heard that.'

'Ah, yes, from our Englishman?'

'I expect so. Which one do you mean?'

'Gregorio.' He looked at her understandingly.

Celina saw that Koronski now knew a great deal more about her than he had the first time they met. She did not mind, for she felt quite at ease with him, and she knew that in a short time she would be able to ask about Gregory.

The young Italian put a whisky gently down in front of her. He and his friend could not keep their over-expressive eyes away from her. They appreciated her *chic*, while intuition told them that some amatory difficulty was in the air. Why should she come here alone like this, unless she was looking for some man? In the presence of the real thing, they were awed and respectful. They sympathized with her, too, for had they not suffered in the same way?

By the time the prince had given her another drink, Celina felt better. What was important was to have escaped from the house, where both Betty and Jango had the power to make her desperate. Here, at any rate, there could be no criticism, either open or implied; here scandal had nibbled so often that it had no power to bite any more.

Koronski drank deeply from his glass. He appeared content, in spite of the gloom radiating from the Indian youth on his right. This, with his financial difficulties, he considered beyond his control and to be due to natural causes, like the weather. Anxiety lay very lightly on him.

'My poor film,' he said. 'Sometimes I am very preoccupied with its future.'

'How far had you got with it?' Celina asked.

'They are doing *doublage* now, in the capital. Here there is no recording studio.'

'Are they?'

The baron turned, his eyes peering sharply at her. 'Did not our friend Gregorio tell you? He went three days back.'

Celina stubbed out her cigarette. 'I – I knew that, of course. I did not know why he went.'

'Do not worry. He will be O.K. He is a lucky one. When the *doublage* is completed, he is paid. He will be free of us.'

'I see. Yes.'

'Most of us must wait. You see, we have a cooperative system . . .'

While he went on talking, Celina was remembering a

sentence spoken lightly and indifferently, but with the final power to hurt: 'When I've raked up enough money, I'll go back to Spain.' Now already he had won something in the state lottery; he had borrowed money from Morris and had taken a great deal from herself. The film company would pay him. Probably he had already bought his ticket.

'I'm sorry.' She interrupted the prince. 'This *doublage*, will it take very long?'

'Perhaps until next week. Do you wish for whisky?'

'Until next week. Thank you, I would love one.'

But this glass turned out to be less helpful than its predecessors. She became very conscious of the close observation of the two Italians. When she looked around her, the place still seemed amiable, but it was no longer anywhere she wanted to be. People had come here after a series of abdications, when they had ceased to compete or even put in an appearance at the usual arenas. Compared with these people, even Jango and Betty lived in extreme situations, on the outer edge of life.

Celina prepared to leave. She had made up her mind to an all-night drive. At the end, he was there or he was not there. Suddenly it was the journey that was important, taking the car out through the suburbs, over the railway lines, and swooping down on to the wide road that led to the capital. She would be there by morning.

Koronski went on talking, but in Italian now. Nelson Vasconcelos, the Indian boy, was still sulking, and when Celina rose to leave he did not move. The others sprang to their feet and bowed her out, and she left, a little drunk – dimly aware of the puddles of comment she had stirred up behind her.

6

Morris woke suddenly, shaken out of a nightmare. His mouth was dry and he had the hard clear wakefulness of one who had been drinking too much gin beforehand. There was a rumbling noise in the distance. Thunder. Perhaps it was lightning that had woken him. He looked at his watch. One thirty. The rumbling noise continued, too regular for thunder, and nearer, and now there was shouting with it. But until he got out of bed he could not tell what direction the sound came from.

He put on a dressing-gown and slippers, and shuffled through to the living-room. All the time the banging continued and at intervals behind it came an inarticulate shout. He opened the window and went on to the balcony. The lights were on in both the servants' rooms.

He wondered what Mrs Kochen's Polish girl was doing. Possibly praying in terror. There was no doubt where the noise came from now. The thunderous banging stopped. In the sharp silence that followed it, a man could be heard muttering and swearing. Then the banging began again.

Morris went back through the flat. He unlocked the front door and hurried down the steps. The lights flashed up in the Kochens' part of the house. He could already hear Mrs Kochen being calmed and restrained by her husband.

The night here was warmer than inside, and very dark. The air felt hot against his face. A strong smell came from the various sorts of foliage that Kochen had cultivated. Big leaves flapped against him, and when he stumbled into a flower-bed he felt he was entering a jungle.

He stood in front of Expedita's room. The man had stopped hammering on the door. He was just inside it, breathing heavily.

Morris found the switch of the wall light. He saw now that the door had been locked on the outside. The man's efforts had shaken the key out on to the ground. He picked up the key and replaced it in the door. Then, not knowing what to expect, he turned it. The Negro almost fell out on top of him.

At this hour of the night, the man seemed enormous. His bare feet were huge, grey and wrinkled like elephant's skin. He wore cotton trousers and his unbuttoned shirt showed the moulded black wall of his chest. His face was rueful and troubled.

'What happened?'

Though they had never even greeted one another, they were suddenly intimates; almost nothing seemed to need explaining.

'Expedita. She's jealous. She fought with me and got the knife out of my belt. She said she was going to kill herself.'

Morris looked past him into the little room. The bed-clothes had been pulled on to the floor and a potted plant had crashed on top of them. Various bits of clothing were scattered around. In the cage that hung at the window, two ruffled lumps of feather slept unmoving on their perch.

'Where is she?'

'She ran out. I heard her go on to the road. That was an hour back. I did not want to cause inconvenience to people,' he said humbly. 'I thought she would come back. Then I got angry.'

'Where would she go?'

'I know where she went. She has a friend – a bad woman, a *macumbeira* and 'mother of the saint' – who lives near here. I don't hold with those people.'

By this time they had moved out beside the house. In his dressing-gown Morris felt at a physical disadvantage, but the Negro beside him gave an impression of gentleness, of being someone large and simple honestly mixed up in his dealings with too many women. He was proffering his situation without apology, and he seemed to think that the other knew all about it already. To Mrs Kochen, however, watching furtively from the window above, he must have appeared quite different. He was the incarnation of her deepest terrors. While he was there her whole being would throb with disquiet and her mouth go sour with loathing. Perhaps she had already forced her husband to telephone the radio patrol-car.

'What are you going to do?'

'I'm going to bring her back.' The Negro turned away and padded softly out of the front gate into the darkness.

Mrs Kochen's voice broke in from overhead. 'What is happening, please?'

'It is all right.'

'We will telephone the police.'

'It is all right, I tell you.'

'All right! We are in danger, Mr Morris.'

He looked up at her, graceless and desperate at the window. 'Please don't interfere. It is my business.'

Mrs Kochen was deaf to reproof. Her mind only warmed up in response to situations; it was quite undisturbed by sarcasm or abuse, or, for that matter, by anything that anyone might say.

'I will make Rachmel to call the radio patrol.' She slammed the window shut.

He was alone outside the house. The wounded air had settled down heavy and black around him, except where a yellow square of light showed that activity continued in the Kochens' flat. He was alone. He had to climb the steps to his flat and go to sleep. The warm night smothered him like inertia, it hemmed him in with the limitations of his own body. Whenever he felt like this, it was his smallness and absurdity that he blamed for getting him into moral situations. Now he even seemed to have difficulty in moving. He shook himself, pushing his way out of a melancholy inanition. He got slowly back to the flat, but when he arrived there he could not go to bed. He went to the balcony and stared in front of him. His mind was sore at the edges.

Somewhere the moon was coming up. The night grew less dark and he watched the dull swirl of clouds overhead. Below him the leafy garden was alive with insects clicking and whirring. He stayed there for about a quarter of an hour. Drugged with sleep, he had forgotten that he had a watch to look at. Then the gate banged outside in the road. He heard footsteps and a noise of sobbing.

Very small and shrunken, Expedita was walking in front, with her face hidden in her hands. The man followed in silence. Now he had the knife.

The door of the servant's room shut. The weeping diminished in importance and became one of the incoherent noises of the night.

The Englishman on the balcony pondered over the scene he had just witnessed. In his mind the whole episode combined tenderness and violence, almost like the sexual act itself. Expedita, a domestic servant, age somewhere over thirty, could call down grief and tragedy; they were at her disposal whenever she had need of them. A few nights ago, through the mediation of her friend the 'mother of the saint', she had summoned her African gods to bring ill-fortune to Mrs Kochen, whom she obviously held responsible for the tangled course of her love. For her Negro lover, the emotions were probably more complicated. To be desired is in itself a clumsy and muddled thing compared with desiring. From a racial habit, his gestures had been apologetic but his attitude unrepentant. His face had only had that ruefulness which is the result of the will's efforts to reject the body's blind triumphs – for, after it was all over, he could still be pleased with himself. He didn't need to call on the gods at all.

Morris heard a sharp whistle.

The man was under the window, standing on the flower-bed with his head framed among the hibiscus leaves.

'Senhor, excuse me.'

He stretched a long arm up through the branches, and handed Morris the knife.

'I don't know whether she wants to kill me or herself. You'd better take it.'

The doorbell rang at noon. It was Kochen, gentle, deprecating, and ready to laugh it off.

'Forgive me, please.'

'Of course, come in.'

'It is about last night. My wife became hysterical. As you can observe, I did not go to the factory this morning. She is resting now.'

'Yes?' There was a silence. He was damned if he would say he was sorry about Mrs Kochen. As far as he was concerned, she was hysterical the whole time.

'Previously,' Kochen went on, 'I believe there was this business of the *despacho*.'

'Yes.'

'You saw it, I think? Well,' Kochen laughed unhappily, 'of course for me – and my wife too, naturally – there is nothing in that. But, as I think I tell you, she suffered very much in the war, and such things affect her imagination. Last night, for example, it was she who wanted to call the police.'

'They didn't come.'

'No, they didn't come.' Kochen giggled. 'As a matter of fact, I only pretended to telephone to them. For the sake of my wife. You see, it costs money to call the radio patrol, and I thought to myself perhaps Mr Morris will not be willing to pay.'

'You were quite right.'

'Yes?'

'Nothing more happened.'

'No.' Kochen scratched the orange fluff on his skull. He sounded miserable. 'Mr Morris, I do not wish to interfere with your affairs, but my wife still is extremely nervous. She feels she cannot bear to be in the same house as –'

'I have already paid my servant. She is leaving this afternoon.'

Morris would have felt happier if the effect of this news had not been exactly what he expected: Kochen blossomed; he became plumper; he beamed.

'I am so glad, Mr Morris. Now all is well, then my wife will be so pleased. I am very grateful.'

'I didn't like her cooking,' Morris said.

In reality there was nothing he could say. How could he explain to Kochen that he could no longer stand an atmosphere of hatred surrounding a place where he was trying to live? Kochen might beam plumply now, but the situation was still with him as long as he and his family stayed in this country. For, from his wife's point of view, it had been a real race-riot. Irrational hatred had gone on accumulating on top of a rational motive for complaint. Finally Mrs Kochen had developed all the symptoms, the burning cheeks and choked throat; she had spoken with the fetid sexual undertone of jealousy masquerading as disgust.

Compared with all this, the knife, which still lay where Morris had placed it early this morning, was a clean and simple thing. He picked it up, balanced it and gingerly fingered the sharp blade. He wondered when its owner would come back to claim it.

As a matter of fact, the Negro never returned to the house, and later Morris used the knife for bread.

Book Four

I

The problem of the lemons had evidently arisen before. These in the basket on the sideboard were the dark-green sort, perfectly hard and spherical, like little rubber balls. They looked unpromising and the first one cut proved, as usual, to be composed only of pips, surrounded by a damp cellulose substance which produced no juice.

Newton threw the lemon down on to the tray among the glasses.

'Darling, I have told you many times not to buy lemons like these.'

'But these are very good lemons, everyone knows that these are the best lemons. In my home they always use these – these *gallegos*. *Papai* and my uncles, they knew how to drink!' She gave a proud scornful laugh. 'With *aguardiente* always these lemons! He does not know!'

Her husband gripped the edge of the sideboard and his scarlet face darkened. He wore only a blue cotton shirt and scoutmaster's shorts; his legs were still thin, and as white as if they had been kept away from the sun.

Her answer were always the same. There was the perpetual appeal against experience, towards local patriotism and remote standards. There was blame and accusation for himself, and, behind it all, blind home sickness.

'Can't you see these lemons have no juice?' he shouted. Then he wiped his scalded forehead. 'Never mind! Never mind! No need to weep about it!' He turned to Robin Morris and said very quietly in English: 'Do you mind having a pink gin?'

'Of course not.'

Mrs Newton was unruffled and showed no sign of weeping. She took up the basket. 'Wait, I will show you.'

Between his teeth, Newton said to Morris: 'I am so sorry about this. Will you go through the balcony door on the left?'

'I expect I can find my way.' The decks were being cleared for a matrimonial dispute. There was no attempt to disguise it even from a comparative stranger.

Mrs Newton held one of the fruit to her nose, and closed her eyes in pleasure. 'These are real *gallegos*, the best lemons. How lovely they smell! They make me remember my father's farm. He had hundreds of lemon trees.'

'Go through, will you,' Newton said more sharply. 'I will come in a few minutes with the drinks.'

Morris found himself in the living-room of the apartment. It had obviously been let furnished; Mrs Newton's table-cloths and ornamental vases did not fit in with the bare lines of the furniture. The whole room seemed uncomfortable, and it was possible that the only pleasant place was the balcony outside. The evening was beginning and the sun was setting fire to the windows of other blocks along the bay. The sea had the colour and texture of quicksilver. Caught in it, all the islands, boats and late bathers seemed to be corroded to a deep blackness.

Celina was lying on a chaise-longue. Her bandaged left foot was propped slightly higher on cushions.

'It's still this scar,' she said, answering his inquiry. 'It's the only thing that refuses to heal.'

Morris sat down in a chair beside her. The last time he had seen Celina had been on the evening of Les's party. Her desperate telephone call had followed a few days later. After that, he had dropped out of touch.

Celina looked well and friendly. Lying in the sun all day had bleached some locks of her hair almost to the colour of sisal. Her skin had always been tanned; now it was so dark that it already had that bluish bloom that blonde women sometimes get. However, the sun had not given calm to her face. Perhaps it wasn't a calm sun, this sun of the Januaries in the capital. For Celina, the city had meant many adventures and unhappinesses. It was true, though, that she was now living in a suburb where none of her former friends, or the friends of her father and brother, lived. She was staying with people she had not known a year before. She was on an island cut off, among foreigners who had few acquaintances. In the same way the suburb itself was cut off from the rest of the city by a wall of rocky hills, covered with jungle and shacks where the Negroes lived.

'Mercedes thinks it must have got infected in that hospital.'

'Which hospital?'

'The first one. It was in a little town near where I crashed. The ambulance took me there that night. The nuns were awfully sweet to me, but I expect they did everything wrong. When I got here it was no better. I didn't want to go to our own doctor; the one I found for myself was not any good. So I thought of Mercedes.'

'I was certainly surprised to hear you were here.'

Celina laughed. 'I expect you were.'

There was a pause while they both considered the reasons why Morris had been surprised.

The Newtons were not rich and Celina was. Even though she had been kind to them in the past, they were not the type she would have as friends. There was an element of exploitation, the same that he himself had felt earlier in his acquaintanceship with Celina.

'Mercedes has been simply wonderful. She looked after me the whole time. Especially at the beginning. As you can guess, I was in a rather terrible state.'

Morris looked away. The exploitation was forgotten. His eyes pricked and he felt suddenly deeply moved. 'Yes, I – I suppose you must have been.' He laughed a little, to show that he knew this was inadequate.

She began again in a firmer voice: 'Mercedes took me completely in hand. It was three weeks before I could really get control of myself, and during that time she did everything for me. She washed me and fed me, and gave me my dope and my injections. She's a wonderful person at her job. I admire her very much.'

A long time back, Newton sitting on a rock by the sea had said: 'I think she saved my life.' Morris gained the impression from all the praise and gratitude that Mercedes performed prodigies of goodness, but all the same remained apart – something of a different species, hardly to be considered on the same level as ordinary human beings.

Newton had not yet appeared. In fact there was a significant silence in the flat behind them. A well-fitting door had been decisively and firmly closed on a conversation. Celina must have guessed this. If you live in a flat with other people you learn about their lives by the shutting of intervening doors, by those stifled silences when you know that in some other room everyone is talking hard.

'When you are in great trouble, as I was, it is difficult to find someone like that.'

'I am sure it is. You were very lucky.'

Celina was quiet for a moment. Then she said: 'I kept telling myself I was lucky. But now I know that in a certain sense it was easy for her.'

'Why? What do you mean?'

'She loves me.'

'Oh?' Morris looked up, surprised: the hardness he had

heard in Celina's voice was on her face as well. He understood what she meant.

'I mean that. She is in some ways a very innocent person, and perhaps, almost certainly, she doesn't know. But she really loves me.'

Cecil Newton appeared on the balcony. His hands were unsteady and the glasses were rattling a little on the tray.

'So you've been talking to our invalid?'

'Yes.'

'She's looking well, don't you think?'

'Yes. I agree with her, she's very fortunate to have all this.'

'That's Celina's special. That one is yours,' Newton said. 'I hope it's to your liking. Cheerio.'

'Cheerio.'

'Cheerio.'

Newton leaned on the parapet and gazed out across the bay. 'Just look at that sunset. It makes life seem worth while somehow, doesn't it?' Obviously Newton was quite simple and sincere about what he felt, but for him any comment on feelings had to be blurted out under pressure. 'This is the best time of the day for me. You see, I don't drink before sundown. Never. I don't know why. No moral scruples attached. It just isn't my way.' He sounded as if he did not expect to be believed.

Celina spoke to him softly: 'Cecil, why don't you sit down and relax? We've got all we want here.'

'Why not? Yes, that's an idea.' He sat down and was quiet, but they could both feel his unhappiness going on and on. It was like the insistent noise of cicadas in the trees below the flat. A moment later, he was talking again.

'So you think Celina's lucky to be here? Frankly, we're lucky to have her. I know one person to whom it's been a godsend. Mercedes. You see, she's not allowed to work as a doctor in this country. She was also without something to do. This has made a world of difference to her.'

'She's been wonderful to me,' Celina said. When Newton was present the praise was easy and conventional.

'It's her whole life, looking after people.'

'She must have been a marvellous doctor,' Celina said.

'I can assure you she was. They had an epidemic of typhus up there among the copper mines. Mercedes worked day and night for two months. Afterwards they gave her medals. I don't think she ever really understood why. You see, they thought she was being noble. As a matter of fact she was doing something that was entirely and completely natural to her. But of course nobody understood that. She was a freak. Women in South America just don't do that sort of thing, do they, Celina?'

'No, they don't.'

Newton turned to Morris. 'I want my wife to be happy in this country. You see, she did so much for me. She gave up everything for me.'

'Yes, you told me.'

'She's been happy looking after Celina. Happier than I have seen her for ages.' Newton was not an insincere man, but now he was playing a role, not for them but for himself to believe.

At that moment Morris saw that Celina was watching him. He was a little scared by the intensity of her look. It set him apart, as the recipient of private knowledge: it began a conspiracy between them. At the same time, her ironic half smile seemed to diminish the importance of the man sitting between them.

This last Morris was unprepared for. He considered Newton with the firm intention of going on liking him and sympathizing with him.

Mrs. Newton came out on to the balcony. She had changed,

and was wearing a wide frilled skirt. She carried a small jug, half-full of lemon juice.

'You see, I have been trying the *gallegos*. They are beauties. You can have lemon juice with your drinks now, like *papai* used to.' She held the jug to Morris. 'You will take some?'

He looked helplessly at his pink gin. 'No, thank you.'

'Oh!' She was offended. 'Cecil, you take some of my lemon juice.'

He shook his head briefly. Mercedes put the jug on the table. 'It is here when you want it. What a pity to waste those lovely *gallegos*!'

Mercedes settled herself into her chair. As though under an obligation, she began to talk. Like many simple women, she believed that conversation to be polite had to be completely trivial, punctuated by little giggles which emphasized the unimportance of what was said. In this way, speaking slowly so that Morris should understand, she touched on the weather, the apartment, and the view from the balcony. She smiled and laughed a great deal.

But behind this her body was restless; it showed that the tension was still affecting her. Her eyes were wandering about for something to settle on. There was disquiet in her gestures.

Silently Celina held out her empty glass.

The giggles and the platitudes stopped at once. It was obvious that Mercedes had taken offence again. They watched her nervously. How many drinks had Celina had? she asked, her eyebrows arched improbably, and her eyes blazing. Didn't she know she was going against the treatment? How could she expect the wound to heal? What was the use of all the trouble, all the slavery, all the sleepless nights Mercedes had gone through, if her advice was to be flouted?

Celina said nothing. She continued to hold out her glass. After a moment or two, Newton got up out of his chair and took the glass from her. He carried it through into the living-room.

When Mrs Newton saw this, she appeared to go a little mad. She gave a strangled cry of rage and frustration. She stood up with a rustle of frills, and her clumsy movement upset the jug of lemon juice. She stared at it, biting her lip, and swirled away through the glass door. Like explosions, other doors banged all over the apartment.

Morris looked miserably at the floor. He felt the dreadful pathos in all Mercedes' gestures. She had lost, she had lost all along.

'You mustn't worry, Robin. This happens all the time.'

'It's the violence I'm not used to.'

'But in this country I am afraid you must get used to it.'

'I hate rows.' He sounded querulous and young.

'It's the only way some people can express themselves. Mercedes doesn't really know what she wants. She is jealous of everyone. She thinks she is being ignored but, you know, she is not easily included in conversations.' Celina laughed and snuggled down into her chair, entirely pleased with herself. 'I spend hours thinking of medical anecdotes to tell her, stories of diseases and accidents and things. But it is an effort.'

After the scene that had just taken place, Morris no longer felt Celina was being malicious. He found himself agreeing with her. The reality of living with limited and headstrong people had often afflicted him. It was the same everywhere: you had to go down a rough road of headaches and recriminations, violent silences and slammed doors.

'Why do you stay here?'

'I am fond of them both. Otherwise, I would be quite alone.'

The appeal was there again. Morris looked across at her. Alone? He still didn't trust her, but her beauty and calm, with all their buried intensities, were a strong enough invitation to forget the small appeals to justice by which one steered one's life.

He went over and sat beside her. Once he had lifted her hand from where it was lying on the arm of the chair, everything was easier. He stopped thinking. His diaphragm was so tense it hurt him, and he heard his breath rushing in and out in a curiously mechanical way. She looked up at him, and her eyes wrinkled at the corners.

While they were kissing, they heard Newton coming back through the room behind them. Morris stood up quickly; he pretended to be examining a ship out at sea. Celina picked up her cigarette.

Their host had changed his clothes: he was wearing a white suit and a tie. His thin hair was smoothed down. He looked humbled and exhausted, like a survivor from somewhere – a shipwreck or a lost safari. 'I've brought you both drinks. I thought you would be ready for them.'

Either the quarrel between the couple was unresolved or he had won it. But he didn't look as if he had won anything in his whole life. Now he took Morris aside and whispered: 'I think, if you don't mind, it would be better if we had dinner out.'

'But –' Morris indicated Celina's bandaged foot.

'Don't worry about me, Robin,' Celina called out. 'I shall be all right here.'

Morris looked back to her. He was still trembling a little with excitement, but Newton was too taken up with himself to notice the reactions of other people. Nor did he make any excuses: in the past year he had become accustomed to improvising plans for the emergencies of his wife's temperament.

Still looking at Celina, Morris finished his drink obediently, and then he followed his host through the flat. Mrs Newton was nowhere to be seen.

2

A solid line of cars, mostly with their radios playing, stretched out along the seafront. The air was warm and the pavements were crowded. The fact that Newton and Morris alone were wearing suits set them off uncomfortably as foreigners. But the attention of the crowd hardly seemed to focus on them at all. The people in the street were like actors who must not look at the camera or the audience. Young girls in tight sweaters and trousers, gently rotating their buttocks, passed with drowsy unseeing eyes, as if their sensuous attention was equally distracted by the ice-creams they sucked at and the man's brown arm across their shoulders; strings of young men swivelled and whispered at passing women; stiff pairs of naval fusiliers paraded at the corners in white forage-caps and scarlet-and-black uniforms. There were Negro and mulatto sailors, and collections of satin-skinned girls who were chaperoned by bored little brothers. To the tune of motor horns, each group approached and retreated like dancers.

In one of the side streets dancing was actually going on. It was two weeks to carnival, and a street band of Negroes with percussion instruments and whistles was beating out rhythms which had infected many of the passers-by. An absurd, uncorseted woman was gyrating on the arm of a small hairy man. Barefooted children hopped like fleas in the gutters.

The younger Englishman was still deeply disturbed by the incident that had just passed. After the still, tense minute on the balcony, the sudden uprush of life from the pavements was overwhelming. He felt his heart scamper and hot water burn in his eyes. But he was quiet. He saw that his friend was unaffected by outside events. Newton observed nothing, he was confronting an entirely different problem, that of existing in the streets of the city. As with human relationships, he managed to make the whole game appear to require more expertise than common sense. He was tense and curt.

'The bus stop is round the corner,' he said.

There, more complications were to be confronted. The bus had to be carefully chosen, for though all of them went to the same place, some took a longer route. Once the two men were on the bus, the right seats had to be selected: at the back you were bumped around, the nearer seats placed you on top of the wheel, and in front you were likely to get the worst of it in a collision.

At length they were settled in the correct place and the bus dived off through the narrow tree-lined streets. By now Newton was braced like a man on a roller-coaster, and with the same slight air of triumph. He felt he was in control over circumstances.

At subsequent stops the bus filled up rapidly with men in coloured shirts. Near the front of the bus, a white woman, as heavily painted as a circus clown, was sitting with a mulatto boy. Their arms were locked tightly, their faces were close and their eyes brushed together in a little idiocy of passion.

The bus went through a tunnel in the rock and coasted along the bleak shore of a bay, where the broken-down skeletons of construction projects shone dimly in the headlights. Then the buildings thickened again. When the bus stopped, the seat behind the lovers was taken by two drunks.

One of them began speaking in a high public voice: '*Credo, meu deus*, it's all hot here. That type who got off had a hot seat.' The word he used was mildly indecent and it fell into a silence.

At once the mulatto boy in front whirled round. His lips were tight and his eyes furious. His lady had been insulted

175

and he demanded an apology. Beside him the female clown giggled feebly.

'What's the matter, my friend? I only said he had a hot seat.'

The boy stood up, but his determination was not strong. The woman could pull him down into his place easily. The other occupants of the bus, however, were on his side. 'Stop the bus!' they shouted. 'Throw him out!' 'Teach him manners!' Someone added more quietly, 'Beat him up.'

The driver stopped the bus, but more people shouted for him to go on. The other drunk persuaded his friend to keep quiet. The bus lurched forward again; for a few minutes the man kept a truculent silence.

But he was soon muttering: 'Why do people make a fuss? All I said was his seat was hot.'

The driver braked once more. The mulatto sprang to his feet and advanced, clenching his fists. The drunk took one look at him and slithered down the steps on to the road. The mulatto went after him.

Someone looking out of the window shouted: 'Go on, give it him!'

'Come on. Let's all give it him.' The men in the bus stood up. Laughing and shouting they got down in to the road. The bus driver was with them.

Now the two Englishmen were left alone with the painted woman whose honour had been attacked. She simpered meaninglessly. It was a moment of complete separation from real life. Outside in the road the obligatory rites were proceeding. But you were set apart, without even an attitude to fall back on. This was the constant and unadmitted condition of those who live habitually abroad – you ended up in a complete moral vacuum.

The men came back into the bus one by one, with satisfied expressions, rolling down their sleeves. The driver settled in his seat and the bus shuddered and roared, preparatory to setting off again.

Morris turned to see out of the window. The drunk was lying motionless in the gutter. His head was at an angle and blood was coming out of his mouth. His friend had disappeared.

Morris looked at Newton. Newton was scarlet-faced, sweating gently. He said in a preoccupied voice: 'I hope Mercedes remembers that she must change Celina's bandages tonight.'

'My wife always refuses to eat in restaurants. I come here by myself.'

Indeed, the waiters seemed to know him better than he knew them. You could imagine him a noticeable figure here, an exotic with his boiled red face, chain-smoking, not minding how long he was kept waiting, and finally eating without looking at the food, while he worked his way round his peculiar private hell.

This evening however, he must have appeared quite different. Across the narrow white tablecloth, he almost beamed at Morris. Outside in the street a band was thumping out its mind-obliterating rhythms, with whistles and percussion and singing. The music caught in a gasping pause, then crashed down again, and the shuffle of dancing feet followed like pebbles after a wave. None of this was affecting Newton. He was betraying his wife: he had a friend.

It was at his suggestion that they were going to eat *pizza* and drink wine – black Portuguese wine that would drive you crazy in this heat. The waiters had all collected near the doorway, where a breeze came from the sea. From time to time they went through unwillingly to the kitchen in the corridors beyond. There the food was drawn out of roaring brick ovens and handed down a chain of dim half-naked figures of inferior status. The wine took less time in arriving;

they both had drunk a glass of it, and devoured a plate of olives, when Newton began to speak again.

'You may not believe it, Robin, but you arrived just in time.'

'Oh?'

'I don't know if I can stick it much longer. As you saw, the situation at the flat is quite impossible. There's bound to be an explosion fairly soon.'

Morris had to make some remark that, without agreeing or disagreeing, would mark time. 'But if, as you told me, your wife is only happy when she has a sick person to look after –'

'Oh, she is. Mercedes really has something to do now. Don't mistake me, I've never seen her better.'

'What about Celina?'

'Celina has nowhere else to go. You know she broke with her family?'

'No, I didn't. I haven't seen her for three or four months.'

'The brother is a complete fanatic. As for the stepmother, well, you saw her when we were there.'

Morris noticed a complete change in Newton since the last time they'd had a serious conversation together. At that time, when people's characters were discussed, the little man had primly kept silence. Either academic philosophy or social background had taught him to be uninterested; he had learnt how to think from the best minds, and how to live from acquaintances in saloon bars. His life seemed to have been a succession of blind steps. He had married, the second time at least, with reckless disregard for the consequences.

But now something had changed his attitude and, with this change, had brought him speculation and disquiet about other people and himself.

'What are you going to do?'

'That's what I'm wondering.'

Morris finished his second glass of wine. 'Why don't you just keep away?'

'Keep away?'

'Make yourself scarce, I mean.'

It would have been his own solution. From his visit to the apartment, he had gained a picture of Newton battered about by intense atmospheric disturbances. It would be hard to say whether Mercedes or Celina possessed the stronger personality. In spite of some fifteen years' difference in age, they were not dissimilar in their equipment: each was energetic, childless, and in some way had her natural scope curbed. Together in that small flat, they used up all the breathing space.

'Go out to meals, or to the cinema. At any rate until Celina is better.'

'Forgive me, but I don't see how that would help.'

From his puzzled expression Morris guessed he had gone too fast. There was something else.

'I thought you knew. I thought it was obvious,' Newton said.

'What?'

'Oh dear, we'll have to go all the way back to the beginning again.'

Morris felt like laughing. The two women never gave the man a chance of this type of conversation; he was relishing it.

At that moment the waiter came up with the round dish. He lifted two slices of *pizza* on to each plate. Morris took the opportunity to order another bottle of wine.

'You see,' Newton said, 'I am deeply in love with Celina.'

Morris stopped cutting his slice. He looked at the tablecloth. The situation was absurd, but of course it was impossible to indicate exactly why. He wondered why he himself felt furiously angry.

'I'm sorry. I certainly didn't know that.'

'Have you ever been in love?'

'Well I –'

Fortunately Newton did not attach any importance to an answer. 'Now you'll understand why I want to do everything I possibly can to help her. I don't want her to leave us, because I know too well what the alternatives are.'

'Does she know?'

'No, thank God.'

Morris felt relieved. But the other went on: 'Luckily she's far too stupid. If she found out, the fur would fly. She'd turn Celina out of the house at once.'

The second bottle of wine had begun to confuse the issue.

'I didn't mean your wife. I meant Celina. Does Celina know?' Morris's voice was strained with anxiety.

'I felt it my duty to tell her,' the other said pompously.

Absurdity refused to go away. Like Chekhov characters on a remote steppe, everything they said was affected by their isolation. Statements boomed out without the tiny adjustments, pressures and ironies that an English background imposes on the expression of feelings and moral attitudes. Morris realized that his interest was no longer detached. How had Celina taken Newton's declaration?

Feeling intolerably inquisitive, he asked: 'What happened?'

'Nothing, of course.'

'What did Celina say?'

Newton looked humble. 'I don't think she took me very seriously. As a matter of fact, after her last experience, she doesn't want anything more to do with men.' Morris pushed aside his knife and fork and wiped his mouth; it is a revelation, a sort of epiphany, when you find that someone else is absolutely and entirely wrong.

When somebody loves another person you cannot really say anything about either of them. Morris tried with:

'She has a very complicated personality.' It sounded all wrong.

'I think she's a wonderful person. If only I'd met her before, before I got mixed up with Mercedes.'

Morris's feelings for Celina were confused by knowing how much she was exploiting the Newtons. He could forgive her anything in her struggle for survival; but could they, if they knew?

'Of course, you hardly know her. She has been at the flat for two months now. She's told us everything.'

'I see.'

'Some of it's not very pretty. She's had a difficult life. Some things she's only told Mercedes. But of course Mercedes told me.'

'You didn't mind?'

'If you love somebody, you only want to help them.' He poured the remainder of the second bottle into Morris's glass. 'I'm afraid she made a mistake telling Mercedes, though. It's difficult to know about these things between women, especially in a country like this.'

'What did your wife do?'

'Nothing, so far. To her, Celina is primarily a case. She hasn't even had time to be jealous of me. She looks after her like a mother.'

This seemed to leave an enormous amount unexplained. Perhaps Newton was accustomed to violence, but certainly this evening Mercedes had been passionately involved. Was this only due to homesickness, or the emotional overflow of someone who had been brought up to value feelings for their own sake? Or was it, as Celina suggested, frustrated love?

'This is only because Celina is her patient, mind you,' Newton said. 'Finally, I think they hate each other's guts.'

'Oh God.'

'Neither of them has nearly reached the stage of admitting that. But Mercedes is terribly possessive. If she should ever suspect my feelings for Celina, then she would use violence. She is a woman of action.'

When they left the restaurant, the streets were still full of people.

Perhaps here at the centre of the city the population was different; perhaps it was the wine he had drunk. But now the crowd was willing him in. Eyes floated across his face that he could not ignore. He wanted to loiter, to feast on each variety of human feature that immigration or mixture of blood had brought here. The men mostly stood along the kerb, while broad-hipped women swayed past, whose faces were dedicated to animal health, painted or naked ugliness, sexuality and pride. From time to time, after a dozen misthrows, the jumble characteristic of Mediterranean and Negro, Nordic and Amerindian, would form suddenly a pattern of beauty – in the shape of a fourteen-year-old child, perhaps, who wandered erect, unspeaking, her lips parted, almost pathetically unconscious of her distinction, through the jungle.

Some of the children and young girls had whistles and carnival hats, and were armed with cylinders of scented ether. These they squirted at people who passed, the children indifferently, as a mockery of pomposity; their elder sisters with sharp intention, as if expressing a little jab of angry lust, a courtship rite of small fierce beasts.

There are no Puritans like the worried : anxiety knocks all the lure out of things. Newton hurried blindly to the next bar, the next station of pilgrimage, and Morris was obliged to follow. And because Newton still saw nobody, nobody seemed to see him.

Morris felt the sudden warm splash of scent pollute his face; it trickled into the corner of his eyes. Stung into sudden irritation, he turned round. She was there, staring at him. The grin of mockery was waning from a small perfect face.

He felt a flush of excitement, forcing him to stillness. His feet were heavy.

With her girl-friends on either side attempting to pull her away, she too was still: a fantastic little figure in tight white trousers and a blouse of some sleazy fabric that imitated leopard skin.

Newton was already far ahead.

'I say!'

Newton waited for him on the corner. 'Yes, what is it?'

The tense look on the other's face made Morris ashamed. He couldn't desert him at this point. When he looked back, he saw that the three girls had already gone.

Meekly he followed his friend into a new street. After a little way, he was astonished to see the trio emerge ahead of him. He realized that they had run round the block, taking a short cut through a shopping arcade.

This time it was her companions who giggled and squirted him with ether. She was silent and proud in the middle. Morris stopped again, divided in a moment of pure decision, as banal as a personage in an allegorical painting. But too quickly he imagined the difficulty of explaining to Newton: Newton's preoccupied incomprehension, delay in understanding, explanations and apologies, and, finally, his slightly offended good wishes. The prospect of all this was too unnerving. Alone, he followed Newton into the bar.

'Well, what am I going to do?'

'Do?'

'Yes.' Newton smiled apologetically. 'You must forgive me, I have had no one else to talk to about this for a long time.'

'Of course I forgive you,' Morris said.

He felt entirely out of his depth, however, as the other plunged deeper into an account of his marriage to Mercedes. Now he was being asked to assent to general truths, the rubbery words from the books. Perhaps, as Newton stated them, they were still true: people's lives, when they get older, tend to conform more to pattern, and the physiology of love is as limited as its vocabulary. Newton was intelligent and detached. The whole notion, however, of intelligence and detachment was nauseating. Morris withdrew in pain from the vision of the rabbit-like man clambering over the worn thighs of his wife. He drank deeply, waiting for this uncomfortable confession to end. He felt a stab of nostalgia for the living street outside.

'So, keep it under your hat. I have decided to leave my wife.'

'I see.' He thought it kinder to avoid those hurt middle-aged eyes. Surely his own face looked untrustworthy, with its dubiousness, its limited ability to understand?

'Are you surprised?'

'Yes, I am. Your really mean it?'

'I do.'

'What about Celina?'

'Celina? But there's nothing there. I love her, but she won't have me. She's wrong in a way. Because I can help her. She needs someone to drink with. Someone who understands her.'

'You'll be alone, then?'

'Yes.'

'I see. You don't think that after a time –?'

'I'll never go back to Mercedes, if that is what you mean. I hate her. In fact, I told you I hated her before, the first or second time I met you.'

'I know you did. I must say I thought it very odd.'

Newton looked intensely at him. 'My God, Robin, you don't know how long it was since I'd met a real human being.'

The young man blushed unnecessarily. All this was one more evidence of the desolation of the other's exile.

'No, it's absolutely no good talking to me about Mercedes. She's gone too far this time. Up there you see she had it all her own way. She could impose anything. But here, in a different country, I can see it all more clearly. I realize now that it was wrong from the start. None of her own country-men would have her: she was too proud, and too ugly. She'd set herself up to equal Carlos – that was her husband – just to get her revenge on him. I was the obvious solution, wasn't I? I was very unhappy then and I was drinking a lot, and I didn't realize what was happening until it was too late. But she made a big mistake in leaving the country. A big mistake. Here she's nobody. She hasn't any money, either.'

'What will she do, then?'

'Oh, there's a lot of things she can do. She's in no diffi-culty. Even if they don't accept her qualifications as a doctor, she can always get some sort of a job in a hospital. There're never enough people for that in these countries.'

'I see.'

'But of course, if she's really sensible, she'll go to her own embassy and ask to be repatriated.'

'If she's as proud as you say, I can't imagine her doing that.'

'To tell you the truth, nor can I. But I'm not worrying about her. She's bound to fall on her feet.'

He began to shake a little; he had spoken over-confidently.

For the first time Morris looked round the place where they were sitting. There was nothing of interest. It was a businessmen's bar: everyone automatically ordered whisky. At all the tables the comrades-in-arms of Rachmel Kochen were drinking to new triumphs of ethical realism. The middle-European waiters spoke American, with English accents.

He turned back to Newton, who was looking miserable. A certain mental agility had carried him too far out of his situation, and he was experiencing an emotional after-effect.

The spirit of Mercedes was at hand, desolate, torn, unjust and, in appearance at any rate, maternal.

'What are you going to do? Ask her for a divorce?'

'There isn't any divorce in this country. And, even if there was, she wouldn't give it me. The moment she knows what I'm up to, she'll hang on as hard as possible. I want a clean break. The only thing to do is to bolt for it.'

'I see.'

'I want you to help me.'

'Me? How?'

'What's this place you are going to? Nova Fronteira. It's miles away, isn't it? If you gave me a letter of introduction I could get a job there.'

'You probably could. It's a fairly grim place, though. Umbrella pines and Polish peasants.'

'I don't care in the least what it's like. You've no idea what it means, to have to live in this hatred and violence the whole time. I don't like violence.'

'Nor do I. But it seems a necessary part of living here. You have to take violence sooner or later.'

'I've taken it. I've gone on taking it. I've had enough.'

'All right,' Morris said, 'I'll help you.'

When Newton arrived home he found his wife sitting alone on the balcony in the darkness. He lit a cigarette and went out to her.

The air was cool now. Lights from aeroplanes and mountain-peaks flickered high up in the vast sky. Three or four ships were stopped at anchor in the broad arena of the bay. In the daytime the dazzling sun held you down to the limits of the apartment. But at night, on the balcony, you were physically in the presence of departure, of escape, of flight.

'What is the matter?' he asked. 'Where is Celina? Did she go to bed?'

There was silence between each of Newton's questions. He hardly noticed this, because he was not able to concentrate very well. He had drunk a fair amount, and he still had a sense of relief and even euphoria from his conversation with Morris, even though he knew it hadn't changed anything.

Their encounter was full of misapprehensions. Newton was an inadequate father-figure, and Morris too young and undeveloped to be of much use as a recipient of confidences; he thought of age, ugliness and lack of social opportunity, and they left him speechless. But exile had meant the same thing to both of them. They had in common a respect for the power that distances have to alleviate the pains of the past.

Mercedes was still silent and he could hardly see her. There was a sense of wrong in the air. He switched on the wall light, blinked a moment from its burning glare, and turned towards her. She was crouched down in the chair, her head twisted away from him.

'You remembered about changing the bandage?'

Mercedes stayed silent a moment longer. Then she got up silently. She wore absurdly feminine finery, high-heeled slippers of mauve silk, a peignoir with down trimmings. She looked, in the grandest sense, terrible.

'Change the bandage? For that one? Listen, it is all finished.'

'Finished?'

'She went away.'

Newton looked at her incredulously. The stabbing shock went through him, and then he felt overwhelmingly sad and tired. The sense of loss was devastating.

After a time he realized that his wife was still talking: 'She got her marching orders, that one, and it was high time too. I do not want people like that in my house. She is not respectable. She is an immoral evil woman, and I do not want her to be here. She told me enough; I am dealing with such women before. Once they are like that they are all the same.'

'Then it was you who sent her away?'

She nodded, then seeing his horror, changed her tone a little. 'Listen, my darling, *you* know how it was. At first I was only trying to help her, since these doctors here know nothing. And I must comfort her, because the emotional state is also important. This man she slept with has deserted her. She hears nothing from him even when her life is in danger; she does not know what to do. Santa Maria, how she wept and wept. And always I am trying to comfort her. It is my work. Is it not true?'

He did not reply.

'But I find out what is happening. She does not want to get better.'

'You are lying!' he shouted. 'She could not walk. You sent her away and she could not walk. When did this happen?'

'Two hours ago. But do not worry. She telephoned a taxi, she will go to an hotel.'

'Without us, she has nobody. Nobody!'

'Yes, I know that.' She laughed. 'That is why she did not want to get better. She wanted to stay here doing harm to us. Always she was trying to come between us. She is crazy for a man – I know that, but I do not say.'

'She is ill. You are a doctor. You drove her out.' His voice was calm now, as if discussion was impossible.

'Cecil, I did everything to cure her. God knows how I work for her. But it is useless, I tell you, I know what she is trying to do. And besides' – Mercedes began to look evil – 'she knew that wound of hers would not heal too easily. Not with that blood she has in her veins. Her blood is dirty. She has a disease. She has –'

Newton stepped forward and struck his wife viciously across the face.

188

The insinuation, like the blow she had gained for it, was only another sign of how far they had got. They had married out of different countries, and now all they shared was the basic brutality of the human state.

Mercedes was still shocked into silence. When she saw that he was not going to hit her again, she began to weep. It seemed hardly to be for the pain or the insult.

'I am so unhappy. O Mother of God, I am so unhappy.'

The tears flowed and flowed as though they would never stop. They fell like blood, continuous, weakening.

And worst of all she looked hideous, so hideous that he wanted to cry out with pity.

3

Mercedes used to tease her with the two bottles of sleeping-tablets, offering them as a reward for attention and affection, then bearing them off and hiding them in her medicine chest. During the retreat from the Newtons' flat, while the elder woman was sobbing somewhere on the balcony, Celina managed to secure the bottles. She held on to them in the taxi, put them down only to sign the hotel register. Before retiring to sleep, she swallowed three tablets, holding the tumbler of water so tightly that her thumb seemed likely to crack it.

Celina woke late on the following day. For the time being she felt calm and methodical, unanxious if solitary. She had a private sitting-room, a desolate space into which her meals were brought. The waiter and the chamber-maid were frankly inquisitive; warned by this, she spoke to them only perfunctorily, and decided not to telephone for a hairdresser and manicurist. The bandage on her foot, too, would need no attention, because Mercedes had renewed it the previous evening.

She ate little, coddling herself, and returned to bed, where she was reading a Gallimard novel, which seemed to come through to her with an almost unnatural clearness, as if she were meeting the personages in a sickbed vision. She put the book down from time to time, and thought about her own life.

Jango was the part of the past that rose up with most persistence. She could see him and hear his voice, not in memory but saying new things. The other people she had been sure about, but her own brother she had loved and hated over and over again. Jango as a strangely unintelligent child; as a skulking and manic adolescent; now as the shaven-headed military puritan, innocently destructive, useless and absurd without a war. He, not *papai*, had deliberately created unhappiness. He, although five years younger, had been Raimundo's friend. It was when Jango began to hate his stepmother that Betty, unconscious of his detestation but feeling uncertainty and lack of trust in the atmosphere, had succumbed to alcoholism and public absurdity.

Poor Jango had to be very violent to be anything at all. There was nothing to distinguish him from anyone else, for the children of the rich here start physically and morally at street level. They are not born taller and with different hair, as in England, or surrounded with moral upholstery, as in other countries.

That night, Celina took some more tablets. She woke the following morning extremely well, and began telephoning her friends.

This afternoon Morris was flying to Nova Fronteira, and in a week from today he would be home, which was what he called his flat at the Kochens'.

While he was shaving, various images of his stay in the capital shifted through his mind : his colleagues in the company offices outvying each other with inside dope about the country, sitting on desks in gartered shirtsleeves and beginning every other sentence with 'of course'; their nice wives pushing sharp little noses round diplomatic cocktail parties. 'H.E.,' they said, 'H.E. and Lady Parkins. She's so sweet.' All this happened apart, in a framed and separate world. You never left such people without a little shock at finding the great drab spectacular city was still there in front of you, and sometimes, for about three blocks, you wanted to run.

Even early in the morning, music drifted up from the streets outside. Carnival in the capital would have a smouldering intensity that rainstorms, municipal mismanagement and police interference could not entirely suppress. He felt jealous of the festival he would miss, as though it were a party to which he hadn't been invited.

Then he remembered the small cockpit of unhappiness in the apartment building along the bay. While he was thinking about Celina, she telephoned him.

She came quickly to the point: she wanted to see him today, before he left.

'But surely it's bad for you to move? I'll go there. I've got time.'

Celina realized that he thought she was still at the Newtons' flat. 'No, Robin, I can walk quite well. When shall I come?'

'Whenever you like. Cecil is meeting me in the bar here at half-past twelve. Didn't he tell you?'

'No, he didn't. I'll explain why, later. I'll be there at twelve, Robin.'

'Very well.' But now he was less enthusiastic. He suspected that something had gone wrong, and that he would be made use of.

The bar was a sort of air-conditioned cave. A long way outside, through glass door after glass door, the street could be seen as a yellow square of sunlight, like the view-finder of a camera, with small people coming and going across it. In here electric light was reflected from biscuit-coloured walls; you sat in the buzz of ventilators in semi-darkness at noon. Three stale cacti were a tribute from the tropic world outside.

Celina's silhouette flickered through the doors. She carried a stick but was walking firmly. Morris sprang up to meet her. She sat where he had been, and they looked at each other for a moment.

Dressed in a light-grey silk suit, she could not, he thought, have looked better. He watched her body up and down, stopping again at the sad intensity of the eyes.

Celina put her gloves on the table. 'Well, Robin, it happened.'

He was still standing. 'There, there. Tell Uncle all about it.' He did not usually speak to her in this way – their conversation had always been plain and denotative, a concession to their mutual foreignness. But now he was not really speaking to her at all, but catching up on feeling about her.

'I left their apartment.'

'Why?'

'We had a scene, Mercedes and I.'

'Oh God.'

She laughed. 'The thing you hate so much, Robin. A truly violent scene, right to the bitter end.'

'I don't mind scenes with people I know,' he said defensively. 'I don't know Mrs Newton and I find her very embarrassing, that's all.'

He went up to the bar and brought back two Tom Collins. He lit Celina's cigarette. She puffed a moment and said: 'When you and Cecil went out to dinner, I knew something was going to happen.'

'Why on earth didn't you say so?'

'I thought that your idea was to be alone. It was obvious that he was longing to talk to you. And you wanted to go with him.'

'I did?' he said hotly.

She smiled. 'I thought you did. The position was a little awkward.'

Then she drank, and bowed her head, looking down at the table. Stillness descended suddenly, as though music had been switched off. He watched her in surprise. Then he saw that she was quivering, shaking under the pressure of wild disintegrating emotion. He laid his hands on her arm and waited. There was nothing he could do, and nowhere to look.

Celina began: 'She came –' Her voice was harsh, terribly broken up. She gave up the attempt to speak. He sat there with his hand squeezing her arm, straining with sympathy.

There was silence. Her hands made the blind motions of opening her handbag and finding a handkerchief, which she held to her face for a moment or two. It was like watching someone swim several lengths of a pool under water. She shook her head, as if trying to blink the pain out of her eyes.

She came to the surface, and they both relaxed.

'I'm so sorry.' Celina pointed to her glass. 'C-could I have another of these?'

When he came back she was calm again. It had been a whole process, a natural cycle: he had watched emotion sprout and run riot and die. He was respectfully quiet, but also totally outside, because he did not yet know what it was all about.

'Can you tell me now?'

'It's nothing. She drank a lot and then she came and – what I told you about, before.'

Morris nodded, a little appalled, as completely out of his depth now as he had been with Newton.

Nervously, Celina stirred the glass with the swizzle stick. She still did not look at him. 'You see I was wrong, Robin. I told you that she was innocent and she is not. I suppose no woman like that ever is, there are so many opportunities. . . . I told her I would leave the flat there and then, and if she did not let me go, I would inform her husband.'

'What did she do?'

'She wept and screamed. But she was thinking quite coolly all the time. She knew she had betrayed herself. And so I got my things and left. Here I am.'

In spite of his great desire to sympathize, to be encouraging, he felt a little gust of despair. Partly it was due to shyness. He had never before had a conversation quite like this with a woman. She belonged to a different country, was half a dozen years his senior: the whole thing was quite different from the experimental frankness of the young. Instincts of sloth and self-preservation made him want to withdraw. To help, you had to go so much further. You had to love.

'Why does she worry about Newton? Why is she so jealous of him?'

'Mercedes must hold on to her man,' Celina said vehemently.

'Why? She has a medical training, she could work.'

'Because of pride. She tried to enter a man's domain and remain a woman. She couldn't, of course. She went against all the traditions of our civilization here. If she loses Cecil she will not be able to live.'

'I see. He's coming here in a moment. What do I say?'

'Robin, he does not know anything of this.' She seemed scared. 'Please –'

'Of course I won't.' He looked down at his hands. 'When we were out the other night, I offered to help him.'

'Please do. He is a nice man. *He* doesn't deserve all this.'

Then they sat in silence, waiting for Newton to arrive. But why had Celina wept? Why? She was experienced. She knew about 'life' – that word which so often indicates those desolate sidings off the main track.

Perhaps she was overwrought and ashamed, because by

chance the same young man had been present at two bad moments in her life. But her weeping had not been a nervous reaction. It had been an intense and private thing, arising from the depths. There was more, there was always more.

'You look as though you need a drink.'

Newton's face was drawn, his hair wispy. He was exhausted; the fiery summer, seizing the advantage of his inattention to it, had set out to destroy him.

'It isn't easy. One has to go on working, with all this business at home.'

Morris returned to the bar. He wanted to leave the other the opportunity of speaking to Celina. In the mirrored wall beyond the barman, he saw them sitting side by side against the bleak decorations: the small provincial-looking man, damaged by intellectualism, who today was sweating inside a tweed coat with leather-patched sleeves, and the blonde pretty woman. They didn't look like any two people who would have met or even known each other by name.

Without turning, Newton said quietly: 'I am so sorry that this had to happen.'

'There was nothing you could do.'

Perhaps their lots were justly apportioned. Celina was younger, she possessed the greater resilience, the buoyancy that would lead her still further into disaster. Newton had suffered a bad shock, he longed for indifference, boredom and peace. In spite of everything, he was the most likely to gain what he desired.

They smiled gently at Morris, but a sickroom atmosphere settled down around them.

'Will you lunch with us?' he asked Newton.

'I telephoned to Mercedes that I was meeting you here, and wouldn't be back.'

'Good.'

They drank more Tom Collins. Though conversation was

difficult, each was convinced of the other's good-will. After Newton had fetched another round, Celina said to him: 'I have just thought of something. Does Mercedes know where Robin is staying?'

'Yes, of course she does. She was there yesterday when I telephoned. In fact, she wouldn't let me out of her sight the whole day.'

'Then she will come here.'

'Perhaps we'd better go,' Morris said quickly. 'I mean, there seems no point in you meeting her again, does there?'

'No. No point at all,' Celina said. But although the two men had finished what they were drinking, she lit a cigarette, stirred her glass, and seemed willing to delay as long as possible. Finally she smiled at the sight of the young man's worried expression, and relented. He jumped to his feet and went to the bar to pay the bill.

Of course, it was too late. Mercedes Newton came through the glass door on top of him. She seemed hesitant and lost, as though she had never penetrated a place like this before. She was heavily made up, her hair was disarranged, and when she recognized him he saw that she trembled with anger and excitement. To him, she no longer appeared pathetic, but monstrous.

'Where are they?' she asked hoarsely.

He indicated her husband and Celina at the table in the corner.

Mercedes lurched straight over to them, bumping into glass-topped tables, setting pin-legged metal chairs screeching on the floor. For a moment she stared down at them, without speaking. Then she sat where Morris had been.

Morris was satiated with all these people: the only thing was to get rid of them, have lunch and catch his plane. But, back at the table, he met a suppressive calming look from Celina.

They sat on in silence. He offered Mrs Newton a drink.

'No, nothing,' she said. With little fussy movements she settled herself into her seat as though preparing for a long bus ride. After some minutes she took a handkerchief from her handbag and began to sob quietly, thus becoming the second woman to weep at this table during the past hour.

'When does your plane leave?' Celina asked.

'14.20,' he said, advancing the time an hour. 'I think we had better go, if we are to have lunch.'

'I am coming with you,' Newton said.

His wife watched him get up. They had been speaking English, but now she understood that he was deserting her.

She burst into a harsh cry: 'Cecil, where are you going?'

'I have been invited to lunch.'

'No, no.'

Her reddened eyes turned beseechingly to Morris. The indifference with which he returned her gaze surprised and disconcerted her. She had been used to gaining everything by tears. Whatever happened, he was not going to ask her to accompany them.

Mercedes gripped her husband's arm. 'No, my darling. Do not go with these people.'

'You can take a taxi home,' Newton said. 'I will give you the money.'

Her hand was still restraining him; it squeezed through the heavy tweed to his flesh and bone. She put her face near his.

'If you go, I will make a scene. You know that I am desperate and will do anything. I will scream and fight and the police will come to calm me. Then I will tell them about this woman here. I will tell everything, everything.'

She sat back, triumphant.

Newton wiped the sweat from his scarlet forehead. Morris looked questioningly at Celina. She avoided his eyes. 'I am sorry about all this,' Newton said finally.

'What is happening? I didn't understand.'

'She is threatening to make a scene if I come with you. What do you think?'

Already the disarray and drama surrounding Mrs Newton had caused comment. The barman, who had watched them intermittently all along, since they were the only customers, now came out into the room. This, however, was only to see if they were going to drink again. But now two of the German reception clerks watched from the doorway.

'Perhaps you had better stay,' Morris said. 'I should like to be helpful, but I must catch this aeroplane.'

Newton looked saddened and disappointed, as though he had been let down. 'Yes, I see. I was forgetting this is tough on you. I'll stay with her. Good-bye then.'

'Good-bye.'

Newton was left defeated and powerless. Mercedes still kept her strong hand locked on his arm.

In the taxi Celina said: 'Poor man, I am so sorry for him. But he should have asserted himself.'

'And let her make a scene?'

She looked at him sharply and unsympathetically, and then seemed to convince herself that he was asking out of curiosity, without accusation. 'Perhaps. It does not matter very much now.'

Outside the Senate house the taxi swerved between traffic, and they were thrown together; he held on to her shoulder. Through the low windows the lines of shops had ceased and now the bays began to unfold again, one after the other, blazing with sunlight, each with its little groups of half-naked figures, black or terra-cotta, outlined on the stone wall against the sea. The beneficent effect of drink, the stream of carnival songs from the car-radio, and the world of brightness outside should have made everything easy and cheerful.

But Morris went on: 'What was she going to have a scene about, anyway?'

'About me.'

The young man snorted. 'I should have thought it was the other way around. If you wanted, you might make quite a scene about her.'

'No.'

He turned round in surprise, but when he saw her face he decided not to say anything after all. Why should he be inquisitive? One of the things he was learning was that everything that appears simple and and clear in human relations is always a little damaged and wrong. If, in fact, Celina had not told him the truth today, before Newton's arrival, it was better to be bland and good mannered about it.

Nevertheless, he felt depressed during lunch. He had looked forward to a guilty sense of relief, a truancy from the emotional crises of this morning. He had thought they might laugh a lot, and instead they drank a bottle of wine sadly. It improved their spirits only by separating and isolating each moment, and making them forget what had gone before.

'Where are you spending carnival?' Celina asked suddenly.

'Nova Fronteira, I suppose. It'll be frightfully dull – just the Country Club.'

'I don't know what I shall do. I cannot dance this year, because of my foot.'

He stared at her in astonishment. 'Were you going to dance?'

'I always dance at carnival. Usually I get tickets for the ball at the municipal theatre.'

This impressed him as a sort of disloyalty to her own unhappiness. Perhaps he had overestimated her. That same acquiescence, which had irritated him when he had first seen her with Cowan, made her strangely resilient to experience. She bowed her head and it passed over; carnival came round and she danced. He wondered how the Newtons would spend their time: they at least took their despair desperately.

He poured more wine, but the seed of melancholy had been sown and had sprouted.

Afterwards, they drove to the airport.

He squeezed her arm under his own. 'You must come and see me at home.'

'No, Robin. I can't go there.'

'Why on earth not?'

'Because of my family.'

'There are two million people in the city.'

'And it is a very small place, in spite of that. I don't want to go there, Robin, I am sorry.'

During the past few minutes his emotions had been rushing ahead with him. Now he was brought up short, hurt and irritated. He wanted to help her and she was resisting at all turns.

In the echoing hall of the airport they stood, suffering a desolate anti-climax. The blurted instructions from the loud-speakers jarred their nerves. Nothing could diminish Celina's calm beauty, but now his heart sank again as he watched her. She was determined to be unhappy and finally there was nothing he wanted to do about it.

He was thankful when the passengers for Nova Fronteira were called; his last few remarks had received no reply. She stared emptily ahead, and they moved together towards the turnstile.

He turned and kissed Celina on the mouth: only then did he feel her relax, with a buried sigh. But it was a moment falsified by drink and sadness and departure.

The shuffling dismal group followed the stewardess out into the sun. All around him, at the bottom of the steps into the plane, businessmen were crossing themselves brusquely, an irritated settling up of accounts; a fat Spanish woman broke into a wail of nervousness, until patted into silence by her husband and son.

He spent the first deaf moments in his seat thinking about

Celina. The engines roared and silenced again and again. Then out of the window he saw the shadow of the plane bouncing and scuttling along the brown grass and the airport buildings, and reappearing, a black cross aureoled in trembling light, within the tawny waters of the bay.

Gasping, the plane clambered on to a higher shelf of air, and they slid out serenely between the mountain-sized granite rocks that protected the capital city.

4

In a certain street at the foot of these mountains, the big houses were all overshadowed by ancient evergreen trees.

This street, though inhabited by people of similar incomes, represented a different world from the smart apartment blocks near the sea. There all the trees had been put to the axe, and the sun entered with North-American blankness through unshuttered walls of glass. Here the whole district spoke of middle-class respectability, tradition and decay. Long tracks of green and brown, from dripping branches and rusty balconies, stained the plaster façades of the houses. The gardens flourished like Victorian ferneries and the enormous trees were encampments of parasitic vegetation. There were even orchids sprouting on the telephone wires.

People in this street were hospitable among their colleagues and immediate families, and a number of cars always stood outside the wrought-iron gates. In some of these the radios were playing softly, while in others the chauffeurs were asleep – those who later were to be witnesses.

At three in the afternoon the street was further darkened by a sky which threatened torrential rain. The reunion in Jacinto Moreira's house was almost at an end. The wife, Dona Evangelina, and the three pretty daughters were smiling decoratively, while in the tiled hall and on the portico outside the last conferences were going on.

These conferences repeated the same pattern that you would see on any street corner. The men stood closely together in groups of three or four; hands were thrust on hearts to protest sincerity or were jerked loosely to indicate moral disapproval; voices were raised in assertions of indignation or pugnacity. And now that the guests were beginning to go away, sooner or later an arm would creep round a neighbouring shoulder. At the moment of farewell the embrace tightened; in an ecstasy of complicity and mutual comprehension, the two men stood close together, each feeling the other's fierce breath on his face, each absentmindedly beating the other's back with the fat palms of his hands. Without all this, the political business of the party could not continue. Nothing was without its purpose, and these meetings were a brothel of fraternity – finally, you had to pay for everything.

In uniform, Jango Fonseca stood waiting for the guests to depart. The eyes of Jacinto's daughters were never far away from him. In this house he was crowned and garlanded, far more than he had ever been in his own home. The daughters lit candles for him in the cathedral, and whenever Jacinto or one of his colleagues saw him alone, they would squeeze his shoulders affectionately: 'All will be well, *rapaz*,' they said, 'all will be well.' By now it was as if they had squeezed the power of thought entirely out of Jango: his eyes were bright, his lips quivered, he seemed to be in church the whole time. And, even though Dona Evangelina wanted him for one of her daughters, both she and her husband gave him the sort of smiles that are bestowed on someone with a vocation for the priesthood.

When the last guest had driven away, Jango fetched the briefcases which contained the Federal Deputy's note-books. Today was the debate on finance, and this was one of the fundamental questions on which Jacinto Moreira based his attack on the government. Today he would expose the whole precarious situation: he had evidence of vast loans obtained by bribery of the president's younger brother, and the personal bodyguard who had been in charge at the palace since the early years of the dictatorship. The list of names was there, and the attested documents of several monetary transactions.

Jango's face was grim as he brought out the two brief-cases, but his seriousness disappeared when he said good-bye to the three girls. He teased them all gently and promised the eldest, Maria do Carmo, that he would return later to escort her to the ball at the Italian Embassy. It was difficult to have a preference among the girls, they were all pretty and charming and they had all been brought up to get married as quickly as possible. His choice of the eldest was helped by the fact that it was obviously the correct thing to do.

Jacinto Moreira's face was blank, owl-like with heavy spectacles, coldly preoccupied. For some weeks all his energies had been screwed up to the work of destruction, to the catharsis of a political 'show-down'. He kissed his family briefly. They were used to this – it was Jango who filled the emotional gap, acting as an intermediary from whom they learnt what was going on in Jacinto's mind. Without him the family might have been faced with the same failure as the Fonsecas. But Jango's efforts were easier here than in his own home; these were women of good will, who knew what was expected of them.

'Where's the sergeant?' he asked. As usual, he had brought a platoon with him to the house.

'Poor man, he's in the kitchen still, having his lunch,' Maria do Carmo said.

'Will you tell him to wait here till we return? We won't need him, the car is just at the gate and the Chamber of Deputies is under guard.'

'All right.'

'I'll see you tonight then.' He patted her shoulder.

The girl smiled dazedly at him. 'I'll see you tonight.'

Outside the wind was still bringing dark clouds across the street. Twigs and seedpods were pattering on the hard tops of the stationary cars. At the end of the long corridor of jacaranda trees, a black saloon slid into sight across the street corner. The driver backed and advanced, as if he was trying to keep the gate of Moreira's house in sight.

Jacinto took the briefcases from his young friend. Together they walked down the steps on to the pavement.

The first shot was deafening. It shattered the tension of the silent afternoon. It bit a corner from the plaster wall beside them. Jacinto Moreira ducked back among the evergreen plants behind the wall.

Out in the street Jango drew his revolver, still clutching the handle of the car door with his left hand. He was breathless, feverish with fear and excitement. He edged along to where he could get a clear view. A man in a brown suit crouched behind the mudguard of the car on the opposite side of the road. Jango fired once, and there was a little whine of pain. Then suddenly he saw the other. There was a pause like the pause on the stage when somebody has missed a cue, and he felt his breath rush back into his mouth. Through the windows of Jango's car and the other, through four thicknesses of glass, they stared each other in the eyes. The man was standing upright on the opposite pavement, a huge *cafuso* – half-Indian, half-Negro.

The man was from the palace, the chief of the president's bodyguard. His name was in Jacinto's briefcase.

Beyond the line of cars, the man began to retreat down the street. Jango was following him; he knew he had only to wait. Hardly a minute had passed since the first shot; his platoon would be out immediately. He felt the fallen twigs snapping on the pavement under his feet. Then he passed a gap between two cars. The man in the brown suit fired several times and Jango's head struck the kerbstone.

The quickly pattering footsteps dwindled away, and at the end of the street the black saloon roared and vanished.

A few minutes later, the first raindrops fell and snuffed out the ring of candles that had already been placed round the body on the pavement.

5

When Morris arrived back from Nova Fronteira, he found Kochen and his son in deck-chairs in the front garden. They were playing chess. In this part of the country the rainy season had come to an end, and after a day of drought the air was turning blue in the early evening.

Kochen greeted him with enthusiasm, and, after inquiring about the journey, he announced importantly: 'We are now a house of only men.'

'How is that?'

'My wife is away. She went to visit her relatives in a German town in the south. She was very very tired.' From the sly way Kochen spoke of it, Morris was expected to have his own ideas for the reasons, or perhaps the genuineness of Mrs Kochen's tiredness.

'So we are alone, two old bachelors who look after ourselves. We have everything that we like and we fix ourselves up very well.' He giggled with satisfaction, and put his arm round his son's shoulder. The son grinned and looked at the ground, but he appeared self-possessed, not shy.

'When you are ready, come and have a drink. We drink very good drink – even he is learning to drink.' He patted the boy again.

Morris had been a little apprehensive about his return to

the city, but it was extraordinary how peaceful he felt. In the past week he had shed all his anxieties on various flights through the interior, and he arrived home renewed. He unlocked the door of the flat and pulled in his suitcase. A woman had been in several times to clean, and the rooms smelt fresh and sharp with polish. He went through and undid the shutters on to the balcony; through the hibiscus bushes, which had sprouted high in his absence, the late light filtered greenly into the room. A large accumulation of letters lay fanned out on the table, and among them he recognized an envelope in Cecil Newton's handwriting; quickly and automatically he pushed it away under the others, all of which he left unopened.

When he had had a shower and changed into fresh clothes, he went down to Kochen's flat.

'The boy has gone out to the stores. He will be back soon. Do you play chess?'

'I'm afraid I don't.'

'We are playing together every evening. Always I used to win, but now from time to time he beats me. He is intelligent, that boy. Previously I was not thinking so, because of these bad schools we have here. Besides, his mother does not want him to be intelligent, only to get on in the business world. I say yes, do that, all well and good, but not only. My own family was intellectual. My father knew Alfred Adler, I think I told you. Speak frankly to me, please, Mr Morris, and tell me if you like that cocktail.'

'It's very good.'

'I think so.' He giggled again. 'It is stronger than the one you had the last time you were here.'

The orchid season was ended and the clusters of tough slippery leaves had been exiled to the veranda outside. But there was still a faint marshy stink about the room, and beyond Kochen's beaming face stood a large new aquarium, where thin shreds of silver glittered among ribbons of weed.

Rubber tubing led to other tanks placed in different parts of the room. In this rather clinical atmosphere they conversed about the outer world.

'I think you have been on a business trip, Mr Morris. And how is economic imperialism?'

When Kochen spoke of the oil companies his tone was cynical and over-assertive – that of the boy from a minor public school who is anxious to prove that all schools are equally deficient in good qualities. Morris helped him with an ironic account of his recent travels.

'We may conclude, then, that you had a satisfactory trip?'

'Very satisfactory.'

'I am glad. Here we have not been so calm. My poor wife, she was very nervous, all because of the boy. I tell her, do not be silly, it is natural at his age, as in Poland. And, besides, she is a clean girl.'

'Who is that?'

'This Polish girl we have. She is taking him into the bath-room, locking the door and making love to him.'

Morris remembered Mrs Kochen's anxieties about Expedita. He could not help smiling.

'For me, too, it is funny. All this fuss! First she sends the girl away, cursing her in all languages, in Polish and German and Yiddish. The girl, who has been brought up here, does not understand any of it. Then my wife goes to her bed and weeps the whole night!' Kochen shook his head incredulously. 'She tells me it is because of this *despacho*, you remember. Misfortune has come to our house. Tch Tch! So I tell her, you are tired, my darling, you have been working too hard at the factory accounts, you go away now and visit your sister in the south.' He stood up and flapped his hands as though he was shooing a large bird out of the house. 'We are all men here now, we can look after ourselves! Another drink?'

'Thank you.'

'Misfortune, indeed!' Kochen went on, filling the little glasses on the sideboard. 'At least we know now that he will not be one of these.' He pushed his tongue into his cheek, placed one hand on his hip and stuck out the opposite buttock. Morris burst out laughing.

After this the boy came back; he had bought matjes herring, boiled salt beef and pumpernickel. While they were eating they drank beer, and Kochen discussed whether Shakespeare was in fact the Earl of Oxford. Then he pulled out a gramophone which had been hidden under one of the aquaria, and put on a recording of a Haydn string quartet.

Later, in his own flat, Morris found himself sufficiently encouraged to read his correspondence. He began with Newton's letter; in this way for the first time he learned that the young officer, whose assassination a few days ago still threatened to bring about an Army *coup-d'état*, was in fact Celina's puritanical brother. She was overwhelmed by the news: just before it happened, Newton wrote, she had moved into a small furnished flat, and since then he had visited her several times – to drink with her, since it seemed quite impossible now to dissuade her from drinking. Perhaps at last, Morris thought, his friend's saloon-bar wisdom had a practical application.

His eyes raced furiously down the pages, with their harsh impact of misery. Newton was a born disaster-monger; his news always seemed to be that everything was turning out as badly as possible. His absences had led to further strife with Mercedes, and he wanted the letters of introduction in Nova Fronteira as soon as possible.

Among the other letters was an invitation from Tinka to go and play tennis on the previous Sunday. He telephoned her the next day, but was told that she had gone away for a few weeks.

Book Five

I

Now she too knelt, following the others. Her hands clasped the rosary that she had just bought.

After a few moments her knees felt pinched on the paving-stones of the square. All around came the noise of prayers, the low murmurs of the desperate, the louder voices of those who heckle and clamour for divine attention. Cars were hooting in the streets beyond, and now more people surged out into the square. There was a squeaking scrape of wheel chairs and wooden carts carrying those too ill to walk. Jostled by the crowd, a man dropped a big straw-covered wine flask; exploding, gushing on to the dirty stones, it was seen to have been full of water.

She closed her eyes once more, but it was of no use. Trying to pray, she only smelt the stink of filth and poverty – those things that no one bothers about, since they are well on this side of prayer.

Against a violent sky, on the edge of the plateau that formed the site of this small country town, stood the church; a blank face with a round window and two square towers, all of it freshly painted with strong yellow ochre. Many of the low buildings that made up the town were of the same colour. There were no trees and, except for the square, the streets were unpaved. This town was the same as a hundred others, which only change when the landscape changes; from here, the same man-devastated scenery of dust and eucalyptus went on for half a continent.

In one of the towers a bell began clanking, clanking; waves

of emotion heaved through the waiting crowd. Everyone who could walk pushed further and further forward, with a cordon of police holding them back. Then two priests emerged from the church door and stood in the small area fenced by the policemen's arms.

The younger priest stepped back to the wall. Now Father Belotti was standing alone; he turned towards the crowd a white face, which life seemed to have worn down beyond all expression of feelings.

From the healthy ones who could push as close as this there came a gasp of shock. Perhaps they blamed themselves with the knowledge that it was their pains and their prayers that had exhausted the priest and brought him to this state. During the past six weeks, the parish had become the most celebrated in the whole country. Father Belotti had performed miracles, and might still do so, for as yet the Church had made no official declaration on the subject. But a statement would be made any day now; this was why the people, who often have more faith than is licitly allowed them, came crowding here before it would be too late.

A young mechanic, bright-eyed and insolently healthy, pushed a microphone in front of the tragic face. A crunching of static issued from loudspeakers at the far side of the square.

From there, they saw only a bone-white hand raised in benediction. Women fell on their knees, men and boys held up jars and bottles to receive a blessing on the water. Suddenly a child screamed; there were sobbing cries of prayers. Pushing each other back, a cluster of women cleared a space on the pavement.

'A miracle ! He is walking ! He is walking !'

In the middle a small boy in leg-irons, with his skin slack and grained by sickness, staggered for a minute or two. Then, neat as a skittle, he pitched over, yelling in pain. The weeping women gathered him up again and hid him in their shawls.

The door of the church closed; the priest had gone.

Mercedes Newton picked her way back through the crowd. She passed the lines of stalls hung with beads, holy images, and the white tallow models of boy babies, legs, arms, noses and obscurer organs, made as offerings for the church. She had been crying a little, and looked tired.

The taxi-drivers, heavy bull-like men in caps of cotton tartan, had taken over the only bar in the town. There they drank and ate, gesticulated, quarrelled and scratched themselves: at first sight it seemed as though the holiness of the town had stimulated them to greater barbarism. Like the sellers of images and holy water, the drivers took pride in extorting ever-increasing prices from the pilgrims. There wasn't much time, they shouted, hectoring the passers-by from their taxi-rank near the Senate House in the capital, the Father might die, the Church might stop him working. Forcing their battered Chevrolets along the dusty road through the eucalyptus woods, they could make the sixty-mile trip twice a day and three times on Sundays and religious feasts. But there were holy images and pictures fixed to the dashboards of each taxi, and their owners had an endless store of convincing anecdotes to tell the passengers. They were believers from more than self-interest, for a sort of miracle had happened to them as well.

Many people travelled in small groups; it was easy for a single person like Mercedes Newton to find an extra seat in a taxi.

For some time after they set off, she sat stiffly upright, but soon the twisting road began to shake the occupants of the car together. Next to her was a young woman, with that expression of calm dignity which fits naturally on to some mulatto faces. A baby slept in her arms; she had covered its faces with an embroidered shawl.

Mercedes could not resist the child. Her foreign accent

211

made the others in the car turn to stare. The girl answered simply, in a quiet voice.

'I wanted the Father to bless him.'

For explanation she drew back the shawl, and her young maternal face saddened a little as she gazed down at what she had revealed – the grey skin, the cold boiled-looking eyes of an idiot.

Mrs Newton winced violently. She was too tired and too unhappy to hide the shock of disgust that sprang up through her. The mother withdrew herself, making herself smaller on the seat, and the elder woman felt bitterly ashamed. Mercedes had been a doctor, she had worked with these people. It was now, when she had no work, that her whole life was on her hands, that the sense of intolerable cruelty smote her hardest. Whether it was cruelty of God or man – this hereditary disease that men give their children – did not concern her any more.

While the young woman crooned to her child, Mercedes wept in silence. Nobody paid attention: worse despair happened every day on the way back from the place of miracles. Mercedes was a long way from her own country and her proper life. Injured pride had already made her miserable, and incidents like this one affected her further. Without knowing it, she was always the victim, not of Celina or her husband, but of the violence of her own feelings. As Morris had guessed, she had already lost everything. She would go on battling ignorantly for pride and possession. This afternoon, kneeling in the town square before the yellow church, praying for the first time for many years, she found that she had nothing to pray for: she had been too used to fighting for herself.

Mercedes arrived back in the city in the middle of the evening, and a bus took her home along the bay. The lights were glittering with a hard ugly glare in the tamed sea water. The open-air cafés were full; it was the time of evening when all arrangements have been made and you know for certain whether you are to be alone or not.

Mercedes had reached a similar point in her whole life. Unknown to her, decisions had already been reached that condemned her to work and solitude for her remaining years. When she arrived at the apartment, she found that Newton's suitcases had gone, and on the sideboard there was his apologetic and inadequate letter.

A few days later, Mrs Newton arrived at the Fonsecas' house in the other city, and was shown on to the veranda, where Betty was sitting with an elderly English woman. A liqueur bottle stood on a small table between them, and a stack of cigarette stubs was sending pale fumes into the quiet air.

Mrs Fonseca stood up and came forward. Shaking her head from side to side, she peered through her dark spectacles at the newcomer. Then, with a start of surprise, she recognized her.

Mercedes Newton wore one of the bright dresses she had always chosen. It was her face that was violently altered. By now it had become a gaunt mask of exhaustion, with burning eyes, the cheeks sunken, and tinted hair springing wildly in all directions from a lined forehead. Make-up was smeared on her eyes and mouth, which twitched in pain. She waited there in accusing silence, a harpy-like embodiment of grief and rage.

'My dear, my dear,' Betty muttered, horrified. Her soft sympathies were aroused; she took the woman's arm and led her gently to a chair. 'What can have happened?'

For days now Mercedes had led the life of a captured animal, shaken by storms of feeling, staring out on an alien human world. At last she had conquered her pride and made the decision to come here. Now, suddenly in a relaxed atmosphere, she broke down. The two women watched her.

'Should I offer her a liqueur, Ethel?'

'Cognac is better,' her friend Mrs Camargo replied. 'But wait till we see what it's all about. Who is she, anyway? I've never seen her before, to my knowledge.'

'She and her husband dined here two or three times. Celina took them up, I remember. Then they moved and we haven't seen them in ages. So many terrible things happened. You know we never see anyone now, Ethel.'

Mrs Camargo, the gruff-voiced mother of Sidney Camargo of the lads' apartment, knew very well. There were many disaffected women in the foreign colony, usually neglected by husbands caught up in commercial life; to their large vulgar houses she was often the only visitor from outside. Herself the survivor of a variety of marriages, she was an expert at this sort of thing. She had a strong appetite and an encyclo-paedic memory for the unhappiness of others, and though women spoke against her, they valued Ethel's company at moments of crisis and despair.

'She speaks Spanish! Let me find out about it, will you?'

One of Mrs Camargo's husbands had been Argentinian. While Mercedes recounted her version of her story, Mrs Camargo was beside her, nodding understandingly but without comment. Betty Fonseca watched them the whole time, tormented by curiosity, unable to understand a word that was being said.

'I think some cognac would help, Betty.'

'But what goes on? What is it?'

'Her husband. He's run away from her.'

'Oh God, don't say. He seemed – I don't know – such a quiet good man. Isn't that just terrible?'

'A little cognac, please.'

Obediently Mrs Fonseca went in through the glass doors. Oswaldo had lost all interest in trying to control his wife's habits, and there was always plenty of drink to be found in the house. And, perhaps because of this, Betty herself was drinking rather less than she had done formerly.

Mercedes took a small sip of the brandy, and immediately went on talking.

'Thank God you were here, honey,' Betty said, trying to interrupt once more. 'What would I have done? You know I can't understand these languages.'

Mrs Camargo lit another cigarette and did not reply.

Mercedes had opened her handbag and was leafing through her husband's letters; from time to time she separated a page, folding it back so that only a few selected sentences were revealed. These she pointed out to the new friend beside her.

The other looked up speculatively at Betty. 'Oh dear, this is all very complicated, isn't it?' she said in English. 'I see now why she wanted to come here.'

'Honey, what is it? We hardly know the woman.'

'She thinks her husband went off with Celina.'

Betty looked bewildered. 'But that's incredible. She hardly knew him either. And, well, he was so much older. And, you know I'm not snobby, honey, but he was just a teacher – you know what I mean.'

'We've been having a real heart-to-heart here, Betty. They know each other quite well. In fact Celina has been their guest for some time.'

'Oh God, is that true? Is she all right? We never heard what happened. You see, she fought terribly with her father and – and poor Jango.'

Ethel ignored these comments and went on: 'This woman – what is your name, dear? – Mercedes has had a medical training. She used to run a clinic in her own country, but she can't practise here. So she agreed to look after Celina, after this motor accident. Out of pure friendship!'

'What happened? Tell me, she's all right?'

'According to Mercedes, yes. More than that, in fact. She's

215

had quite a nice time, really, living in their flat, never paying anything, then running off with the husband.'

Betty snorted, looking hard at Mercedes. 'Well, honey, you can inform her I just don't believe it. She's a damn liar. The poor girl is not here to defend herself, but I'll defend her.' She shakily poured herself another liqueur.

Ethel said: 'There was more than that involved between them.'

'What more? I know it's all goddam lies. Celina was straight. She held her head high.'

'Perhaps, darling. But when she went there first, she was going to have a baby.'

'Oh, God save us.'

'That's all over now. This one here helped her to get rid of it.'

Betty obviously accepted this as the truth. For a minute she muttered to herself, shaking her head, then burst out: 'Honey, you can surely tell her there's no reason for her to come here. If Celina's having an affair with her man, they wouldn't be doing it here, would they?'

She waited while Ethel translated this to Mercedes. It was beginning to grow dark under the palm trees in front of them. Farther down the hill the city was coming to life. Betty felt ill and old. Ethel's attention had been taken away from her. Their quiet gossiping afternoon with the liqueur bottle had been ruined by this intrusion from outside, with its agonizing reminder of all the failures that had happened in this house.

'Tell her to go away. Hasn't everyone been hurt enough already? Tell her to get out or I'll tell her. She understands that much English.'

'She'll go, darling, when she's ready. There's someone else she wants to see. What was his name?' She asked Mercedes.

'Mr Morris.' Mercedes again searched her handbag. 'Here is his letter for my husband.'

'That's it. Morris, who's he? She met him here.'

'Oh God, that boy!' Betty cackled and coughed. 'He's a friend of Celina's too. Ethel, do you think this is getting us any place? Hasn't she got people here, someone we can leave her with?'

'No, she says she never knew anyone here. Only this Morris, who was a friend of her husband's. He didn't have any Spanish-speaking friends. She never went out, except to come to this house.'

'What'll you do?'

'Take her to see this Morris she talks about.'

'All right, darling. But come back. I shall be all alone this evening. You know I can't stand to be alone.'

2

And so tonight when he walked into the drive, humming contentedly to himself, three women were waiting for him at the bottom of the steps to his flat. In the dim electric light he recognized Mrs Kochen and the massive silhouette of Mercedes Newton. The third woman, grey-haired and sturdy, was unknown to him.

As he approached, they stopped talking. He looked from one to another. As a group, there was nothing much to be said for them. They were just women; he felt slightly uncomfortable, like a lone European in a group of Japanese.

From the pressure of their silence he guessed at once that something disastrous had happened.

'You were looking for me?'

Nobody replied, but after a moment Mrs Kochen patted Mercedes on the shoulder, and scuffed away on her slippers into the darkness. Since her return from the south, she did not speak or even look at Morris.

'Mr Morris? My name is Ethel Camargo.'

'Oh yes. Will you come in?'

He opened the doors for them to pass into the flat. They stood in darkness while he found the switch.

'Please sit down.'

For the first time he could see Mrs Newton clearly. His glance quickened with curiosity, then for a moment he was so overwhelmed with pity that he could not speak. Her face had changed as it might have done in one's worst dreams. Surely, he thought, even the dead cannot look as different as this from their living selves. Perhaps she was going mad.

He trembled as he sat down. 'I think I know what has happened,' he said to Mrs Camargo.

'Her husband has left her.'

'He told me he was going to.'

They both spoke hardly above a whisper, which established the atmosphere of an operating theatre.

'She thinks he is with Celina Fonseca.'

'He's not. According to him, that had nothing to do with it. He's not with her.'

Mercedes spoke for the first time.

'I'm sorry, I didn't understand.'

'She says that you know where her husband is.'

Morris writhed and twisted his feet. 'Why does she think that?'

'She found a letter you wrote to her husband. Also he told her that you were helping him to get a new job.'

The young man felt a sudden spurt of hatred for Newton, his clumsiness, his abuse of offers of help, his forcing other men to lie for him.

'I gave him letters of introduction because I was sorry for him. He had good reasons for wanting to leave her. If she finds him because of me, I shall be responsible for what happens.'

'What would happen?'

'He'd kill himself.'

Mrs Camargo gave the comfortable snort with which women usually, perhaps rightly, greet this suggestion. He felt put down, childish.

'Will you tell us where he is?'

Morris shuddered all over. 'No.' He stood up, trying to avoid that terrible head staring at him from the opposite chair.

'What is this poor woman to do?'

'Why doesn't she go to the consul-general? Or the police?'

'She can't do that,' Mrs Camargo said.

'Why not?'

'It would be useless. Her husband would never forgive her. She wants him back.'

He walked up and down the room. 'Look, I can't help you. Besides, you have only heard one side of the story. I think her husband was right, but I'm not arguing about right and wrong. He was a friend of mine and so I tried to help him. Please excuse me, I have to go out now.'

'I hope you realize what you are doing to this poor woman, Mr Morris.'

'I realize quite well, but there is still nothing I can do about it.'

The two women left his flat in silence.

At the Municipal Theatre, Tinka was waiting for him.

'It's just going to begin,' she said.

She was wearing a woollen stole which, on her small figure, looked as large as a motoring rug. Her face was pink: she had arrived early and, standing alone in the white and gilded foyer, had already received the attentions of various loitering young men.

'I'm so sorry; when I got home I found I had visitors.'

Morris was sweating, and he felt as absent-minded as if he had been drunk. When Tinka stopped in the doorway to get a programme, he bumped into her back. Later he found that he couldn't listen to the music with any attention: it merely hurried his painful thoughts along faster. His knee was shaking like a part of a motor-bicycle, and sweat was creeping out all over him.

He watched the girl at his side. She sat with her chin raised, as though her small round face was a cup to catch every note that the pianist played. Her profile was as neat as a young cat's. When the first piece had ended, she turned excitedly to him, then stopped.

'Are you all right?' she asked.

'Yes, of course. Do I look peculiar?' He put his elbow on his knee to stop it vibrating.

'A little bit.'

During the interval they went into the bar.

They made conversation about the music for a while, and then Tinka asked again: 'You're sure you're all right? I mean, you don't want to go or anything?'

'No, of course not. This drink was really what I needed. As a matter of fact, I've just had really rather a frightful time and I'm longing to tell you about it.'

At that moment the electric buzzer sounded, and they returned to their seats.

Afterwards in a restaurant Morris gave Tinka a brief, nameless, slightly-censored account of what had happened.

'Poor woman.'

'That's what everyone says. All the girls gang up.'

'Well, you said you were sorry for her.'

'I'm sorry for everyone, but most of all for him. He was a nice man. I can't explain exactly why, but he was. He can't be having much of a time now. The place he's gone to is like the first human colony in outer space.'

'What's it called?'

'Do you mind if I don't tell you? It's just that, if I tell anyone its name, I shall tell everyone.'

'I see.' Tinka seemed a little irritated by this, however. Later she said in a patronizing voice: 'I must say you do know some odd people.'

'These aren't very odd, Tinka, really.'

'The other day I saw that film man who was at Daph's engagement party. He's odd, all right. You know, the one with the girl.'

'Oh God, Gregory.'

'Yes.' She looked at Morris as though waiting for him to defend Gregory Cowan.

'You're sure it was him? Everyone thinks he's in Europe.'

'It was him all right. At Sears Roebuck, the day before yesterday. He came up and spoke to me. Is he still with that girl?'

'No, he's not.'

When telling his story, he had forgotten that Tinka had met one of the chief personalities. Celina's entry into both episodes seemed somehow to make her less defensible. Perhaps it was only when she was there near you that you knew there was no question of defence, only of acceptance. But the moment he had thought this, he realized that it was no longer true.

'Do you think you will ever see any of them again?' Tinka asked.

'I hope not.'

'Why?'

'Tired and bored, really. No, it's all this business of helping people. I've come to the conclusion that it's quite wrong to help people without loving them first. Do you understand?'

'I think so,' Tinka said uncertainly.

'Perhaps you helped me find out this.'

'Did I?'

'Yes.'

Tinka wriggled a little in her chair. 'Oh, good.'

Then they talked of other things, and were happy for the rest of the evening.

After this, Morris thought himself better equipped for the next occasion that he met Mercedes Newton. He soon found out that he was wrong.

It was midday, and this time she was alone by the gateway.

'Mr Morris, I am desperate. You must tell me where he is.'

'No.'

'You must tell me. I think perhaps I am going mad.'

'Go to the police if you want to find him.'

'No, no. You must tell me. You must tell me.'

He saw that she was brimming over with violence. She seized hold of his sleeve and her strong fingers were like teeth on the cloth. She glared at him furiously, enraged by his young face, which had closed up and set, in the English fashion, against passion and publicity, her two great weapons.

'Please go away,' he said. 'I cannot help you.'

Mercedes was pushing him back against the flowering hedge. Leaves and twigs were snapping behind him and he lurched forward in order to keep his balance.

'Let me go.'

But by now he was less certain. Something in his upbringing had made him feel pathos in the middle-aged far more than in the young. They were the people you had always to disappoint; the young were your own rivals. For him, no Butterfly could be too stout or elderly to prevent him weeping at her Pinkerton's desertion.

However, he managed to tear himself away, with her sobs and prayers still following him. He went up to his flat.

He found his daily servant in the midst of desolation. All the drawers were opened, all his books had been dragged out on to the floor.

The woman – he had hardly seen her before; she was on loan from friends – was profusely apologetic and almost in despair.

'Senhor Robin, forgive me. It was the lady downstairs who told me to let her in. She said that that one was a friend of yours.'

'You could not know. What was she trying to do?'

'She pulled all the books out. When I spoke to her, she said she was finding a letter you wanted to give her. Also, she drank whisky.'

'I see.'

'She kept saying "Letter, letter". Then, when I saw what she was doing, I told her to go away.'

Morris sat down for a moment. He was surprised at the violence of his reaction. Mrs Newton's behaviour made him feel furiously angry, and at the same time defiled, as though strangers had made love in his bed.

He told the servant not to continue cooking lunch; he did not know when he would be back.

The street was quiet and neutral in the noon sun. Murmurs of traffic came from the middle distance. The only living thing in sight was a Japanese boy from a dry-cleaner's, carrying coat-hangers. Morris walked to the nearest corner. Half-way down the next block, he caught sight of Mercedes. Her heavy body was stumbling along and – for some reason this seemed worst of all – she had taken off her high-heeled shoes.

As he approached, he felt himself crying out silently, howling inside with chagrin.

She did not seem surprised to see him again. Her animosity against him had quietened down. He knew immediately that it would be a hopeless waste of effort to tax her with the way she had treated his house. She was grey-faced and looked quite mad.

'Where is Mrs Camargo? Why isn't she here to help

you?' He repeated the question twice before he got her attention.

'That woman? She is bad, she has had three husbands. They are all like that here. Almighty God will punish them.'

Morris realized that Mercedes Newton was entirely isolated by now, as completely alone as if she had been in the middle of a desert. Individual people could no longer be expected to go the long distances to meet her; she would have to be dealt with by official machinery.

He told her briefly that he was going to take her to the British Consulate, and that whatever happened she must never come back to his house again or he would call the police. He could not be sure that she understood anything he said.

After some delay he found a taxi. The driver was ironically curious at the spectacle of Mercedes, who at that moment was replacing her shoes; it was the usual absurdity of a young man with an older woman, increased by the fact that the woman was neither handsome nor apparently rich. Worse, Mrs Newton wept all the way to the consulate. Morris sat a foot and a half away from her. The driver watched them both in his mirror.

At the consulate, a queue of visa-seekers looked them up and down. Morris spoke quickly to one of the secretaries. 'She is the wife of a British subject. Will you make sure that the consul sees her?'

Then he left, plunging downstairs out of a bad dream into the daylight of the street.

3

The soreness, the wincing memories of the situation, began to fade away. From Nova Fronteira Newton did not write. Through official channels Mercedes was returned to the capital, where she was given employment at the Anglo-American hospital.

At the beginning of winter, the weather was hot and rainless. The days began already staled, with no dew or mist, into a world of smoking asphalt, a whole city that had the perpetual smell of Woolworth's. Dust clouds, foul and stinging with the wind, met you at the corners of the huge buildings.

A month passed. It was the phase of Tinka. Morris spent two Sundays at the house outside the suburbs, watching her exercise her horse. He was celebrated by her spaniels and cross-questioned on oil politics by her father. In this way he began to retreat from the city. Occasionally it surprised him, on the rare evenings when he found himself in the centre, at the hour when the male crowds, the Farouks and Charlie Chaplins, were overcrowding the pavements and seething in the portals of cinemas. He had forgotten that things went like this, that here, in the enormous democracy of a well-pressed suit, a white shirt and a pack of cigarettes, you were the master of your little fate, that you could stand on a corner talking of women and football until anything that might conceivably happen frequently did.

Mostly he saw this from taxi windows going to other places. The gnawing cinema loneliness, the drunken wanderings from night-club to night-club, the visits to Maria Aparecida had retreated into a dim and different past.

Celina had begun to be a part of this, when she emerged suddenly, after lunch on a Saturday, and asked for a drink.

He had not remembered her to be quite like this. She had

changed, not a great deal, but it was as though you saw for the first time in a mirror the reflection of someone you know well: she was a little blurred, and had lost a certain symmetry.

He gave her the drink – Celina had asked for gin – and they sat together in his green-reflecting room, talking and not often looking at one another.

'I didn't know your address.'

'Well, you must come soon and see my apartment. It is really beautiful, with a view right along the bay. I hardly ever want to go out, even at carnival. Anyway, carnival was very weak this year.'

'Don't people always say that?'

'I suppose they do.' She curled her legs together and made herself comfortable. 'How long it is since I've seen you, Robin! What a time that was! Do you remember the awful scene in that bar? What happened to her, I wonder?'

'You missed the worst part.'

'Tell me.'

He described his final encounter with Mercedes.

'Poor Robin. I had to keep clear. You know, she swore to kill me.'

Laughing, she appeared self-satisfied and callous. He felt angry and wanted to break this down.

'I was very, very sorry for her,' he said. 'You should have seen her when she came here. I never knew that feelings could destroy a person in that way, physically.'

But Celina was not listening. She drained her glass and held it out for him. 'No, really she was a terrible woman. I have never met anyone else like her before. What on earth made him keep on with her?' Morris, his back turned, did not answer. 'I mean, I know he married her from pity, to get her out of a mess. But why go on, when it was no good?'

'Loneliness, I imagine.'

He mixed the gin fizz and handed it to her. He made another for himself.

'Are you lonely, Robin?' She was being winsome. Today for the first time he found her a little dreadful, as only humourless people can be. With him she had never used this manner before.

He said quickly: 'Me? No, I have several friends.'

'Girls?'

'One girl.'

'I see.' She was silent for a moment. 'You're quite right, of course, loneliness is a very serious thing. Do you know why I came here?'

'No.' He did not want to know the answer to her question. Gregory Cowan was in the city; it was only a matter of time before she spoke of him.

'I wanted to see my father, to make peace with him. You see, he must be one of the loneliest people in the world. He sees no one at all.'

'I suppose so. I'm very sorry.'

'I miss Jango terribly, terribly. Perhaps you think it is foolish to say that. I had not seen him for some time and, if he had lived, I might never have seen him again. Even so, I miss him. I used to think that in the end I might come back and help him in some way. Not because I believed any of it, but because he did. But it would have meant coming back too far. The bosom of the family, and the Church! Am I talking too much?'

'No.' He was sure now that she had not seen Cowan.

'Tell me, really.'

'I was thinking that perhaps you haven't had any one to talk to for a long time.'

She looked offended. He knew then that she was desperately lonely, and was scared of admitting it.

'But I know a lot of people, Robin.'

'Perhaps not the right ones. People who are shockable.'

'Oh dear, am I shocking?'

Morris had gone too fast, but he wanted to go on. His desire to speak the truth still had with it a little lust to hurt.

'I didn't mean that. But friends must be people who can understand that anything can happen to human beings. Then, whatever happens to you or me, they can remain our friends without having to lie to themselves.'

'Enough has happened to me,' Celina said.

'You need friends. Not just – people.'

'But why should I worry about people, Robin? You don't think I've done anything wrong, do you? I told you all about that woman Mercedes.'

He did not answer. She drank nervously, feeling his silence to be judicial.

'Have you got any new gramophone records, Robin?'

'Yes. Would you like to hear them?'

'I would love to. But please first get me a drink.'

Drinking with Celina, he wanted to blunt the agonizingly sharp edges of their encounter. He put gin in the glasses up to the same level, but made sure that hers was already full of ice.

The stack of records began slipping down. The gay unapologetic tunes of the carnival street bands followed one after the other.

Later, he saw that Celina was no longer listening. Her lips were moving and he realized that she was talking, half to herself. He switched down the volume, and went beside her.

'... I had never seen the man before. He was sitting on the arm of the sofa. I don't know how he got there. I must have left the door of the apartment open.'

'Go on.'

'He asked me what the music was. I was so confused that I just held out the printed cover. He came nearer to see it. Then he attacked me.' She was plunged in unhappy silence for a minute, and then she continued in a different voice:

'Of course I fought and fought. You know I have a revolver? Well, I got it out and I drove him away.'

Morris put his arm round her, holding it closer against the heaving disquiet of her body. 'Everything was all right. You mustn't worry about it any more, that's all.'

'You see now. This is what it means to be a lonely woman in a country like this.'

'Yes.'

'Poor Robin! All my stories!' She laughed painfully. 'You don't want to be bothered with me, do you?' She was still inside his arm.

'You know, if I can help you –'

'Let's have some music, shall we?'

Outside, the evening had darkened between the leaves. They had played nearly all his records. A defect on the last one caused the turntable to continue hissing round. They left it there, staring in front of them.

Suddenly Celina said: 'If you write to Cecil, please don't tell him I was like this.'

'What do you mean?'

'Like this!' she cried out with sudden childish impatience, waving her glass and her cigarette from side to side.

He pretended not to understand, but he himself was feeling desolate, the victim of contagious melancholia. Worse, at that moment the room was filled with a shrill demented clatter. It was seven o'clock; his alarm clock had gone off. On awaking that morning he must have rewound the wrong switch.

Celina appeared to notice nothing. She pushed herself in front of him.

'Robin. It was no use. I thought –'

'Yes?'

'Can't you see? Can't you see?' She was looking quite drunk and her eyes were blurred over with moisture. 'It is not true, what I told you about that man.'

229

'What?'

'That man. He stayed the whole night. I didn't know a man could do that to a woman. He stayed the whole night. In the morning there were scratches right down his belly.'

She was in tears now, and there was nothing to say. He leant her head against him. He felt her breasts and the cage of ribs, and his face dropped into the warm corner between neck and shoulder. When she grew calmer, he raised his head and they kissed too hard, confusedly.

'No, Robin,' she said after a time.

'Yes.'

'This is only because you are sorry for me. What about your girl?'

'Please.'

Celina sat upright, smoothing her hair. 'No, it would not work.' She heard noises outside and turned to him quickly. 'Who is that?'

'It's only my cook, coming in to make the dinner.'

'Is it as late as that?'

'Yes. No.' He thought for a minute. 'I'm going to tell her to go away. We'll have dinner in the city. Please. And afterwards we can come back here.'

She smiled at him, wrinkling her eyes, which were still wet. 'Perhaps, Robin. Perhaps.'

Morris watched her, surprised once again at her physical beauty. Her mind was hurrying on – he could not flatter himself as a bringer of comfort. She was not happy and she was not even calm.

'Give me an hour, Robin. I must go to the hotel and bath and change, telephone some people – lots of things.'

'Telephone what people?'

'Just people.'

'All right.' He dismissed the last of his suspicions – Celina did not even know that Gregory Cowan was back in the country. Besides, now that they were deciding things together, the tempo had grown quicker and lighter and all the tensions of the afternoon were relieved.

'I'll get you a taxi now. I'll come and fetch you in an hour's time.'

'Oh, Robin, you do know how to help people. Your flat was the only place I could have come today.'

'Then you must come back after dinner.'

She smiled without answering. When he helped her into the car he saw that her eyes were full of affection. He thought she looked happier now than he had seen her do for a long time.

Alone in the sitting-room, he stood in the presence of the slight desolation that the afternoon had left with its passing, the bowl of melting ice, the clogged ashtrays, the long-playing records shuffled and separated from their sleeves. Now that he had stopped talking he began to feel drunk; nevertheless, his confidence began to trickle away in anxiety. He had to brace himself into a sense of well-being.

Since he had first met Celina, he had always thought, the next time I meet her she will be different. There had been Cowan, and there had been the Newtons – and always hidden complexities that remained unexplained. But today it seemed that she *was* different: he had begun by hating her, by wanting to punish her, and had ended like this, tingling with anticipation.

He shaved carefully, and put on a fresh tropical suit and a new silk tie. A refilled glass, perched on the soap-dish, made things easier.

While he shaved he watched his face in the mirror, and thought about Celina and Newton. His own life, even running out to Maria Aparecida or going to concerts with Tinka, had been entirely different from theirs. In them, he had watched the desolation that passion had made: he had been a spectator of the game. He had watched Cowan play with passion and run away, and himself had helped Newton run away from it. He had seen Celina near destruction and Mrs Newton destroyed. Gregory Cowan, with his inane meaningless eye and steady hand, had been the least damaged. He had had luck in this, as he had done in the state lottery, the Animal Game.

And now if Morris was taking his part with Celina, it was fundamentally because he did not care any more.

An hour later he was at the hotel.

He had bumped into a glass wall before he saw a pair of bronze shapes floating at stomach level; they were the door handles. Inside, the carpeting was soft and spongy; air conditioning chilled the roots of his hair.

There was no sign of Celina in the foyer. A reception-desk and a travel-agent's counter curved away into the background. Everywhere there were new boxes of cactus plants, with their furry shapes sticking out of the dry earth like the paws of buried carrion. A mobile stirred restlessly overhead. The whole style of the place seemed designed to make Europeans, unless they were students of architecture, vaguely depressed and unhappy.

Morris found the bar and sat there with a waterish Martini. Celina was very late. He thought his watch had stopped, but he found it to be in agreement with a circle of dots and dashes on the mirrored wall.

Ten minutes later he went to the reception-desk. There were three Austrians behind it, all in black suits and with bright blond hair. One of them bent towards him.

Morris told him Celina's room number. 'Could you put me through to her?'

'But she is already gone out.'

'Are you sure?'

'About twenty minutes back. With an English gentleman.'

His mind was stunned with incredulity. He stood there,

being ridiculous, for three or four minutes before he remembered the next question to be asked.

'She left a message.'

'No, no message,' the Austrian said smugly.

Bitched! Morris pushed his way out into the street and stood on the kerb watching the traffic. Coming back from its paralysis, his mind began to hurt.

He began walking along without trying to think. But he soon told himself that Celina's telephone calls had been responsible. She had found someone who knew Gregory Cowan. Morris did not doubt for a moment that he was the Englishman who had come to fetch her.

After another ten minutes of walking, he began to feel an enormous sensation of relief.

He went into a café and telephoned Tinka.

More about Penguins

If you have enjoyed reading this book you may wish to know that *Penguinews* appears every month. It is an attractively illustrated magazine containing a complete list of books published by Penguins and still in print, together with details of the month's new books. A specimen copy will be sent free on request.

Penguinews is obtainable from most bookshops; but you may prefer to become a regular subscriber at 4s. for twelve issues. Just write to Dept EP, Penguin Books Ltd, Harmondsworth, Middlesex, enclosing a cheque or postal order, and you will be put on the mailing list.

Some other books published by Penguins are described on the following pages.

Note : *Penguinews* is not available in the U.S.A., Canada or Australia.

Another Penguin by Frank Tuohy

The Ice Saints

The Ice Saints tells the other side of the story of the Iron Curtain – the moment for a Polish family when a unit from the West seems to give hope of a new life in this glittering world outside. Here is the agony of ordinary people trapped in the biggest issues of our time.

The Ice Saints was awarded the Geoffrey Faber Memorial Prize for the best novel of 1963–4 and the James Tait Black Memorial Prize for the best novel of 1964.

Not for sale in the U.S.A.

The Garrick Year

Margaret Drabble

Theatrical marriages – glamorous . . . scandalous . . .
bitchy . . . brief? Or are they in fact just like anyone
else's?

This novel takes the lid off one such marriage: inside
we find Emma married to an egocentric actor playing a
year's season at a provincial theatre festival. David her
husband, and Wyndham the producer.
The mixture turns rapidly to acid.

Not for sale in the U.S.A.

The Whisperers

Robert Nicolson

Lonely, slightly dotty, old Mrs Ross escapes from the
Glasgow slums into her own private world – her forays
outside it being limited to the National Assistance Board
and the reading room of the Public Library. Suddenly
she is pitched into the even madder world of
psychiatrists and criminals, a world in which dignity
and compassion have no meaning.

Not for sale in the U.S.A.

The Writing Today ... Series

An interesting new venture by Penguins which aims to inform the English-speaking reader of new developments in the literature of other countries.

The following volumes are available or in preparation

The New Writing in the U.S.A.*
African Writing Today
Latin American Writing Today
South African Writing Today
German Writing Today

Not for sale in the U.S.A.